THE
MIDNIGHT
LIBRARY

Also by Matt Haig

THE MIDNIGHT LIBRARY

MATT HAIG

VIKING

VIKING

An imprint of Penguin Random House LLC

penguinrandomhouse.com

First published in hardcover in Great Britain by
Canongate Books, Ltd., Edinburgh, in 2020.

First published in the United States by Viking in 2020.

Grateful acknowledgment is made for permission to reprint the following:
Excerpt from *The Unabridged Journals of Sylvia Plath*
by Sylvia Plath, edited by Karen V. Kukil, copyright © 2000 by the Estate of
Sylvia Plath. Used by permission of Anchor Books, an imprint of the Knopf
Doubleday Publishing Group, a division of Penguin Random House LLC,
and Faber and Faber Ltd. All rights reserved.

Excerpt from *Marriage and Morals*, by Bertrand Russell.
Copyright © 1929, renewed 1956, by Bertrand Russell.
Reproduced by permission of Taylor & Francis Group through PLSclear.

Library of Congress Control Number: 2020940583
ISBN 9780525559474 (hardcover)
ISBN 9780525559481 (ebook)

Printed in the United States of America
1   3   5   7   9   10   8   6   4   2

To all the health workers.
And the care workers.
Thank you.

I can never be all the people I want and live all the lives I want. I can never train myself in all the skills I want. And why do I want? I want to live and feel all the shades, tones and variations of mental and physical experience possible in my life.

Sylvia Plath

'Between life and death there is a library,' she said. 'And within that library, the shelves go on for ever. Every book provides a chance to try another life you could have lived. To see how things would be if you had made other choices . . . Would you have done anything different, if you had the chance to undo your regrets?'

A Conversation About Rain

Nineteen years before she decided to die, Nora Seed sat in the warmth of the small library at Hazeldene School in the town of Bedford. She sat at a low table staring at a chess board.

'Nora dear, it's natural to worry about your future,' said the librarian, Mrs Elm, her eyes twinkling.

Mrs Elm made her first move. A knight hopping over the neat row of white pawns. 'Of course, you're going to be worried about the exams. But you could be anything you want to be, Nora. Think of all that possibility. It's exciting.'

'Yes. I suppose it is.'

'A whole life in front of you.'

'A whole life.'

'You could do anything, live anywhere. Somewhere a bit less cold and wet.'

Nora pushed a pawn forward two spaces.

It was hard not to compare Mrs Elm to her mother, who treated Nora like a mistake in need of correction. For instance, when she was a baby her mother had been so worried Nora's left ear stuck out more than her right that she'd used sticky tape to address the situation, then disguised it beneath a woollen bonnet.

'I *hate* the cold and wet,' added Mrs Elm, for emphasis.

Mrs Elm had short grey hair and a kind and mildly crinkled oval face sitting pale above her turtle-green polo neck. She was quite old. But she was also the person most on Nora's wavelength in the entire school, and even on days when it wasn't raining she would spend her afternoon break in the small library.

'Coldness and wetness don't always go together,' Nora told her. 'Antarctica is the driest continent on Earth. Technically, it's a desert.'

'Well, that sounds up your street.'

'I don't think it's far enough away.'

'Well, maybe you should be an astronaut. Travel the galaxy.'

Nora smiled. 'The rain is even worse on other planets.'

'Worse than Bedfordshire?'

'On Venus it is pure acid.'

Mrs Elm pulled a paper tissue from her sleeve and delicately blew her nose. 'See? With a brain like yours you can do anything.'

A blond boy Nora recognised from a couple of years below her ran past outside the rain-speckled window. Either chasing someone or being chased. Since her brother had left, she'd felt a bit unguarded out there. The library was a little shelter of civilisation.

'Dad thinks I've thrown everything away. Now I've stopped swimming.'

'Well, far be it from me to say, but there is more to this world than swimming really fast. There are many different possible lives ahead of you. Like I said last week, you could be a glaciologist. I've been researching and the—'

And it was then that the phone rang.

'One minute,' said Mrs Elm, softly. 'I'd better get that.'

A moment later, Nora watched Mrs Elm on the phone. 'Yes. She's here now.' The librarian's face fell in shock. She turned away from Nora, but her words were audible across the hushed room: 'Oh no. No. Oh my God. Of course . . .'

Nineteen Years Later

The Man at the Door

Twenty-seven hours before she decided to die, Nora Seed sat on her dilapidated sofa scrolling through other people's happy lives, waiting for something to happen. And then, out of nowhere, something actually did.

Someone, for whatever peculiar reason, rang her doorbell.

She wondered for a moment if she shouldn't get the door at all. She was, after all, already in her night clothes even though it was only nine p.m. She felt self-conscious about her over-sized ECO WORRIER T-shirt and her tartan pyjama bottoms.

She put on her slippers, to be slightly more civilised, and discovered that the person at the door was a man, and one she recognised.

He was tall and gangly and boyish, with a kind face, but his eyes were sharp and bright, like they could see through things.

It was good to see him, if a little surprising, especially as he was wearing sports gear and he looked hot and sweaty despite the cold, rainy weather. The juxtaposition between them made her feel even more slovenly than she had done five seconds earlier.

But she'd been feeling lonely. And though she'd studied enough existential philosophy to believe loneliness was a fundamental part of being a human in an essentially meaningless universe, it was good to see him.

'Ash,' she said, smiling. 'It's Ash, isn't it?'

'Yes. It is.'

'What are you doing here? It's good to see you.'

A few weeks ago she'd been sat playing her electric piano and he'd run down Bancroft Avenue and had seen her in the window here at 33A and given her a little wave. He had once – years ago – asked her out for a coffee. Maybe he was about to do that again.

'It's good to see you too,' he said, but his tense forehead didn't show it.

When she'd spoken to him in the shop, he'd always sounded breezy, but now his voice contained something heavy. He scratched his brow. Made another sound but didn't quite manage a full word.

'You running?' A pointless question. He was clearly out for a run. But he seemed relieved, momentarily, to have something trivial to say.

'Yeah. I'm doing the Bedford Half. It's this Sunday.'

'Oh right. Great. I was thinking of doing a half-marathon and then I remembered I hate running.'

This had sounded funnier in her head than it did as actual words being vocalised out of her mouth. She didn't even hate running. But still, she was perturbed to see the seriousness of his expression. The silence went beyond awkward into something else.

'You told me you had a cat,' he said eventually.

'Yes. I have a cat.'

'I remembered his name. Voltaire. A ginger tabby?'

'Yeah. I call him Volts. He finds Voltaire a bit pretentious. It turns out he's not massively into eighteenth-century French philosophy and literature. He's quite down-to-earth. You know. For a cat.'

Ash looked down at her slippers.

'I'm afraid I think he's dead.'

'What?'

'He's lying very still by the side of the road. I saw the name on the collar, I think a car might have hit him. I'm sorry, Nora.'

She was so scared of her sudden switch in emotions right then that she kept smiling, as if the smile could keep her in the world she had just been in, the one where Volts was alive and where this man she'd sold guitar songbooks to had rung her doorbell for another reason.

Ash, she remembered, was a surgeon. Not a veterinary one, a general human one. If he said something was dead it was, in all probability, dead.

'I'm so sorry.'

Nora had a familiar sense of grief. Only the sertraline stopped her crying. 'Oh God.'

She stepped out onto the wet cracked paving slabs of Bancroft Avenue, hardly breathing, and saw the poor ginger-furred creature lying on the rain-glossed tarmac beside the kerb. His head grazed the side of the pavement and his legs were back as if in mid-gallop, chasing some imaginary bird.

'Oh Volts. Oh no. Oh God.'

She knew she should be experiencing pity and despair for her feline friend – and she was – but she had to acknowledge something else. As she stared at Voltaire's still and peaceful expression – that total absence of pain – there was an inescapable feeling brewing in the darkness.

Envy.

String Theory

Nine and a half hours before she decided to die, Nora arrived late for her afternoon shift at String Theory.

'I'm sorry,' she told Neil, in the scruffy little windowless box of an office. 'My cat died. Last night. And I had to bury him. Well, someone helped me bury him. But then I was left alone in my flat and I couldn't sleep and forgot to set the alarm and didn't wake up till midday and then had to rush.'

This was all true, and she imagined her appearance – including make-up-free face, loose makeshift ponytail and the same second-hand green corduroy pinafore dress she had worn to work all week, garnished with a general air of tired despair – would back her up.

Neil looked up from his computer and leaned back in his chair. He joined his hands together and made a steeple of his index fingers, which he placed under his chin, as if he was Confucius contemplating a deep philosophical truth about the universe rather than the boss of a musical equipment shop dealing with a late employee. There was a massive Fleetwood Mac poster on the wall behind him, the top right corner of which had come unstuck and flopped down like a puppy's ear.

'Listen, Nora, I like you.'

Neil was harmless. A fifty-something guitar aficionado who liked cracking bad jokes and playing passable old Dylan covers live in the store.

'And I know you've got mental-health stuff.'

'Everyone's got mental-health stuff.'

'You know what I mean.'

'I'm feeling much better, generally,' she lied. 'It's not clinical. The doctor says it's situational depression. It's just that I keep on having new . . . situations. But I haven't taken a day off sick for it all. Apart from when my mum . . . Yeah. Apart from that.'

Neil sighed. When he did so he made a whistling sound out of his nose. An ominous B flat. 'Nora, how long have you worked here?'

'Twelve years and . . .' – she knew this too well – '. . . eleven months and three days. On and off.'

'That's a long time. I feel like you are made for better things. You're in your late thirties.'

'I'm thirty-five.'

'You've got so much going for you. You teach people piano . . .'

'One person.'

He brushed a crumb off his sweater.

'Did you picture yourself stuck in your hometown working in a shop? You know, when you were fourteen? What did you picture yourself as?'

'At fourteen? A swimmer.' She'd been the fastest fourteen-year-old girl in the country at breaststroke and second-fastest at freestyle. She remembered standing on a podium at the National Swimming Championships.

'So, what happened?'

She gave the short version. 'It was a lot of pressure.'

'Pressure makes us, though. You start off as coal and the pressure makes you a diamond.'

She didn't correct his knowledge of diamonds. She didn't tell him that while coal and diamonds are both carbon, coal is too impure to be able, under whatever pressure, to become a diamond. According to science, you start off as coal and you end up as coal. Maybe that was the real-life lesson.

She smoothed a stray strand of her coal-black hair up towards her ponytail.

'What are you saying, Neil?'

'It's never too late to pursue a dream.'

'Pretty sure it's too late to pursue that one.'

'You're a very well qualified person, Nora. Degree in Philosophy . . .'

Nora stared down at the small mole on her left hand. That mole had been through everything she'd been through. And it just stayed there, not caring. Just being a mole. 'Not a *massive* demand for philosophers in Bedford, if I'm honest, Neil.'

'You went to uni, had a year in London, then came back.'

'I didn't have much of a choice.'

Nora didn't want a conversation about her dead mum. Or even Dan. Because Neil had found Nora's backing out of a wedding with two days' notice the most fascinating love story since Kurt and Courtney.

'We all have choices, Nora. There's such a thing as free will.'

'Well, not if you subscribe to a deterministic view of the universe.'

'But why *here*?'

'It was either here or the Animal Rescue Centre. This paid better. Plus, you know, music.'

'You were in a band. With your brother.'

'I was. The Labyrinths. We weren't really going anywhere.'

'Your brother tells a different story.'

This took Nora by surprise. 'Joe? How do you—'

'He bought an amp. Marshall DSL40.'

'When?'

'Friday.'

'He was in Bedford?'

'Unless it was a hologram. Like Tupac.'

He was probably visiting Ravi, Nora thought. Ravi was her brother's best friend. While Joe had given up the guitar and moved to London, for a crap IT job he hated, Ravi had stuck to Bedford. He played in a covers band now, called Slaughterhouse Four, doing pub gigs around town.

'Right. That's interesting.'

Nora was pretty certain her brother knew Friday was her day off. The fact prodded her from inside.

'I'm happy here.'

'Except you aren't.'

He was right. A soul-sickness festered within her. Her mind was throwing itself up. She widened her smile.

'I mean, I am happy with the job. Happy as in, you know, satisfied. Neil, I need this job.'

'You are a good person. You worry about the world. The homeless, the environment.'

'I need a job.'

He was back in his Confucius pose. 'You need freedom.'

'I don't want freedom.'

'This isn't a non-profit organisation. Though I have to say it is rapidly becoming one.'

'Look, Neil, is this about what I said the other week? About you needing to modernise things? I've got some ideas of how to get younger peo—'

'No,' he said, defensively. 'This place used to just be guitars. String Theory, get it? I diversified. Made this work. It's just that when times are tough I can't pay you to put off customers with your face looking like a wet weekend.'

'What?'

'I'm afraid, Nora' – he paused for a moment, about the time it takes to lift an axe into the air – 'I'm going to have to let you go.'

To Live Is to Suffer

Nine hours before she decided to die, Nora wandered around Bedford aimlessly. The town was a conveyor belt of despair. The pebble-dashed sports centre where her dead dad once watched her swim lengths of the pool, the Mexican restaurant where she'd taken Dan for fajitas, the hospital where her mum had her treatment.

Dan had texted her yesterday.

Nora, I miss your voice. Can we talk? D x

She'd said she was *stupidly hectic* (big lol). Yet it was impossible to text anything else. Not because she didn't still feel for him, but because she did. And couldn't risk hurting him again. She'd ruined his life. *My life is chaos*, he'd told her, via drunk texts, shortly after the would-be wedding she'd pulled out of two days before.

The universe tended towards chaos and entropy. That was basic thermodynamics. Maybe it was basic existence too.

You lose your job, then more shit happens.

The wind whispered through the trees.

It began to rain.

She headed towards the shelter of a newsagent's, with the deep – and, as it happened, *correct* – sense that things were about to get worse.

Doors

Eight hours before she decided to die, Nora entered the newsagent's.

'Sheltering from the rain?' the woman behind the counter asked.

'Yes.' Nora kept her head down. Her despair growing like a weight she couldn't carry.

A *National Geographic* was on display.

As she stared now at the magazine cover – an image of a black hole – she realised that's what she was. A black hole. A dying star, collapsing in on itself.

Her dad used to subscribe. She remembered being enthralled by an article about Svalbard, the Norwegian archipelago in the Arctic Ocean. She'd never seen a place that looked so *far away*. She'd read about scientists doing research among glaciers and frozen fjords and puffins. Then, prompted by Mrs Elm, she'd decided she wanted to be a glaciologist.

She saw the scruffy, hunched form of her brother's friend – and their own former bandmate – Ravi by the music mags, engrossed in an article. She stood there for a fraction too long, because when she walked away she heard him say, 'Nora?'

'Ravi, hi. I hear Joe was in Bedford the other day?'

A small nod. 'Yeah.'

'Did he, um, did you see him?'

'I did actually.'

A silence Nora felt as pain. 'He didn't tell me he was coming.'

'Was just a fly-by.'

'Is he okay?'

Ravi paused. Nora had once liked him, and he'd been a loyal friend to her brother. But, as with Joe, there was a barrier between them. They hadn't parted on the best of terms. (He'd thrown his drumsticks on the floor of a rehearsal room and stropped out when Nora told him she was out of the band.) 'I think he's depressed.'

Nora's mind grew heavier at the idea her brother might feel like she did.

'He's not himself,' Ravi went on, anger in his voice. 'He's going to have to move out of his shoebox in Shepherd's Bush. What with him not being able to play lead guitar in a successful rock band. Mind you, I've got no money either. Pub gigs don't pay these days. Even when you agree to clean the toilets. Ever cleaned pub toilets, Nora?'

'I'm having a pretty shit time too, if we're doing the Misery Olympics.'

Ravi cough-laughed. A hardness momentarily shadowed his face. 'The world's smallest violin is playing.'

She wasn't in the mood. 'Is this about The Labyrinths? Still?'

'It meant a lot to me. And to your brother. To all of us. We had a deal with Universal. Right. There. Album, singles, tour, promo. We could be Coldplay now.'

'You hate Coldplay.'

'Not the point. We could be in Malibu. Instead: *Bedford*. And so, no, your brother's not ready to see you.'

'I was having *panic attacks*. I'd have let everyone down in the end. I told the label to take you on without me. I agreed to write the songs. It wasn't my fault I was engaged. I was with Dan. It was kind of a deal-breaker.'

'Well, yeah. How did that work out?'

'Ravi, that isn't fair.'

'Fair. Great word.'

The woman behind the counter gawped with interest.

'Bands don't last. We'd have been a meteor shower. Over before we started.'

'Meteor showers are fucking beautiful.'

'Come on. You're still with Ella, aren't you?'

'And I could be with Ella *and* in a successful band, with *money*. We had that chance. Right *there*.' He pointed to the palm of his hand. 'Our songs were *fire*.'

Nora hated herself for silently correcting the 'our' to 'my'.

'I don't think your problem was stage fright. Or wedding fright. I think your problem was *life fright*.'

This hurt. The words took the air out of her.

'And I think *your* problem,' she retaliated, voice trembling, 'is blaming others for your shitty life.'

He nodded, as if slapped. Put his magazine back.

'See you around, Nora.'

'Tell Joe I said hi,' she said, as he walked out of the shop and into the rain. 'Please.'

She caught sight of the cover of *Your Cat* magazine. A ginger tabby. Her mind felt loud, like a Sturm und Drang symphony, as if the ghost of a German composer was trapped inside her mind, conjuring chaos and intensity.

The woman behind the counter said something to her she missed.

'Sorry?'

'Nora Seed?'

The woman – blonde bob, bottle tan – was happy and casual and relaxed in a way Nora no longer knew how to be. Leaning over the counter, on her forearms, as if Nora was a lemur at the zoo.

'Yep.'

'I'm Kerry-Anne. Remember you from school. The swimmer. Super-brain. Didn't whatshisface, Mr Blandford, do an assembly on you once? Said you were going to end up at the Olympics?'

Nora nodded.

'So, did you?'

'I, um, gave it up. Was more into music . . . at the time. Then life happened.'

'So what do you do now?'

'I'm . . . between things.'

'Got anyone, then? Bloke? Kids?'

Nora shook her head. Wishing it would fall off. Her own head. Onto the floor. So she never had to have a conversation with a stranger ever again.

'Well, don't hang about. Tick-tock tick-tock.'

'I'm *thirty-five*.' She wished Izzy was here. Izzy never put up with any of this kind of shit. 'And I'm not sure I want—'

'Me and Jake were like rabbits but we got there. Two little terrors. But worth it, y'know? I just feel *complete*. I could show you some pictures.'

'I get headaches, with . . . phones.'

Dan had wanted kids. Nora didn't know. She'd been petrified of motherhood. The fear of a deeper depression. She couldn't look after herself, let alone anyone else.

'Still in Bedford, then?'

'Mm-hm.'

'Thought you'd be one who got away.'

'I came back. My mum was ill.'

'Aw, sorry to hear that. Hope she's okay now?'

'I better go.'

'But it's still raining.'

As Nora escaped the shop, she wished there were nothing but doors ahead of her, which she could walk through one by one, leaving everything behind.

How to Be a Black Hole

Seven hours before she decided to die, Nora was in free fall and she had no one to talk to.

Her last hope was her former best friend Izzy, who was over ten thousand miles away in Australia. And things had dried up between them too.

She took out her phone and sent Izzy a message.

Hi Izzy, long time no chat. Miss you, friend. Would be WONDROUS to catch up. X

She added another 'X' and sent it.

Within a minute, Izzy had seen the message. Nora waited in vain for three dots to appear.

She passed the cinema, where a new Ryan Bailey film was playing tonight. A corny cowboy-romcom called *Last Chance Saloon*.

Ryan Bailey's face seemed to always know *deep and significant things*. Nora had loved him ever since she'd watched him play a brooding Plato in *The Athenians* on TV, and since he'd said in an interview that he'd studied philosophy. She'd imagined them having deep conversations about Henry David Thoreau through a veil of steam in his West Hollywood hot tub.

'Go confidently in the direction of your dreams,' Thoreau had said. 'Live the life you've imagined.'

Thoreau had been her favourite philosopher to study. But who seriously goes confidently in the direction of their dreams? Well, apart from Thoreau. He'd gone and lived in the woods, with no contact from the outside world, to just sit there and write and chop wood and fish. But life was probably simpler two centuries ago in Concord, Massachusetts, than modern life in Bedford, Bedfordshire.

Or maybe it wasn't.

Maybe she was just really crap at it. At life.

Whole hours passed by. She wanted to have a purpose, something to give her a reason to exist. But she had nothing. Not even the small purpose of picking up Mr Banerjee's medication, as she had done that two days ago. She tried to give a homeless man some money but realised she had no money.

'Cheer up, love, it might never happen,' someone said.

Nothing ever did, she thought to herself. *That was the whole problem.*

Antimatter

Five hours before she decided to die, as she began walking home, her phone vibrated in her hand.

Maybe it was Izzy. Maybe Ravi had told her brother to get in touch.

No.

'Oh hi, Doreen.'

An agitated voice. 'Where *were* you?'

She'd totally forgotten. *What time is it?*

'I've had a really crap day. I'm so sorry.'

'We waited outside your flat for an hour.'

'I can still do Leo's lesson when I get back. I'll be five minutes.'

'Too late. He's with his dad now for three days.'

'Oh, I'm sorry. I'm so sorry.'

She was a waterfall of apologies. She was drowning in herself.

'To be honest, Nora, he's been thinking about giving up altogether.'

'But he's so good.'

'He's really enjoyed it. But he's too busy. Exams, mates, football. Something has to give . . .'

'He has a real talent. I've got him into bloody Chopin. Please—'

A deep, deep sigh. 'Bye, Nora.'

Nora imagined the ground opening up, sending her down through the lithosphere, and the mantle, not stopping until she reached the inner core, compressed into a hard unfeeling metal.

*

Four hours before she decided to die, Nora passed her elderly neighbour, Mr Banerjee.

Mr Banerjee was eighty-four years old. He was frail but was slightly more mobile since his hip surgery.

'It's terrible out, isn't it?'

'Yes,' mumbled Nora.

He glanced at his flowerbed. 'The irises are out, though.'

She looked at the clusters of purple flowers, forcing a smile as she wondered what possible consolation they could offer.

His eyes were tired, behind their spectacles. He was at his door, fumbling for keys. A bottle of milk in a carrier bag that seemed too heavy for him. It was rare to see him out of the house. A house she had visited during her first month here, to help him set up an online grocery shop.

'Oh,' he said now. 'I have some good news. I don't need you to collect my pills any more. The boy from the chemist has moved nearby and he says he will drop them off.'

Nora tried to reply but couldn't get the words out. She nodded instead.

He managed to open the door, then closed it, retreating into his shrine to his dear dead wife.

That was it. No one needed her. She was superfluous to the universe.

Once inside her flat the silence was louder than noise. The smell of cat food. A bowl still out for Voltaire, half eaten.

She got herself some water and swallowed two anti-depressants and stared at the rest of the pills, wondering.

Three hours before she decided to die, her whole being ached with regret, as if the despair in her mind was somehow in her torso and limbs too. As if it had colonised every part of her.

It reminded her that everyone was better off without her. You get near a black hole and the gravitational pull drags you into its bleak, dark reality.

The thought was like a ceaseless mind-cramp, something too uncomfortable to bear yet too strong to avoid.

Nora went through her social media. No messages, no comments, no new followers, no friend requests. She was antimatter, with added self-pity.

She went on Instagram and saw everyone had worked out how to live, except her. She posted a rambling update on Facebook, which she didn't even really use any more.

Two hours before she decided to die, she opened a bottle of wine.

Old philosophy textbooks looked down at her, ghost furnishings from her university days, when life still had possibility. A yucca plant and three tiny, squat potted cacti. She imagined being a non-sentient life form sitting in a pot all day was probably an easier existence.

She sat down at the little electric piano but played nothing. She thought of sitting by Leo's side, teaching him Chopin's Prelude in E Minor. Happy moments can turn into pain, given time.

There was an old musician's cliché, about how there were no wrong notes on a piano. But her life was a cacophony of nonsense. A piece that could have gone in wonderful directions, but now went nowhere at all.

Time slipped by. She stared into space.

After the wine a realisation hit her with total clarity. She wasn't made for this life.

Every move had been a mistake, every decision a disaster, every day a retreat from who she'd imagined she'd be.

Swimmer. Musician. Philosopher. Spouse. Traveller. *Glaciologist.* Happy. Loved.

Nothing.

She couldn't even manage 'cat owner'. Or 'one-hour-a-week piano tutor'. Or 'human capable of conversation'.

The tablets weren't working.

She finished the wine. All of it.

'I miss you,' she said into the air, as if the spirits of every person she'd loved were in the room with her.

She called her brother and left a voicemail when he didn't pick up.

'I love you, Joe. I just wanted you to know that. There's nothing you could have done. This is about me. Thank you for being my brother. I love you. Bye.'

It began to rain again, so she sat there with the blinds open, staring at the drops on the glass.

The time was now twenty-two minutes past eleven.

She knew only one thing with absolute certainty: she didn't want to reach tomorrow. She stood up. She found a pen and a piece of paper.

It was, she decided, a very good time to die.

Dear Whoever,

I had all the chances to make something of my life, and I blew every one of them. Through my own carelessness and misfortune, the world has retreated from me, and so now it makes perfect sense that I should retreat from the world.

If I felt it was possible to stay, I would. But I don't. And so I can't. I make life worse for people.

I have nothing to give. I'm sorry.

Be kind to each other.

Bye,
Nora

00:00:00

At first the mist was so pervasive that she could see nothing else, until slowly she saw pillars appear on either side of her. She was standing on a path, some kind of colonnade. The columns were brain-grey, with specks of brilliant blue. The misty vapours cleared, like spirits wanting to be unwatched, and a shape emerged.

A solid, rectangular shape.

The shape of a building. About the size of a church or a small supermarket. It had a stone facade, the same colouration as the pillars, with a large wooden central door and a roof which had aspirations of grandeur, with intricate details and a grand-looking clock on the front gable, with black-painted Roman numerals and its hands pointing to midnight. Tall dark arched windows, framed with stone bricks, punctuated the front wall, equidistant from each other. When she first looked it seemed there were only four windows, but a moment later there were definitely five of them. She thought she must have miscounted.

As there was nothing else around, and since she had nowhere else to be, Nora stepped cautiously towards it.

She looked at the digital display of her watch.

00:00:00

Midnight, as the clock had told her.

She waited for the next second to arrive, but it didn't. Even as she walked closer to the building, even as she opened the wooden door, even as she stepped inside, the display didn't change. Either something was wrong with her watch, or something was wrong with time. In the circumstances, it could have been either.

What's happening? she wondered. *What the hell is going on?*

Maybe this place would hold some answers, she thought, as she walked inside. The place was well lit, and the floor was light stone – somewhere between light yellow and camel-brown, like the colour of an old page – but the windows she had seen on the outside weren't there on the inside. In fact, even though she had only taken a few steps forward she could no longer see the walls at all. Instead, there were bookshelves. Aisles and aisles of shelves, reaching up to the ceiling and branching off from the broad open corridor Nora was walking down. She turned down one of the aisles and stopped to gaze in bafflement at the seemingly endless amount of books.

The books were everywhere, on shelves so thin they might as well have been invisible. The books were all green. Greens of multifarious shades. Some of these volumes were a murky swamp green, some a bright and light chartreuse, some a bold emerald and others the verdant shade of summer lawns.

And on the subject of summer lawns: despite the fact that the books looked old, the air in the library felt fresh. It had a lush, grassy, outdoors kind of smell, not the dusty scent of old tomes.

The shelves really did seem to go on for ever, straight and long towards a far-off horizon, like lines indicating one-point perspective in a school art project, broken only by the occasional corridor.

She picked a corridor at random and set off. At the next turn, she took a left and became a little lost. She searched for a way out, but there was no sign of an exit. She attempted to retrace her steps towards the entrance, but it was impossible.

Eventually she had to conclude she wasn't going to find the exit.

'This is abnormal,' she said to herself, to find comfort in the sound of her own voice. 'Definitely abnormal.'

Nora stopped and stepped closer to some of the books.

There were no titles or author names adorning the spines. Aside from the difference of shade, the only other variation was size: the books were of similar height but varied in width. Some had spines two inches wide, others significantly less. One or two weren't much more than pamphlets.

She reached to pull out one of the books, choosing a medium-sized one in a slightly drab olive colour. It looked a bit dusty and worn.

Before she had pulled it clean from the shelf, she heard a voice behind her and she jumped back.

'Be careful,' the voice said.

And Nora turned around to see who was there.

The Librarian

'Please. You have to be careful.'

The woman had arrived seemingly from nowhere. Smartly dressed, with short grey hair and a turtle-green polo neck jumper. About sixty, if Nora had to pin it down.

'Who are you?'

But before she had finished the question, she realised she already knew the answer.

'I'm the librarian,' the woman said, coyly. 'That is who.'

Her face was one of kind but stern wisdom. She had the same neat cropped grey hair she'd always had, with a face that looked precisely as it always did in Nora's mind.

For there, right in front of her, was her old school librarian.

'Mrs Elm.'

Mrs Elm smiled, thinly. 'Perhaps.'

Nora remembered those rainy afternoons, playing chess.

She remembered the day her father died, when Mrs Elm gently broke the news to her in the library. Her father had died suddenly of a heart attack while on the rugby field of the boys' boarding school where he taught. She was numb for about half an hour, and had stared blankly at the unfinished game of chess. The reality was simply too big to absorb at first, but then it had hit her hard and sideways, taking her off the track she'd known. She had hugged Mrs Elm so close, crying into her polo neck until her face was raw from the fusion of tears and acrylic.

Mrs Elm had held her, stroking and smoothing the back of her head like a baby, not offering platitudes or false comforts or anything other than concern. She remembered Mrs Elm's voice telling her at the time: 'Things will get better, Nora. It's going to be all right.'

It was over an hour before Nora's mother came to pick her up, her brother stoned and numb in the backseat. And Nora had sat in the front next to her mute, trembling mother, saying that she loved her, but hearing nothing back.

'What is this place? Where am I?'

Mrs Elm smiled a very formal kind of smile. 'A library, of course.'

'It's not the school library. And there's no exit. Am I dead? Is this the afterlife?'

'Not exactly,' said Mrs Elm.

'I don't understand.'

'Then let me explain.'

The Midnight Library

As she spoke, Mrs Elm's eyes came alive, twinkling like puddles in moonlight.

'Between life and death there is a library,' she said. 'And within that library, the shelves go on for ever. Every book provides a chance to try another life you could have lived. To see how things would be different if you had made other choices ... Would you have done anything different, if you had the chance to undo your regrets?'

'So, I *am* dead?' Nora asked.

Mrs Elm shook her head. 'No. Listen carefully. *Between* life and death.' She gestured vaguely along the aisle, towards the distance. 'Death is outside.'

'Well, I should go there. Because I want to die.' Nora began walking.

But Mrs Elm shook her head. 'That isn't how death works.'

'Why not?'

'You don't *go* to death. Death comes to you.'

Even death was something Nora couldn't do properly, it seemed.

It was a familiar feeling. This feeling of being incomplete in just about every sense. An unfinished jigsaw of a human. Incomplete living and incomplete dying.

'So why am I not dead? Why has death not come to me? I gave it an open invitation. I'd wanted to die. But here I am, still existing. I am still aware of things.'

'Well, if it's any comfort, you are very possibly *about* to die. People who pass by the library usually don't stay long, one way or the other.'

When she thought about it – and increasingly she had been thinking about it – Nora was only able to think of herself in terms of the things she wasn't. The things she hadn't been able to become. And there really were quite a lot of things she hadn't become. The regrets which were on permanent repeat in her mind. *I haven't become an Olympic swimmer. I haven't become a glaciologist. I haven't become Dan's wife. I haven't become a mother. I haven't become the lead singer of The Labyrinths. I haven't managed to become a truly good or truly happy person. I haven't managed to look after Voltaire.* And now, last of all, she hadn't even managed to become dead. It was pathetic really, the amount of possibilities she had squandered.

'While the Midnight Library stands, Nora, you will be preserved from death. Now, you have to decide how you want to live.'

The Moving Shelves

The shelves on either side of Nora began to move. The shelves didn't change angles, they just kept on sliding horizontally. It was possible that the shelves weren't moving at all, but the books were, and it wasn't obvious why or even *how*. There was no visible mechanism making it happen, and no sound or sight of books falling off the end – or rather the *start* – of the shelf. The books slid by at varying degrees of slowness, depending on the shelf they were on, but none moved fast.

'What's happening?'

Mrs Elm's expression stiffened and her posture straightened, her chin retreating a little into her neck. She took a step closer to Nora and clasped her hands together. 'It is time, my dear, to begin.'

'If you don't mind me asking – begin *what*?'

'Every life contains many millions of decisions. Some big, some small. But every time one decision is taken over another, the outcomes differ. An irreversible variation occurs, which in turn leads to further variations. These books are portals to all the lives you could be living.'

'What?'

'You have as many lives as you have possibilities. There are lives where you make different choices. And those choices lead to different outcomes. If you had done just one thing differently, you would have a different life story. And they all exist in the Midnight Library. They are all as real as this life.'

'Parallel lives?'

'Not always parallel. Some are more . . . *perpendicular*. So, do you want to live a life you could be living? Do you want to do something differently? Is there anything you wish to change? Did you do anything wrong?'

That was an easy one. 'Yes. Absolutely everything.'

The answer seemed to tickle the librarian's nose.

Mrs Elm quickly rummaged for the paper tissue that was stuffed up the inside sleeve of her polo neck. She brought it quickly to her face and sneezed into it.

'Bless you,' said Nora, watching as the tissue disappeared from the librarian's hands the moment she'd finished using it, through some strange and hygienic magic.

'Don't worry. Tissues are like lives. There are always more.' Mrs Elm returned to her train of thought. 'Doing one thing differently is often the same as doing *everything* differently. Actions can't be reversed within a lifetime, however much we try . . . But you are no longer *within* a lifetime. You have popped outside. This is your opportunity, Nora, to see how things could be.'

This can't be real, Nora thought to herself.

Mrs Elm seemed to know what she was thinking.

'Oh, it is real, Nora Seed. But it is not quite reality as you understand it. For want of a better word, it is *in-between*. It is not life. It is not death. It is not the real world in a conventional sense. But nor is it a dream. It isn't one thing or another. It is, in short, the Midnight Library.'

The slow-moving shelves came to a halt. Nora noticed that on one of the shelves, to her right, at shoulder height, there was a large gap. All the other areas of the shelves around her had the books tightly pressed side-by-side, but here, lying flat on the thin, white shelf, there was only one book.

And this book wasn't green like the others. It was grey. As grey as the stone of the front of the building when she had seen it through the mist.

Mrs Elm took the book from the shelf and handed it to Nora.

She had a slight look of anticipatory pride, as if she'd handed her a Christmas present.

It had seemed light when Mrs Elm was holding it, but it was far heavier than it looked. Nora went to open it.

Mrs Elm shook her head.

'You always have to wait for my say-so.'

'Why?'

'Every book in here, every book in this entire library – except one – is a version of your life. This library is yours. It is here for you. You see, everyone's lives could have ended up an infinite number of ways. These books on the shelves are your life, all starting from the same point in time. Right now. Midnight. Tuesday the twenty-eighth of April. But these midnight possibilities aren't the same. Some are similar, some are very different.'

'This is crackers,' said Nora. 'Except *one*? This one?' Nora tilted the stone-grey book towards Mrs Elm.

Mrs Elm raised an eyebrow. 'Yes. That one. It's something you have written without ever having to type a word.'

'What?'

'This book is the source of all your problems, and the answer to them too.'

'But what is it?'

'It is called, my dear, *The Book of Regrets*.'

Nora stared at it. She could see it now. The small typeface embossed on the cover.

The Book of Regrets

'Every regret you have ever had, since the day you were born, is recorded in here,' Mrs Elm said, tapping her finger on the cover. 'I now give you permission to open it.'

As the book was so heavy Nora sat down cross-legged on the stone floor to do so. She began to skim through it.

The book was divided into chapters, chronologically arranged around the years of her life. 0, 1, 2, 3, all the way up to 35. The chapters got much longer as the book progressed, year by year. But the regrets she accumulated weren't specifically related to that year in question.

'Regrets ignore chronology. They float around. The sequence of these lists changes all the time.'

'Right, yes, that makes sense, I suppose.'

She quickly realised they ranged from the minor and quotidian ('I regret not doing any exercise today') to the substantial ('I regret not telling my father I loved him before he died').

There were continual, background regrets, which repeated on multiple pages. 'I regret not staying in The Labyrinths, because I let down my brother.' 'I regret not staying in The Labyrinths, because I let down myself.' 'I regret not doing more for the environment.' 'I regret the time I spent on social media.' 'I regret not going to Australia with Izzy.' 'I regret not having more fun when I was younger.' 'I regret all those arguments with Dad.' 'I regret not working with animals.' 'I regret not doing Geology at University instead of Philosophy.' 'I regret not learning how to be a happier person.' 'I regret feeling so much guilt.' 'I regret not sticking at Spanish.' 'I regret not choosing science subjects in my A-levels.' 'I regret not becoming a glaciologist.' 'I regret not getting married.' 'I regret not applying to do a Master's degree in Philosophy at Cambridge.' 'I regret not keeping healthy.' 'I regret moving to London.' 'I regret not going to Paris to teach English.' 'I regret not finishing the novel I started at university.' 'I regret moving out of London.' 'I regret having a job with no prospects.' 'I regret not being a better sister.' 'I regret not having a gap year after university.' 'I regret disappointing my father.' 'I regret that I teach piano more than I play it.' 'I regret my financial mismanagement.' 'I regret not living in the countryside.'

Some regrets were a little fainter than others. One regret shifted from practically invisible to bold and back again, as if it was flashing on and off, right there as she looked at it. The regret was 'I regret not yet having children.'

'That is a regret that sometimes is and sometimes isn't,' explained Mrs Elm, again somehow reading her mind. 'There are a few of those.'

From the age of 34 onwards, in the longest chapter at the end of the book, there were a lot of Dan-specific regrets. These were quite strong and bold, and played in her head like an ongoing fortissimo chord in a Haydn concerto.

'I regret being cruel to Dan.' 'I regret breaking up with Dan.' 'I regret not living in a country pub with Dan.'

As she stared down at the pages, she thought now of the man she had so nearly married.

Regret Overload

She'd met Dan while living with Izzy in Tooting. Big smile, short beard. Visually, a TV vet. Fun, curious. He drank quite a bit, but always seemed immune to hangovers.

He had studied Art History and put his in-depth knowledge of Rubens and Tintoretto to incredible use by becoming head of PR for a brand of protein flapjacks. He did, however, have a dream. And his dream was to run a pub in the countryside. A dream he wanted to share with her. With Nora.

And she got carried away with his enthusiasm. Got engaged. But suddenly she had realised she didn't want to marry him.

Deep down, she was scared of becoming her mother. She didn't want to replicate her parents' marriage.

Still staring blankly at *The Book of Regrets*, she wondered if her parents had ever been in love or if they had got married because marriage was something you did at the appropriate time with the nearest available person. A game where you grabbed the first person you could find when the music stopped.

She had never wanted to play that game.

Bertrand Russell wrote that 'To fear love is to fear life, and those who fear life are already three-parts dead'. Maybe that was her problem. Maybe she was just scared of living. But Bertrand Russell had more marriages and affairs than hot dinners, so perhaps he was no one to give advice.

When her mum died three months before the wedding Nora's grief was immense. Though she had suggested that the date should be put back, it somehow never was, and Nora's grief fused with depression and anxiety and the feeling that her life was out of her own control. The wedding seemed such a symptom of this chaotic feeling, that she felt tied to a train track, and the only way she could loosen the ropes and free herself was to pull out of the wedding. Though, in reality, staying in Bedford and being single, and letting Izzy down about their Australia plans, and starting work at String Theory, and getting a cat, had all felt like the opposite of freedom.

'Oh no,' said Mrs Elm, breaking Nora's thoughts. 'It's too much for you.'

And suddenly she was back feeling all this contrition, all that pain of letting people down and letting herself down, the pain she had tried to escape less than an hour ago. The regrets began to swarm together. In fact, while staring at the open pages of the book, the pain was actually worse than it had been wandering around Bedford. The power of all the regrets simultaneously emanating from the book was becoming agony. The weight of guilt and remorse and sorrow too strong. She leaned back on her elbows, dropped the heavy book and squeezed her eyes shut. She could hardly breathe, as if invisible hands were around her neck.

'Make it stop!'

'Close it now,' instructed Mrs Elm. 'Close the book. Not just your eyes. *Close it*. You have to do it yourself.'

So Nora, feeling like she was about to pass out, sat back up and placed her hand under the front cover. It felt even heavier now but she managed to close the book and gasped in relief.

Every Life Begins Now

'Well?'

Mrs Elm had her arms folded. Though she looked identical to the Mrs Elm Nora had always known, her manner was definitely a little more brusque. It was Mrs Elm but also somehow *not* Mrs Elm. It was quite confusing.

'Well what?' Nora said, still gasping, still relieved she could no longer feel the intensity of all her regrets simultaneously.

'Which regret stands out? Which decision would you like to undo? Which life would you like to try on?'

She said that, precisely. *Try on.* As if this was a clothes shop and Nora could choose a life as easily as a T-shirt. It felt like a cruel game.

'That was agony. I felt like I was about to be strangled. What is the point of this?'

As Nora looked up, she noticed the lights for the first time. Just naked bulbs hanging down from wires attached to the ceiling, which seemed like a normal kind of light-grey ceiling. Except it was a ceiling that reached no walls. Like the floor here, it went on for ever.

'The point is there is a strong possibility that your old life is over. You wanted to die and maybe you will. And you will need somewhere to go to. Somewhere to land. Another life. So, you need to think hard. This library is called the Midnight Library, because every new life on offer here begins now. And now is midnight. It begins now. All these futures. That's what is here. That's what your books represent. Every other immediate present and ongoing future you could have had.'

'So there are no pasts in there?'

'No. Just the consequence of them. But those books are also written. And I know them all. But they are not for you to read.'

'And when does each life end?'

'It could be seconds. Or hours. Or it could be days. Months. More. If you have found a life you truly want to live, then you get to live it until you die of old age. If you really want to live a life hard enough, you don't have to worry. You will stay there as if you have always been there. Because in one universe you *have* always been there. The book will never be returned, so to speak. It becomes less of a loan and more of a gift. The moment you decide you want that life, really want it, then everything that exists in your head now, including this Midnight Library, will eventually be a memory so vague and intangible it will hardly be there at all.'

One of the lights flickered overhead.

'The only danger,' continued Mrs Elm, more ominously, 'is when you're here. *Between lives.* If you lose the will to carry on, it will affect your root life – your original life. And that could lead to the destruction of this place. You'd be gone for ever. You'd be dead. And so would your access to all this.'

'That's what I want. I want to be dead. I would be dead because I want to be. That's why I took the overdose. I want to die.'

'Well, maybe. Or maybe not. After all, you're still here.'

Nora tried to get her head around this. 'So, how do I return to the library? If I'm stuck in a life even worse than the one I've just left?'

'It can be subtle, but as soon as disappointment is felt in full, you'll come back here. Sometimes the feeling creeps up, other times it comes all at once. If it never arrives, you'll stay put, and you will be happy there, by definition. It couldn't be simpler. So: pick something you would have done differently, and I will find you the book. That is to say, the life.'

Nora stared down at *The Book of Regrets* lying closed on the yellow-brown floor tiles.

She remembered chatting late at night with Dan about his dream of owning a quaint little pub in the country. His enthusiasm had been infectious, and it had almost become her dream too. 'I wish I hadn't left Dan. And that I was still in a relationship with him. I regret us not staying together and working towards that dream. Is there a life where we are still together?'

'Of course,' said Mrs Elm.

The books in the library began to move again, as though the shelves were conveyor belts. This time, though, instead of going as slow as a wedding march they moved faster and faster and faster, until they couldn't really be seen as individual books at all. They just whirred by in streams of green.

Then, just as suddenly, they stopped.

Mrs Elm crouched down and took a book from the lowest shelf to her left. The book was one of the darker shades of green. She handed it to Nora. It was a lot lighter than *The Book of Regrets*, even though it was a similar size. Again, there was no title on the spine but a small one embossed on the front, precisely the same shade as the rest of the book.

It said: *My Life.*

'But it's not my life . . .'

'Oh Nora, they are all your lives.'

'What do I do now?'

'You open the book and turn to the first page.'

Nora did so.

'O-*kay*,' said Mrs Elm, with careful precision. 'Now, read the first line.'

Nora stared down and read.

She walked out of the pub
into the cool night air . . .

And Nora had just enough time to think to herself, 'Pub?' After that, it was happening. The text began to swirl and soon became indecipherable, in fast motion, as she felt herself weaken. She never knowingly let go of the book, but there was a moment where she was no longer a person reading it, and a consequent moment where there was no book – or library – at all.

The Three Horseshoes

Nora was standing outside in crisp, clean air. But unlike in Bedford, it wasn't raining here.

'Where am I?' she whispered to herself.

There was a small row of quaint stone terraced houses on the other side of the gently curving road. Quiet, old houses, with all their lights off, nestled at the edge of a village before fading into the stillness of the countryside. A clear sky, an expanse of dotted stars, a waning crescent moon. The smell of fields. The two-way twit-twoo of tawny owls. And then quiet again. A quiet that had a presence, that was a force in the air.

Weird.

She had been in Bedford. Then in that strange library. And now she was here, on a pretty village road. Without hardly even moving.

On this side of the road, golden light filtered out of a downstairs window. She looked up and saw an elegantly painted pub sign creaking softly in the wind. Overlapping horseshoes underneath carefully italicised words: *The Three Horseshoes.*

In front of her, there was a chalkboard standing on the pavement. She recognised her own handwriting, at its neatest.

THE THREE HORSESHOES
Tuesday Night – Quiz Night
8.30 p.m.
'True knowledge exists in knowing that you know nothing.'
– Socrates (after losing our quiz!!!!)

This was a life where she put four exclamation marks in a row. That was probably what happier, less uptight people did.

A promising omen.

She looked down at what she was wearing. A denim shirt with sleeves rolled halfway up her forearms and jeans and wedge-heeled shoes, none of which she wore in her actual life. She had goosebumps from the cold, and clearly wasn't dressed to be outside for long.

There were two rings on her ring finger. Her old sapphire engagement ring was there – the same one she had taken off, through trembles and tears, over a year ago – accompanied by a simple silver wedding band.

Crackers.

She was wearing a watch. Not a digital one, in this life. An elegant, slender analogue one, with Roman numerals. It was about a minute after midnight.

How is this happening?

Her hands were smoother in this life. Maybe she used hand cream. Her nails shone with clear polish. There was some comfort in seeing the familiar small mole on her left hand.

Footsteps crunched on gravel. Someone was heading towards her down the driveway. A man, visible from the light of the pub windows and the solitary streetlamp. A man with rosy cheeks and grey Dickensian whiskers and a wax jacket. A Toby jug made flesh. He seemed, from his overly careful gait, to be slightly drunk.

'Goodnight, Nora. I'll be back on Friday. For the folk singer. Dan said he's a good one.'

In this life she probably knew the man's name. 'Right. Yes, of course. Friday. It should be a great night.'

At least her voice sounded like her. She watched as the man crossed the road, looking left and right a few times despite the clear absence of traffic, and disappearing down a lane between the cottages.

It was really happening. This was actually it. This was the pub life. This was the dream made reality.

'This is so very weird,' she said into the night. 'So. Very. Weird.'

A group of three left the pub then too. Two women and a man. They smiled at Nora as they walked past.

'We'll win next time,' one of the women said.

'Yes,' replied Nora. 'There's always a next time.'

She walked up to the pub and peeked through the window. It seemed empty inside, but the lights were still on. That group must have been the last to leave.

The pub looked very inviting. Warm and characterful. Small tables and timber beams and a wagon wheel attached to a wall. A rich red carpet and a wood-panelled bar full of an impressive array of beer pumps.

She stepped away from the window and saw a sign just beyond the pub, past where the pavement became grass.

Quickly, she trotted over and read what it said.

LITTLEWORTH
Welcomes Careful Drivers

Then she noticed in the top centre of the sign a little coat of arms around which orbited the words *Oxfordshire County Council*.

'We did it,' she whispered into the country air. 'We *actually* did it.'

This was the dream Dan had first mentioned to her while walking by the Seine in Paris, eating macarons they had bought on the Boulevard Saint-Michel.

A dream not of Paris but of rural England, where they would live together.

A pub in the Oxfordshire countryside.

When Nora's mum's cancer aggressively returned, reaching her lymph nodes and rapidly colonising her body, that dream was put on hold and Dan moved with her from London back to Bedford. Her mum had known of their engagement and had planned to stay alive long enough for the wedding. She had died four months too soon.

Maybe this was it. Maybe this was the life. Maybe this was first-time lucky, or second-time lucky.

She allowed herself an apprehensive smile.

She walked back along the path and crunched over the gravel, heading towards the side door the drunken, whiskery man in the wax jacket had recently departed from. She took a deep breath and stepped inside.

It was warm.

And quiet.

She was in some kind of hallway or corridor. Terracotta floor tiles. Low wood panelling and, above, wallpaper full of illustrations of sycamore leaves.

She walked down the little corridor and into the main pub area which she had peeked at through the window. She jumped as a cat appeared out of nowhere.

An elegant, angular chocolate Burmese purring away. She bent down and stroked it and looked at the engraved name on the disc attached to the collar. *Voltaire.*

A different cat, with the same name. Unlike her dear beloved ginger tabby, she doubted this Voltaire was a rescue. The cat began to purr. 'Hello, Volts Number Two. You seem happy here. Are we all as happy as you?'

The cat purred a possible affirmation and rubbed his head against Nora's leg. She picked him up and went over to the bar. There was a row of craft beers on the pumps, stouts and ciders and pale ales and IPAs. *Vicar's Favourite. Lost and Found. Miss Marple. Sleeping Lemons. Broken Dream.*

There was a charity tin on the bar for Butterfly Conservation.

She heard the sound of clinking glass. As if a dishwasher was being filled. Nora felt anxiety constrict her chest. A familiar sensation. Then a spindly twenty-something man in a baggy rugby top popped up from behind the bar, hardly giving any attention to Nora as he gathered the last remaining used glasses and put them in the dishwasher. He switched it on then pulled down his coat from a hook, put it on and took out some car keys.

'Bye, Nora. I've done the chairs and wiped all the tables. Dishwasher's on.'

'Ah, thanks.'

'Till Thursday.'

'Yes,' Nora said, feeling like a spy about to have her cover blown. 'See you.'

A moment after the man left, she heard footsteps rising up from somewhere below, heading across the tiles she had just walked down, coming from the back of the pub. And then he was there.

He looked different.

The beard had gone, and there were more wrinkles around his eyes, dark circles. He had a nearly finished pint of dark beer in his hand. He still looked a bit like a TV vet, just a few more series down the line.

'Dan,' she said, as if he was something that needed identifying. Like a rabbit by the road. 'I just want to say I am so proud of you. So proud of us.'

He looked at her, blankly. 'Was just turning the chiller units off. Got to clean the lines tomorrow. We've left it a fortnight.'

Nora had no idea what he was talking about. She stroked the cat. 'Right. Yes. Of course. The lines.'

Her husband – for in this life, that was who he was – looked around at all the tables and upside-down chairs. He was wearing a faded *Jaws* T-shirt. 'Have Blake and Sophie gone home?'

Nora hesitated. She sensed he was talking about people who

worked for them. The young man in the baggy rugby top was presumably Blake. There didn't seem to be anyone else around.

'Yes,' she said, trying to sound natural despite the fundamental bizarreness of the circumstances. 'I think they have. They were pretty on top of things.'

'Cool.'

She remembered buying him the *Jaws* T-shirt on his twenty-sixth birthday. Ten years previously.

'The answers tonight were something else. One of the teams – the one Pete and Jolie were on – thought Maradona painted the Sistine ceiling.'

Nora nodded and stroked Volts Number Two. As if she had any idea who on earth Pete and Jolie were.

'To be fair, it was a tricky one tonight. Might take them from another website next time. I mean, who actually knows the name of the highest mountain in the Kara-whatsit range?'

'Karakoram?' Nora asked. 'That would be K2.'

'Well, obviously you know,' he said, a little too abruptly. A little too tipsily. 'It's the kind of thing you would know. Because while most people were into rock music you were into *actual rocks* and stuff.'

'Hey,' she said. 'I was literally in a band.'

A band, she remembered then, that Dan had hated her being in.

He laughed. She recognised the laugh, but didn't entirely like it. She had forgotten how often during their relationship Dan's humour hinged on other people, specifically Nora. When they'd been together, she had tried not to dwell on this aspect of his personality. He'd had so many other aspects – he had been so lovely to her mum when she was ill, and he could talk at ease about anything, he was so full of dreams about the future, he was attractive and easy to be around, and he was passionate about art and always stopped to chat to the homeless. He cared about the world.

A person was like a city. You couldn't let a few less desirable parts put you off the whole. There may be bits you don't like, a few dodgy side streets and suburbs, but the good stuff makes it worthwhile.

He had listened to a lot of annoying podcasts that he thought Nora should listen to, and laughed in a way that grated on her, and gargled loudly with mouthwash. And yes, he hogged the duvet and could occasionally be arrogant in his opinions on art and film and music, but there was nothing overtly *wrong* with him. Well – now that she thought about it – he'd never been supportive of her music career, and had advised her that being in The Labyrinths and signing a music deal would be bad for her mental health, and that her brother was being a bit selfish. But at the time she had viewed that not so much as a red flag but a green one. Her thinking was: he cared, and it was nice to have someone who cared, who wasn't bothered about fame and superficialities, and could help navigate the waters of life. And so when he had asked her to marry him, in the cocktail bar on the top floor of the Oxo Tower, she had agreed and maybe she had always been right to agree.

He stepped forward into the room, placed his pint down momentarily and was now on his phone, looking up better pub quiz questions.

She wondered how much he had drunk tonight. She wondered if the dream of owning a pub had really been a dream of drinking an endless supply of alcohol.

'What is the name of a twenty-sided polygon?'

'I don't know,' Nora lied, not wanting to risk a similar reaction to the one she'd received a moment ago.

He put the phone in his pocket.

'We did well, though. They all drank loads tonight. Not bad for a Tuesday. Things are looking up. I mean, there's something to tell the bank tomorrow. Maybe they'll give us an extension on the loan . . .'

He stared at the beer in his glass, swilled it around a little, then downed it.

'Though I've got to tell A.J. to change the lunch menu. No one in Littleworth wants to eat candied beetroot and broad bean salad and corn cakes. This isn't pissing Fitzrovia. And I know they're going down well, but I think those wines you chose aren't worth it. Especially the Californian ones.'

'Okay.'

He turned and looked behind him. 'Where's the board?'

'What?'

'The chalkboard. Thought you'd brought it in?'

So *that* was what she had been outside for.

'No. No. I'm going to do it now.'

'Thought I saw you go out.'

Nora smiled away her nerves. 'Yes, well, I did. I had to . . . I was worried about our cat. Volts. Voltaire. I couldn't find him so I went outside to look for him and then I found him, didn't I?'

Dan was back behind the bar, pouring himself a scotch.

He seemed to sense she was judging him. 'This is only my third. Fourth, maybe. It's quiz night. You know I get nervous doing the compering. And it helps me be funny. And I was funny, don't you reckon?'

'Yes. Very funny. Total funniness.'

His face fell into a serious mode. 'I saw you talking to Erin. What did she say?'

Nora wasn't sure how best to answer this. 'Oh, nothing much. The usual stuff. You know Erin.'

'The usual stuff? I didn't think you'd ever spoken to her before.'

'I meant the usual stuff that people say. Not what Erin says. Usual people stuff . . .'

'How's Will doing?'

'Er, really well,' Nora guessed. 'He says hi.'

Dan's eyes popped wide with surprise. 'Really?'

49

Nora had no idea what to say. Maybe Will was a baby. Maybe Will was in a coma. 'Sorry, no, he didn't say hi. Sorry, I'm not thinking. Anyway, I'll . . . go and get the board.'

She put the cat down on the floor and headed back out. This time she noticed something she had missed on entering.

A framed newspaper article from the *Oxford Times* with a picture of Nora and Dan standing outside the Three Horseshoes. Dan had his arm around her. He was wearing a suit she had never seen before and she was in a smart dress she would never have worn (she rarely wore dresses) in her original life.

PUB OWNERS MAKE DREAM A REALITY

They had, according to the article, bought the pub cheaply and in a neglected state and then renovated it with a mix of a modest inheritance (Dan's) and savings and bank loans. The article presented a success story, though it was two years old.

She stepped outside, wondering whether a life could really be judged from just a few minutes after midnight on a Tuesday. Or maybe that was all you needed.

The wind was picking up. Standing out on that quiet village street, the gusts pushed the board a little along the path, nearly toppling it over. Before she picked it up, she felt a buzz from a phone in her pocket. She hadn't realised it was in there. She pulled it out. A text message from Izzy.

She noticed that her wallpaper was a photo of herself and Dan somewhere hot.

She unlocked the phone using facial recognition and opened the message. It was a photo of a whale rising high out of the ocean, the white spray soaking the air like a burst of champagne. It was a wonderful photo and just seeing it caused her to smile.

Izzy was typing.

Another message appeared:

This was one of the pics I took yesterday from the boat.

And another:

Humpback mother

Then another photo: two whales this time, their backs breaking the water.

With calf

The last message also included emojis of whales and waves.

Nora felt a warm glow. Not just from the pictures, which were indisputably lovely, but from the contact with Izzy.

When Nora backed out of her wedding to Dan, Izzy had insisted that she come to Australia with her.

They'd mapped it all out, a plan to live near Byron Bay and get jobs on one of the whale-watching boat cruises.

They had shared lots of clips of humpback whales in anticipation of this new adventure. But then Nora had wobbled and backed out. Just like she had backed out of a swimming career, and a band, and a wedding. But unlike those other things, there hadn't even been a *reason*. Yes, she had started working at String Theory and, yes, she felt the need to tend to her parents' graves, but she knew that staying in Bedford was the worse option. And yet she picked it. Because of some strange predictive homesickness that festered alongside a depression that told her, ultimately, she didn't *deserve* to be happy. That she had hurt Dan and that a life of drizzle and depression in her hometown was her punishment, and she hadn't the will or clarity or, hell, the *energy* to do anything.

So, in effect, she swapped her best friend for a cat.

In her actual life, she had never fallen out with Izzy. Nothing that dramatic. But after Izzy had gone to Australia, things had faded between them until their friendship became just a vapour trail of sporadic Facebook and Instagram likes and emoji-filled birthday messages.

She looked back through the text conversations between her and Izzy and realised that even though there was still ten thousand miles between them, they had a much better relationship in this version of things.

When she returned to the pub, carrying the sign this time, Dan was nowhere to be seen so she locked the back door and waited a while, in the pub hallway, working out where the stairs were, and unsure if she actually wanted to follow her tipsy sort-of husband up there.

She found the stairs at the rear of the building, through a door that said *Staff Only*. As she stepped on the beige raffia carpet heading towards the stairs, just after a framed poster of *Things You Learn in the Dark* – one of their favourite Ryan Bailey movies which they had watched together at the Odeon in Bedford – she noted a smaller picture on a sweet little window sill.

It was their wedding photo. Black and white, reportage-style. Walking out of a church into a shower of confetti. It was difficult to see their faces properly but they were both laughing and it was a shared laugh, and they seemed – as far as a photograph can tell you anything – to be in love. She remembered her mum talking about Dan. ('He's a good one. You're so lucky. Keep hold of him.')

She saw her brother Joe too, shaven-headed and looking genuinely happy, champagne glass in hand and his short-lived, disastrous investment-banker boyfriend, Lewis, by his side. Izzy was there, and Ravi too, looking more like an accountant than a drummer, standing next to a bespectacled woman she'd never seen before.

While Dan was in the toilet Nora located the bedroom. Although they evidently had money worries – the nervous appointment with the bank confirmed that – the room was expensively furnished.

Smart window blinds. A wide, comfortable-looking bed. The duvet crisp and clean and white.

There were books either side of the bed. In her actual life she hadn't had a book by her bed for at least six months. She hadn't read *anything* for six months. Maybe in this life she had a better concentration span.

She picked up one of the books, *Meditation for Beginners*. Underneath it was a copy of a biography of her favourite philosopher, Henry David Thoreau. There were books on Dan's bedside table too. The last book she remembered him reading had been a biography of Toulouse-Lautrec – *Tiny Giant* – but in this life he was reading a business book called *Zero to Hero: Harnessing Success in Work, Play and Life* and the latest edition of *The Good Pub Guide*.

She felt different in her body. A little healthier, a little stronger, but tense. She patted her stomach and realised that in this life she worked out a bit more. Her hair felt different too. She had a heavy fringe, and – feeling it – she could tell her hair was longer at the back. Her mind felt a little woozy. She must have had at least a couple of glasses of wine.

A moment later she heard the toilet flush. Then she heard gargling. It seemed to be a bit noisier than necessary.

'Are you all right?' Dan asked, when he came into the bedroom. His voice, she realised, didn't sound like she remembered. It sounded emptier. A bit colder. Maybe it was tiredness. Maybe it was stress. Maybe it was beer. Maybe it was marriage.

Maybe it was something else.

It was hard to remember, exactly, what he had sounded like before. What he had been like, precisely. But that was the nature of memory. At university she had done an essay drily titled 'The Principles of Hobbesian Memory and Imagination'. Thomas Hobbes had viewed memory and imagination as pretty much the same thing, and since discovering that she had never entirely trusted her memories.

Outside the window the streetlamp's yellow glow illuminated the desolate village road.

'Nora? You're acting strange. Why are you just standing in the middle of the room? Are you getting ready for bed or are you doing some kind of standing meditation?'

He laughed. He thought he was funny.

He went over to the window and pulled the curtains. Then he took off his jeans and put them on the back of a chair. She stared at him and tried to feel the attraction she had once felt so deeply. It seemed to require a Herculean effort. She hadn't expected this.

Everyone's lives could have ended up an infinite number of ways.

He collapsed heavily on the bed, a whale into the ocean. Picked up *Zero to Hero*. Tried to focus. Put it down. Picked up a laptop by the bed, shoved an earphone into his ear. Maybe he was going to listen to a podcast.

'I'm just thinking about something.'

She began to feel faint. As if she was only half there. She remembered Mrs Elm talking about how disappointment in a life would bring her back to the library. It would feel, she realised, altogether too strange to climb into the same bed with a man she hadn't seen for two years.

She noticed the time on the digital alarm clock. 12:23.

Still with the earphone in his ear, he looked at her again. 'Right, listen, if you don't want to make babies tonight you can just say, you know?'

'What?'

'I mean, I know we'll have to wait another month until you are ovulating again . . .'

'We're trying for a baby? I want a baby?'

'Nora, what's with you? Why are you strange today?'

She took off her shoes. 'I'm not.'

A memory came to her, related to the *Jaws* T-shirt.

A tune, actually. 'Beautiful Sky'.

The day she had bought Dan the *Jaws* T-shirt had been the day she had played him a song she had written for The Labyrinths. 'Beautiful Sky'. It was, she was convinced, the best song she had ever written. And – more than that – it was a happy song to reflect her optimism at that point in her life. It was a song inspired by her new life with Dan. And he had listened to it with a shruggish indifference that had hurt at the time and which she would have addressed if it hadn't been his birthday.

'Yeah,' he'd said. 'It's okay.'

She wondered why that memory had stayed buried, only to rise up now, like the great white shark on his fading T-shirt.

There were other things coming back to her now too. His over-the-top reaction when she'd once told him about a customer – Ash, the surgeon and amateur guitar player who came into String Theory for the occasional songbook – casually asking Nora if she wanted to go for a coffee some time.

(*'Of course I said no. Stop shouting.'*)

Worse, though, was when an A&R man for a major label (or rather, a boutique former indie label with Universal behind them) wanted to sign The Labyrinths. Dan had told her that it was unlikely they'd survive as a couple. He'd also heard a horror story from one of his university friends who'd been in a band that signed to a label and then the label ripped them off and they'd all become unemployed alcoholics or something.

'I could take you with me,' she said. 'I'd get it in the contract. We could go everywhere together.'

'Sorry, Nora. But that's *your* dream. It's not mine.'

Which hurt even more with hindsight, knowing how much – before the wedding – she'd tried to make his dream of a pub in the Oxfordshire countryside become her dream as well.

Dan had always said his concern was for Nora: she'd been having panic attacks while she was in the band, especially when she got anywhere near a stage. But the concern had been at least a little manipulative, now she thought about it.

'I thought,' he was saying now, 'that you were starting to trust me again.'

'Trust you? Dan, why wouldn't I trust you?'

'You know why.'

'Of course I know why,' she lied. 'I just want to hear you say it.'

'Well, since the stuff with Erin.'

She stared at him like he was a Rorschach inkblot in which she saw no clear image.

'Erin? The one I was speaking to tonight?'

'Am I going to be beaten up for ever about one stupid drunken moment?'

On the street outside, the wind was picking up, howling through trees as if attempting a language.

This was the life she had been in mourning for. This was the life she had beaten herself up for not living. This was the timeline she thought she had regretted not existing in.

'One stupid mistake?' she echoed.

'Okay, two.'

It was multiplying.

'Two?'

'I was in a state. You know, the pressure. Of this place. And I was very drunk.'

'You had sex with someone else and it doesn't seem you have been seeking much . . . atonement.'

'Seriously, why drag all this up? We've been through this. Remember what the counsellor said. About focusing on where we want to go rather than where we have been.'

'Do you ever think that maybe we just aren't right for each other?'

'What?'

'I love you, Dan. And you can be a very kind person. And you were great with my mum. And we used to – I mean, we *have* great conversations. But do you ever feel that we passed where we were meant to be? That we changed?'

She sat down on the edge of the bed. The furthest corner away from him.

'Do you ever feel lucky to have me? Do you realise how close I was to leaving you, two days before the wedding? Do you know how messed up you would have been if I hadn't turned up at the wedding?'

'Wow. Really? You have yourself in quite high esteem there, Nora.'

'Shouldn't I? I mean, shouldn't everyone? What's wrong with self-esteem? And besides, it's true. There's another universe where you send me WhatsApp messages about how messed up you are without me. How you turn to alcohol, although it seems like you turn to alcohol *with* me too. You send me texts saying you miss my voice.'

He made a dismissive noise, somewhere between a laugh and a grunt. 'Well, right now, I am most definitely not missing your voice.'

She couldn't get beyond her shoes. She found it hard – maybe impossible – to take off another item of clothing in front of him.

'And stop going on about my drinking.'

'If you are using drink as an excuse for screwing someone else, I can go on about your drinking.'

'I am a country landlord,' scoffed Dan. 'It's what country land-lords do. Be jovial and merry and willing to partake in the many and manifold beverages we sell. Jeez.'

Since when did he speak like this? Did he always speak like this?

'Bloody hell, Dan. '

He didn't even seem bothered. To seem grateful in any way for the universe he was in. The universe she had felt so guilty for not allowing to happen. He reached for his phone, still with his laptop on the duvet. Nora watched him as he scrolled.

'Is this what you imagined? Is the dream working out?'

'Nora, let's not do this heavy shit. Just get to bloody bed.'

'Are you happy, Dan?'

'No one's happy, Nora.'

'Some people are. You used to be. You used to light up when you talked about this. You know, the pub. Before you had it. This is the life you dreamed of. You wanted me and you wanted *this* and yet you've been unfaithful and you drink like a fish and I think you only appreciate me when you don't have me, which is not a great trait to have. What about *my* dreams?'

He was hardly listening. Or trying to look like he wasn't.

'Big fires in California,' he said, almost to himself.

'Well, at least we're not there.'

He put the phone down. Folded his laptop. 'You coming to bed or what?'

She had shrunk for him, but he still hadn't found the space he needed. No more.

'Icosagon,' she told him.

'What?'

'The quiz. Earlier. The twenty-sided polygon. Well, a twenty-sided polygon is called an icosagon. I knew the answer but didn't tell you because I didn't want you to mock me. And now I don't really care because I don't think me knowing some things that you don't should bother you. And also, I am going to go to the bathroom.'

And she left Dan, with his mouth open, and trod gently on the wide floorboards, out of the room.

She reached the bathroom. Switched a light on. There were tingles in her arms and legs and torso. Like electric static in search of a station. She was fading out, she was sure. There wasn't long left here. The disappointment was complete.

It was an impressive bathroom. There was a mirror. She gasped at her reflection. She looked healthier but also older. Her hair made her look like a stranger.

This was not the life she imagined it to be.

And Nora wished the self in the mirror 'Good luck'.

And the moment after that she was back, somewhere inside the Midnight Library, and Mrs Elm was staring at her from a small distance away with a curious smile.

'Well, how did that go?'

The Penultimate Update Nora Had Posted Before She Found Herself Between Life and Death

Do you ever think 'how did I end up here?' Like you are in a maze and totally lost and it's all your fault because you were the one who made every turn? And you know that there are many routes that could have helped you out, because you hear all the people on the outside of the maze who made it through, and they are laughing and smiling. And sometimes you get a glimpse of them through the hedge. A fleeting shape through the leaves. And they seem so damn happy to have made it and you don't resent them, but you do resent yourself for not having their ability to work it all out. Do you? Or is this maze just for me?

Ps. My cat died.

The Chessboard

The shelves of the Midnight Library were quite still again, as if their movement had never even been a possibility.

Nora sensed they were in a different portion of the library now – not a different room as such, as there seemed to be only one infinitely vast room. It was difficult to tell if she really was in a different part of the library as the books were still green, though she seemed closer to a corridor than where she had been. And from here she could see a glimpse of something new through one of the stacks – an office desk and computer, like a basic makeshift open-plan office positioned in the corridor between the aisles.

Mrs Elm wasn't at the office desk. She was sat at a low wooden table right there in front of Nora, and she was playing chess.

'It was different to how I imagined,' said Nora.

Mrs Elm looked like she was halfway through a game.

'It's hard to predict, isn't it?' she asked, looking blankly in front of her as she moved a black bishop across the board to take a white pawn. 'The things that will make us happy.'

Mrs Elm rotated the chessboard through one hundred and eighty degrees. She was, it appeared, playing against herself.

'Yes,' said Nora. 'It is. But what happens to her? To *me*? How does she end up?'

'How do I know? I only know today. I know a lot about today. But I don't know what happens tomorrow.'

'But she'll be there in the bathroom and she won't know how she got there.'

'And have you never walked into a room and wondered what you came in for? Have you never forgotten what you just did? Have you never blanked out or misremembered what you were just doing?'

'Yes, but I was there for half an hour in that life.'

'And that other you won't know that. She will remember what you just did and said. But as if she did and said them.'

Nora let out a deep exhale. 'Dan wasn't like that.'

'People change,' said Mrs Elm, still looking at the chessboard. Her hand lingered over a bishop.

Nora re-thought. 'Or maybe he was like that and I just didn't see it.'

'So,' wondered Mrs Elm, looking at Nora. 'What *are* you feeling?'

'Like I still want to die. I have wanted to die for quite a while. I have carefully calculated that the pain of me living as the bloody disaster that is myself is greater than the pain anyone else will feel if I were to die. In fact, I'm sure it would be a relief. I'm not useful to anyone. I was bad at work. I have disappointed everyone. I am a waste of a carbon footprint, to be honest. I hurt people. I have no one left. Not even poor old Volts, who died because I couldn't look after a cat properly. I want to die. My life is a disaster. And I want it to end. I am not cut out for living. And there is no point going through all this. Because I am clearly destined to be unhappy in other lives too. That is just me. I add nothing. I am wallowing in self-pity. I want to die.'

Mrs Elm studied Nora hard, as if reading a passage in a book she had read before but had just found it contained a new meaning. 'Want,' she told her, in a measured tone, 'is an interesting word. It means lack. Sometimes if we fill that lack with something else the original want disappears entirely. Maybe you have a lack problem rather than a want problem. Maybe there is a life that you really want to live.'

'I thought that was it. The one with Dan. But it wasn't.'

'No, it wasn't. But that is just one of your possible lives. And one into infinity is a very small fraction indeed.'

'Every possible life I could live has me in it. So, it's not really every possible life.' Mrs Elm wasn't listening. 'Now, tell me, where do you want to go now?'

'Nowhere, please.'

'Do you need another look at *The Book of Regrets*?'

Nora scrunched her nose and gave a minute shake of her head. She remembered the feeling of being suffocated by so much regret. 'No.'

'What about your cat? What was his name again?'

'Voltaire. It was a bit pretentious, and he wasn't really a pretentious cat, so I just called him Volts for short. Sometimes Voltsy, if I was feeling jovial. Which was rare, obviously. I couldn't even finalise a name for a cat.'

'Well, you said you were bad at having a cat. What would you have done differently?'

Nora thought. She had the very real sense that Mrs Elm was playing some kind of game with her, but she also wanted to see her cat again, and not simply a cat with the same name. In fact, she wanted it more than anything.

'Okay. I'd like to see the life where I kept Voltaire indoors. *My* Voltaire. I'd like the life where I didn't try and kill myself and where I was a good cat owner and I didn't let him out onto the road last night. I'd like that life, just for a little while. That life exists, doesn't it?'

The Only Way to Learn Is to Live

Nora looked around and found herself lying in her own bed.

She checked her watch. It was one minute past midnight. She switched on her light. This was her *exact* life, but it was going to be better, because Voltaire was going to be alive in this one. Her real Voltaire.

But where was he?

'Volts?'

She climbed out of bed.

'Volts?'

She looked all over her flat and couldn't find him anywhere. The rain patted against the windows – that much hadn't changed. Her new box of anti-depressants was out on the kitchen unit. The electric piano stood by the wall, silent.

'Voltsy?'

There was her yucca plant and her three tiny potted cacti, there were her bookshelves, with exactly the same mix of philosophy books and novels and untried yoga manuals and rock star biographies and pop science books. An old *National Geographic* with a shark on the cover and a five-month-old copy of *Elle* magazine, which she'd bought mainly for the Ryan Bailey interview. No new additions in a long time.

There was a bowl still full of cat food.

She looked everywhere, calling his name. It was only when she went back into her bedroom and looked under the bed that she saw him.

'Volts!'

The cat wasn't moving.

As her arms weren't long enough to reach him, she moved the bed.

'Voltsy. Come on, Voltsy,' she whispered.

But the moment she touched his cold body she knew, and she was flooded with sadness and confusion. She immediately found herself back in the Midnight Library, facing Mrs Elm, who was sat this time in a comfy chair, deeply absorbed in one of the books.

'I don't understand,' Nora told her.

Mrs Elm kept her eyes on the page she was reading. 'There will be many things you don't understand.'

'I asked for the life in which Voltaire was still alive.'

'Actually, you didn't.'

'What?'

She put her book down. 'You asked for the life where you kept him indoors. That is an entirely different thing.'

'Is it?'

'Yes. Entirely. You see, if you'd have asked for the life where he was still alive I would have had to say no.'

'But why?'

'Because it doesn't exist.'

'I thought every life exists.'

'Every *possible* life. You see, it turns out that Voltaire had a serious case of' – she read carefully from the book – '*restrictive cardio-myopathy*, a severe case of it, which he was born with, and which was destined to cause his heart to go at a young age.'

'But he was hit by a car.'

'There is a difference, Nora, between dying in a road and being hit by a car. In your root life Voltaire lived longer than almost any other life, except the one you've just encountered, where he died only three hours ago. Although he had a tough few early years, the year you had him was the best of his life. Voltaire has had much worse lives, believe me.'

'You didn't even know his name a moment ago. Now you know he had restrictive cardio-whatever?'

'I knew his name. And it wasn't a moment ago. It was the same moment, check your watch.'

'Why did you lie?'

'I wasn't lying. I asked you what your cat's name was. I never said I didn't know what your cat's name was. Do you understand the difference? I just wanted you to say his name, so that you would feel something.'

Nora was hot with agitation now. 'That's even worse! You sent me into that life *knowing* Volts would be dead. And Volts *was* dead. So, nothing changed.'

Mrs Elm's eyes twinkled again. 'Except you.'

'What do you mean?'

'Well, you don't see yourself as a bad cat owner any more. You looked after him as well as he could have been looked after. He loved you as much as you loved him, and maybe he didn't want you to see him die. You see, cats *know*. They understand when their time is up. He went outside *because* he was going to die, and he knew it.'

Nora tried to take this in. Now she thought about it, there hadn't been any external signs of damage on her cat's body. She had just jumped to the same conclusion that Ash had jumped to. That a dead cat on the road was probably dead *because* of the road. And if a surgeon could think that, a mere layperson would think that too. Two plus two equals car accident.

'Poor Volts,' Nora muttered, mournfully.

Mrs Elm smiled, like a teacher who saw a lesson being understood.

'He loved you, Nora. You looked after him as well as anyone could. Go and look at the last page of *The Book of Regrets*.'

Nora could see that the book was lying on the floor. She knelt on the floor beside it.

'I don't want to open it again.'

'Don't worry. It will be safer this time. Just stick to the last page.'

Once she had flicked to the last page, she saw one of her very last regrets – 'I was bad at looking after Voltaire' – slowly disappear from the page. The letters fading like retreating strangers in a fog.

Nora closed the book before she could feel anything bad happen.

'So, you see? Sometimes regrets aren't based on fact at all. Sometimes regrets are just . . .' She searched for the appropriate term and found it. 'A load of *bullshit*.'

Nora tried to think back to her schooldays, to remember if Mrs Elm had said the word 'bullshit' before, and she was pretty sure she hadn't.

'But I still don't get why you let me go into that life if you knew Volts was going to be dead anyway? You could have told me. You could have just told me I wasn't a bad cat owner. Why didn't you?'

'Because, Nora, sometimes the only way to learn is to *live*.'

'Sounds hard.'

'Take a seat,' Mrs Elm told her. 'A proper seat. It's not right, you kneeling on the floor.' And Nora turned to see a chair behind her that she hadn't noticed before. An antique chair – mahogany and buttoned leather, Edwardian maybe – with a brass bookstand attached to one arm. 'Give yourself a moment.'

Nora sat down.

She stared at her watch. No matter how much of a moment she gave herself it stayed being midnight.

'I still don't like this. One life of sadness was enough. What is the point of risking more?'

'Fine.' Mrs Elm shrugged.

'What?'

'Let's do nothing then. You can just stay here in the library with all those lives waiting on the shelves and not choose one.'

Nora sensed Mrs Elm was playing some kind of a game. But she went along with it.

'Fine.'

So Nora just stood there while Mrs Elm picked up her book again.

It seemed unfair to Nora that Mrs Elm could read the lives without falling into them.

Time went by.

Although technically, of course, it didn't.

Nora could have stayed there for ever without getting hungry or thirsty or tired. But she could, it seemed, get bored.

As time stood still, Nora's curiosity about the lives around her slowly grew. It turned out to be near impossible to stand in a library and not want to pull things from the shelves.

'Why can't you just give me a life you know is a good one?' she said suddenly.

'That is not how this library works.'

Nora had another question.

'Surely in most lives I will be asleep now, won't I?'

'In many, yes.'

'So, what happens then?'

'You sleep. And then you wake up in that life. It's nothing to worry about. But if you are nervous, you could try a life where it's another time.'

'What do you mean?'

'Well, it's not night-time everywhere, is it?'

'What?'

'There are an *infinite* number of possible universes in which you live. Are you really saying they all exist on Greenwich Mean Time?'

'Of course not,' said Nora. She realised she was about to cave in and choose another life. She thought of the humpback whales. She thought of the unanswered message. 'I wish I had gone to Australia with Izzy. I would like to experience that life.'

'Very good choice.'

'What? It's a very good life?'

'Oh, I didn't say that. I merely feel that you might be getting better at *choosing*.'

'So, it's a bad life?'

'I didn't say that either.'

And the shelves sped into motion again, then stopped a few seconds afterwards.

'Ah, yes, there it is,' said Mrs Elm, taking a book from the second-to-bottom shelf. She recognised it instantly, which was odd, seeing that it looked almost identical to the others around it.

She handed it to Nora, affectionately, as if it was a birthday gift.

'There you go. You know what to do.'

Nora hesitated.

'What if I am dead?'

'Sorry?'

'I mean, in another life. There must be other lives in which I died before today.'

Mrs Elm looked intrigued. 'Isn't that what you wanted?'

'Well, yes, but—'

'You have died an infinite number of times before today, yes. Car accident, drug overdose, drowning, a bout of fatal food poisoning, choking on an apple, choking on a cookie, choking on a vegan hot dog, choking on a non-vegan hot dog, every illness it was possible for you to catch or contract . . . You have died in every way you can, at any time you could.'

'So, I could open a book and just die?'

'No. Not instantaneously. As with Voltaire, the only lives available here are, well, *lives*. I mean, you could *die* in that life, but you won't have died *before* you enter the life because this Midnight Library is not one of ghosts. It is not a library of corpses. It is a library of possibility. And death is the opposite of possibility. Understand?'

'I think so.'

And Nora stared at the book she had been handed. Conifer

green. Smooth-textured, again embossed with that broad and frustratingly meaningless title **My Life.**

She opened it and saw a blank page, so she moved to the next page and wondered what was going to happen this time. '**The swimming pool was a little busier than normal . . .**'

And then she was there.

Fire

She gasped. The sensations were sudden. The noise and the water. She had her mouth open and she choked. The tang and sting of salt water.

She tried to touch her feet on the bottom of the pool but she was out of her depth so she quickly slipped into breaststroke mode.

A swimming pool, but a salt-water one. Outdoor, beside the ocean. Carved seemingly out of the rock that jutted out of the coastline. She could see the actual ocean just beyond. There was sunshine overhead. The water was cool, but given the heat of the air above her the cool was welcome.

Once upon a time she had been the best fourteen-year-old female swimmer in Bedfordshire.

She had won two races in her age category at the National Junior Swimming Championships. Freestyle 400 metres. Freestyle 200 metres. Her dad had driven her every day to the local pool. Sometimes before school as well as after. But then – while her brother rocked out on his guitar to Nirvana – she traded lengths for scales, and taught herself how to play not just Chopin but classics like 'Let It Be' and 'Rainy Days And Mondays'. She also began, before The Labyrinths were even a figment of her brother's imagination, to compose her own music.

But she hadn't really gone off swimming, just the pressure around it.

She reached the side of the pool. Stopped and looked around. She could see a beach at a lower level in the distance, curving around in a semi-circle to welcome the sea lapping on its sand.

Beyond the beach, inland, a stretch of grass. A park, complete with palm trees and distant dog walkers.

Beyond that, houses and low-rise apartment blocks, and traffic sliding by on a road. She had seen pictures of Byron Bay, and it didn't look quite like this. This place, wherever it was, seemed a little more built-up. Still surferish, but also urban.

Turning her attention back to the pool, she noticed a man smile at her as he adjusted his goggles. Did she know this man? Would she welcome this smile in this life? Having no idea, she offered the smallest of polite smiles in return. She felt like a tourist with an unfamiliar currency, not knowing how much to tip.

Then an elderly woman in a swimming cap smiled at her as she glided through the water towards her.

'Morning, Nora,' she said, not breaking her stroke.

It was a greeting that suggested Nora was a regular here.

'Morning,' Nora said.

She stared out at the ocean, to avoid any awkward chatting. A flock of morning surfers, speck-sized, swam on their boards to greet large sapphire-blue waves.

This was a promising start to her Australian life. She stared at her watch. It was a bright orange, cheap-looking Casio. A happy-looking watch suggestive, she hoped, of a happy-feeling life. It was just after nine a.m. here. Next to her watch was a plastic wristband with a key on it.

So, this was her morning ritual here. In an outdoor swimming pool beside a beach. She wondered if she was here alone. She scanned the pool hopefully for any sign of Izzy, but none was there.

She swam some more.

The thing she had once loved about swimming was the disappearing. In the water, her focus had been so pure that she thought of nothing else. Any school or home worries vanished. The art of swimming – she supposed like any art – was about purity. The more focused you were on the activity, the less focused you were on everything else. You kind of stopped being you and became the thing you were doing.

But it was hard to stay focused when Nora noticed her arms and chest ached. She sensed it had been a long swim and was probably time to get out of the pool. She saw a sign. *Bronte Beach Swimming Pool*. She vaguely remembered Dan, who had been to Australia in his gap year, talking about this place and the name had stuck – Bronte Beach – because it was easy to remember. Jane Eyre on a surfboard.

But here was confirmation of her doubt.

Bronte Beach was in Sydney. But it most definitely wasn't part of Byron Bay.

So that meant one of two things. Either Izzy, in this life, wasn't in Byron Bay. Or Nora wasn't with Izzy.

She noticed she was tanned a mild caramel all over.

Of course, the trouble was, she didn't know where her clothes were. But then she remembered the plastic wristband with a key on it.

57. Her locker was 57. So she found the changing rooms and opened the squat, square locker and saw that her taste in clothes, as well as watches, was more colourful in this life. She had a T-shirt with a pineapple print on it. A whole cornucopia of pineapples. And pink-purple denim shorts. And slip-on checked pumps.

What am I? she wondered. *A children's TV presenter?*

Sun-block. Hibiscus tinted lip balm. No other make-up as such.

As she pulled on her T-shirt, she noticed a couple of marks on her arm. Scar-lines. She wondered, momentarily, if they had been self-inflicted. There was also a tattoo just below her shoulder. A Phoenix and flames. It was a terrible tattoo. In this life, she clearly had no taste. But since when did taste have anything to do with happiness?

She dressed and pulled out a phone from her shorts pocket.

This was an older model than in her married-and-living-in-a-pub life. Luckily, a thumb-reading was enough to unlock it.

She left the changing rooms and walked along a beachside path. It was a warm day. Maybe life was automatically better when the sun shone so confidently in April. Everything seemed more vivid, more colourful and *alive* than it had done in England.

She saw a parrot – a sky-blue and banana-yellow macaw – perched on the top of a bench, being photographed by a couple of tourists. A surfy-looking cyclist passed by holding an orange smoothie, smiling and literally saying, 'G'day.'

This was most definitely not Bedford.

Nora noticed something was happening to her face. She was – could she be? – *smiling*. And naturally, not just because someone expected her to.

Then she noted a piece of graffiti on a low wall which said THE WORLD IS ON FIRE and another that said ONE EARTH = ONE CHANCE and her smile faded. After all, a different life didn't mean a different planet.

She had no idea where she lived or what she did or where she was meant to be heading after the swimming pool, but there was something quite freeing about that. To be existing without any expectation, even her own. As she walked, she googled her own name and added 'Sydney' to see if it brought up anything.

Before she scanned the results she glanced up and noticed a man walking on the path towards her, smiling. A short, tanned man with kind eyes and long thinning hair in a loose ponytail with a shirt that wasn't buttoned correctly.

'Hey, Nora.'

'Hey,' she said, trying not to sound confused.

'What time you start today?'

How could she answer that? 'Uh. Oh. Crap. I've totally forgotten.'

He laughed, a little laugh of recognition, as if her forgetting was quite in character.

74

'I saw it on the rota. I think it might be eleven.'

'Eleven a.m.?'

Kind Eyes laughed. 'What've you been smoking? I want some.'

'Ha. Nothing,' she said, stiffly. 'I've not been smoking anything. I just skipped breakfast.'

'Well, see you this arvo . . .'

'Yes. At the . . . place. Where is it again?'

He laughed, frowningly, and kept walking. Maybe she worked on a whale sight-seeing cruise that operated out of Sydney. Maybe Izzy did too.

Nora had no idea where she (or they) lived, and nothing was coming up on Google, but away from the ocean seemed the right direction. Maybe she was very local. Maybe she had walked here. Maybe one of the bikes she saw locked up outside the pool café had been hers. She rummaged in her tiny clasp wallet and felt her pockets for a key, but there was only a house key. No car keys, no bike keys. So it was a bus or by foot. The house key had no information on it at all, so she sat on a bench with the sun beating hard on the back of her neck and checked her texts.

There were names of people she didn't recognise.

Amy. Rodhri. Bella. Lucy P. Kemala. Luke. Lucy M.

Who are these people?

And a rather unhelpful contact titled, simply: 'Work'. And there was only one recent message from 'Work' and it said:

Where r u?

There was one name she recognised.

Dan.

Her heart sank as she clicked on his most recent message.

Hey Nor! Hope Oz is treating you well. This is going to sound either corny or creepy but I am going to go all out and tell you. I had a dream the other night about our pub. It was such a good dream. We were so happy! Anyway, ignore that weirdness, the point of this is to say: guess where I'm going in May? AUSTRALIA. First time in over a decade. Am coming with work. I'm working with MCA. Would be great to catch up, even for a coffee if you're around. D x

It was so strange she almost laughed. But she coughed instead. (Maybe she wasn't quite so fit in this life, now she thought about it.) She wondered how many Dans there were in the world, dreaming of things they would hate if they actually got them. And how many were pushing other people into their delusional idea of happiness?

Instagram seemed to be the only social media she had here, and she only seemed to post pictures of poems on it.

She took a moment to read one:

FIRE
Every part of her
That changed
That got scraped off
Because of schoolyard laughter
Or the advice of grown-ups
Long gone –
And the pain of friends
Already dead.
She collected those bits off the floor.
Like wood shavings.
And she made them into fuel.
Into **fire**.
And burned.
Bright enough to see **for ever**.

This was troubling, but it was – after all – just a poem. Scrolling through some emails, she found one to Charlotte – a ceilidh band flautist with earthy humour who'd been Nora's only friend at String Theory before she had moved back up to Scotland.

Hi Charl!
Hope all is fine and dandy.
   Pleased the birthday do went well. Sorry I couldn't be there. All is well in sunny Sydney. Have finally moved into the new place. It's right near Bronte Beach (beautiful). Lots of neighbourhood cafes and charm. I also have a new job.
   I go swimming in a saltwater pool every morning and every evening I drink a glass of Australian wine in the sunshine. Life is good!
   Address:
2/29 Darling Street
Bronte
NSW 2024
AUSTRALIA
Nora
X

Something was rotten. The tone of vague, distant perkiness, as if writing to a long-lost aunt. The *Lots of neighbourhood cafes and charm*, as though it was a TripAdvisor review. She didn't speak to Charlotte – or indeed *anyone* – like that.

There was also no mention of Izzy. *Have finally moved into the new place.* Was that *we* have or *I* have? Charlotte knew of Izzy. Why not mention her?

She would soon find out. Indeed, twenty minutes later she was standing in the hallway of her apartment, staring at four bags of rubbish that needed taking out. The living room looked small and depressing. The sofa tatty and old. The place smelt slightly mouldy.

There was a poster on the wall for the video game *Angel* and a vape pen on a coffee table, with a marijuana leaf sticker on it. A woman was staring at a screen, shooting zombies in the head.

The woman had short blue hair and for a moment Nora thought it might be Izzy.

'Hi,' Nora said.

The woman turned. She was not Izzy. She had sleepy eyes and a vacant expression, as if the zombies she was shooting had slightly infected her. She was probably a perfectly decent person but she was not anyone Nora had ever seen in her life. She smiled.

'Hey. How's that new poem coming along?'

'Oh. Yeah. It's coming along really well. Thanks.'

Nora walked around the flat in a bit of a daze. She opened a door at random and realised it was the bathroom. She didn't need the toilet, but she needed a second to think. So she shut the door and washed her hands and stared at the water spiral down the plughole the wrong way.

She glanced at the shower. The dull yellow curtain was dirty in a vague student-house kind of way. That's what this place reminded her of. A student house. She was thirty-five and, in this life, living like a student. She saw some anti-depressants – fluoxetine – beside the basin, and picked up the box. She read *Prescription for N. Seed* at the top of the label. She looked down at her arm and saw the scars again. It was weird, to have your own body offer clues to a mystery.

There was a magazine on the floor next to the bin, *National Geographic*. The one with the black hole on its cover that she had been reading in another life, on the other side of the world, only yesterday. She sensed it was her magazine, given she had always liked reading it, and had been known – even in recent times – to buy it on the occasional spontaneous whim as no online version ever did the photos justice.

She remembered being eleven years old and looking at the photos of Svalbard, the Norwegian archipelago in the Arctic, in her dad's copy. It had looked so vast and desolate and powerful and she had wondered what it would have been like to be among it, like the scientist-explorers in the article, spending their summer doing some kind of geological research. She cut out the pictures and they ended up on the pinboard in her bedroom. And for many years, at school, she had tried hard at science and geography just so she could be like the scientists in the article and spend her summers among frozen mountains and fjords, as puffins flew overhead.

But after her dad died, and after reading Nietzsche's *Beyond Good and Evil*, she decided that a) Philosophy seemed to be the only subject that matched her sudden inward intensity and b) she wanted to be a rock star more than a scientist anyway.

After leaving the bathroom, she returned to her mysterious flatmate.

She sat on the sofa and waited for a few moments, watching.

The woman's avatar got shot in the head.

'Piss off, you zombie fuckface,' the woman snarled happily at the screen.

She picked up the vape pen. Nora wondered how she knew this woman. She was assuming they were flatmates.

'I've been thinking about what you said.'

'What did I say?' Nora asked.

'About doing some cat-sitting. You know, you wanted to look after that cat?'

'Oh yeah. Sure. I remember.'

'Bad fucking idea, man.'

'Really?'

'Cats.'

'What about them?'

'They've got a parasite. Toxoplas-something.'

Nora knew this. She had known this since she was a teen, doing her work experience at Bedford Animal Rescue Centre. 'Toxoplasmosis.'

'That's it! Well, I was listening to this podcast, right . . . and there's this theory that this international group of billionaires infected the cats with it so that they could take over the world by making humans dumber and dumber. I mean, think about it. There are cats *everywhere*. I was talking to Jared about this and Jared said, "Jojo, what are you smoking?" And I was like, "The stuff you gave me" and he said, "Yeah, I know." Then he told me about the grass-hoppers.'

'Grasshoppers?'

'Yeah. Did you hear about grasshoppers?' Jojo asked.

'What about them?'

'They are all killing themselves. Because this parasitic worm grows inside them, to become like a full-grown aquatic creature, and as it grows it takes over the brain function of the grasshopper, so the grasshopper thinks, "Hey, I really like water" and so they divebomb into water and die. And it's happening all the time. Google it. Google "grasshopper suicide". Anyway, the point is, the elites are killing us via cats and so you shouldn't be near them.'

Nora couldn't help thinking how different this life was to her imagined version of it. She had pictured herself and Izzy on a boat near Byron Bay, marvelling at the magnificence of humpback whales, and yet she was here in a small pot-scented apartment in Sydney, with a conspiracy theorist as a flatmate who wouldn't even let her near a cat.

'What happened to Izzy?'

Nora realised she had just asked the question out loud.

Jojo looked confused. 'Izzy? Your old friend Izzy?'

'Yeah.'

'The one who died?'

The words came so fast Nora could hardly absorb them.

'Um, what?'

'The car crash girl?'

'What?'

Jojo looked confused, as curls of smoke wisped across her face. 'You okay, Nora?' She held out the joint. 'Wanna toke?'

'No, I'm okay thanks.'

Jojo chuckled. 'Makes a change.'

Nora grabbed her phone. Went online. Typed 'Isabel Hirsh' into the search box. Then clicked 'News'.

There it was. A headline. Above a picture of Izzy's tanned face, smiling.

BRITISH WOMAN KILLED
IN NSW ROAD COLLISION

A woman, 33, was killed and three people hospitalised south of Coffs Harbour last night when the woman's Toyota Corolla collided with a car travelling in the opposite direction on the Pacific Highway.

The female driver, identified as British citizen Isabel Hirsh, died at the scene of the accident just before 9pm. She was the only person in the Toyota.

According to her flatmate, Nora Seed, Isabel had been driving from Brisbane back to Byron Bay, to attend Nora's birthday party. Isabel had recently started working for Byron Bay Whale Watching Tours.

'I am totally devastated,' Nora said. 'We travelled to Australia together only a month ago and Izzy had planned to stay here for as long as possible. She was such a force of life that it feels impossible to imagine the world without her in it. She was so excited about her new job. It is so unbearably sad and hard to comprehend.'

The passengers of the other car all suffered injuries, and the driver – Chris Dale – had to be airlifted to the hospital at Baringa.

New South Wales Police are asking anyone who witnessed the collision to come forward to help with their enquiries.

'Oh my God,' she whispered to herself, feeling faint. 'Oh, Izzy.'

She knew that Izzy wasn't dead in all her lives. Or even most of them. But in this one it was real, and the grief Nora felt felt real too. The grief was familiar and terrifying and laced with guilt.

Before she could properly process anything, the mobile rang. It said 'Work'.

A man's voice. A slow drawl. 'Where are you?'

'What?'

'You were meant to be here half an hour ago.'

'Where?'

'The ferry terminal. You're selling tickets. I've got the correct number, right? This is Nora Seed I'm talking to?'

'It's one of them,' sighed Nora, as she gently faded away.

Fish Tank

The shrewd-eyed librarian was back at her chessboard and hardly looked up as Nora arrived back.

'Well, that was terrible.'

Mrs Elm smiled, wryly. 'It just shows you, doesn't it?'

'Shows me what?'

'Well, that you can choose choices but not outcomes. But I stand by what I said. It was a good choice. It just wasn't a desired outcome.'

Nora studied Mrs Elm's face. Was she *enjoying* this?

'Why did I stay?' Nora asked. 'Why didn't I just come home, after she died?'

Mrs Elm shrugged. 'You got stuck. You were grieving. You were depressed. You know what depression is like.'

Nora understood this. She thought of a study she had read about somewhere, about fish. Fish were more like humans than most people think.

Fish get depression. They had done tests with zebrafish. They had a fish tank and they drew a horizontal line on the side of it, halfway down, in marker pen. Depressed fish stayed below the line. But give those same fish Prozac and they go above the line, to the top of their tanks, darting about like new.

Fish get depressed when they have a lack of stimulation. A lack of *everything*. When they are just there, floating in a tank that resembles nothing at all.

Maybe Australia had been her empty fish tank, once Izzy had gone. Maybe she just had no incentive to swim above the line. And maybe even Prozac – or fluoxetine – wasn't enough to help her rise up. So she was just going to stay there in that flat, with Jojo, and never move until she was made to leave the country.

Maybe even suicide would have been too *active*. Maybe in some lives you just float around and expect nothing else and don't even try to change. Maybe that was most lives.

'Yes,' said Nora, aloud now. 'Maybe I got stuck. Maybe in every life I am stuck. I mean, maybe that's just who I am. A starfish in every life is still a starfish. There isn't a life where a starfish is a professor of aerospace engineering. And maybe there isn't a life where I'm not stuck.'

'Well, I think you are wrong.'

'Okay, then. I would like to try the life where I am not stuck. What life would that be?'

'Aren't you supposed to tell *me*?'

Mrs Elm moved a queen to take a pawn, then turned the board around. 'I'm afraid I am just the librarian.'

'Librarians have knowledge. They guide you to the right books. The right worlds. They find the best places. Like soul-enhanced search engines.'

'Exactly. But you also have to know what you like. What to type into the metaphorical search box. And sometimes you have to try a few things before that becomes clear.'

'I haven't got the stamina. I don't think I can do this.'

'The only way to learn is to live.'

'Yes. So you keep saying.'

Nora exhaled heavily. It was interesting to know that she could exhale in the library. That she felt entirely in her body. That it felt normal. Because this place was definitely *not* normal. And the real physical her wasn't here. It couldn't be. And yet it was, to all intents and purposes, because she was – in some sense – there. Standing on a floor, as if gravity still existed.

'Okay,' she said. 'I would like a life where I am successful.'

Mrs Elm tutted disapprovingly. 'For someone who has read a lot of books, you aren't very specific with your choice of words.'

'Sorry.'

'Success. What does that mean to you? Money?'

'No. Well, maybe. But that wouldn't be the defining feature.'

'Well, then, what is success?'

Nora had no idea what success was. She had felt like a failure for so long.

Mrs Elm smiled, patiently. 'Would you like to consult again with *The Book of Regrets*? Would you like to think about those bad decisions that turned you away from whatever you feel success is?'

Nora shook her head quickly, like a dog shaking off water. She didn't want to be confronted with that long interminable list of mistakes and wrong turns again. She was depressed enough. And besides, she knew her regrets. Regrets don't leave. They weren't mosquito bites. They itch for ever.

'No, they don't,' said Mrs Elm, reading her mind. 'You don't regret how you were with your cat. And nor do you regret not going to Australia with Izzy.'

Nora nodded. Mrs Elm had a point.

She thought of swimming in the pool at Bronte Beach. How good that had felt, in its strange familiarity.

'From an early age you were encouraged to swim,' said Mrs Elm.

'Yes.'

'Your dad was always happy to take you to the pool.'

'It was one of the few things that had made him happy,' Nora mused.

She had associated swimming with her father's approval and enjoyed the wordlessness of being in the water because it was the opposite of her parents screaming at each other.

'Why did you quit?' asked Mrs Elm.

'As soon as I started winning swimming races, I became *seen* and I didn't want to be seen. And not only seen but seen in a swimsuit at the exact age you are self-obsessing about your body. Someone said I had boy's shoulders. It was a stupid thing but there were lots of stupid things and you feel them all at that age. As a teenager I'd have happily been invisible. People called me "The Fish". They didn't mean it as a compliment. I was shy. It was one of the reasons why I preferred the library to the playing field. It seems a small thing, but it really helped, having that space.'

'Never underestimate the big importance of small things,' Mrs Elm said. 'You must always remember that.'

Nora thought back. Her teenage combination of shyness and visibility had been a problematic mix, but she was never bullied, as such, probably because everyone knew her brother. And Joe, while never exactly tough, was always considered cool and popular enough for his most immediate blood relation to be immune to schoolyard tyranny.

She won races in local and then national competitions, but as she reached fifteen it became too much. The daily swims, length after length after length.

'I had to quit.'

Mrs Elm nodded. 'And the bond you'd developed with your dad frayed and almost snapped completely.'

'Pretty much.'

She pictured her father's face, in the car, on a drizzle-scratched Sunday morning outside Bedford Leisure Centre, as she told him she didn't want to swim in competitions any more. That look of disappointment and profound frustration.

'But you could make a success of your life,' he had said. Yes. She remembered it now. 'You're never going to be a pop star, but this is something *real*. It's right in front of you. If you keep training, you'll end up at the Olympics. I know it.'

She had been cross with him saying that. As if there was a very thin path to a happy life and it was the path he had decided for her. As if her own agency in her own life was automatically wrong.

But what she didn't fully appreciate at fifteen years of age was just how bad regret could feel, and how much her father had felt that pain of being so near to the realisation of a dream he could almost touch it.

Nora's father, it was true, had been a difficult man.

As well as being highly critical of everything Nora did, and everything Nora wanted and everything Nora believed, unless it was related to swimming, Nora had also felt that simply to be in his presence was to commit some kind of invisible crime. Ever since the ligament injury that thwarted his rugby career, he'd had a sincere conviction that the universe was against him. And Nora was, at least *she* felt, considered by him as part of that same universal plan. From that moment in that car park she had felt she was really just an extension of the pain in his left knee. A walking wound.

But maybe he had known what would happen. Maybe he could foresee the way one regret would lead to another, until suddenly that was all she was. A whole book of regrets.

'Okay, Mrs Elm. I want to know what happened in the life where I did what my father wanted. Where I trained as hard as I possibly could. Where I never moaned about a five a.m. start or a nine p.m. finish. Where I swam every day and never thought about quitting. Where I didn't get sidelined by music or writing unfinished novels. Where I sacrificed everything else on the altar of freestyle. Where I didn't give up. Where I did everything right in order to reach the Olympics. Take me to where I am in *that* life.'

For a moment it seemed as though Mrs Elm hadn't been taking any notice of Nora's mini-speech, as she kept frowning at the chessboard, working out how to out-manoeuvre herself.

'The rook is my favourite piece,' she said. 'It's the one that you think you don't have to watch out for. It is straightforward. You keep your eye on the queen, and the knights, and the bishop, because they are the sneaky ones. But it's the rook that often gets you. The straightforward is never quite what it seems.'

Nora realised Mrs Elm was probably not talking just about chess. But the shelves were moving now. Fast as trains.

'This life you've asked for,' explained Mrs Elm, 'is a little bit further away from the pub dream and the Australian adventure. Those were closer lives. This one involves a lot of different choices, going back further in time. And so the book is a little further away, you see?'

'I see.'

'Libraries have to have a system.'

The books slowed. 'Ah, here we are.'

This time Mrs Elm didn't stand up. She simply raised her left hand and a book flew towards her.

'How did you do that?'

'I have no idea. Now here's the life you asked for. Off you go.'

Nora took hold of the book. Light, fresh, lime-coloured. She turned to the first page. And this time she was aware of feeling absolutely nothing at all.

The Last Update That Nora Had Posted Before She Found Herself Between Life and Death

I miss my cat. I'm tired.

The Successful Life

She had been asleep.

A deep, dreamless nothing, and now – thanks to the ring of a phone alarm – she was awake and didn't know where she was.

The phone told her it was 6:30 a.m. A light switch beside the bed appeared, thanks to the glow of the screen. Switching it on, she could see she was in a hotel room. It was rather plush, in a bland and blue and corporate kind of way.

A tasteful semi-abstract sub-Cezanne painting of an apple – or maybe a pear – was framed on the wall.

There was a half-empty cylinder-shaped glass bottle of still mineral water beside the bed. And an unopened collection of shortbread biscuits. Some printed-out papers too, stapled together. A timetable of some sort.

She looked at it.

ITINERARY FOR NORA SEED OBE, GUEST SPEAKER,
GULLIVER RESEARCH INSPIRING SUCCESS
SPRING CONFERENCE

8.45 a.m. Meet Priya Navuluri (Gulliver Research) and
Rory Longford (Celebrity Speakers) and J in lobby,
InterContinental Hotel

9.00 a.m. Soundcheck.

9.05 a.m. Tech run-through.

9.30 a.m. Nora to wait in VIP area or watch first speaker in main hall (JP Blythe, inventor of MeTime app and author of *Your Life, Your Terms*)

10.15 a.m. Nora to deliver talk

10.45 a.m. Audience Q + A

11.00 a.m. Meet and greet

11.30 a.m. Finish

Nora Seed OBE.
Inspiring Success.

So, there *was* a life in which she was a success. Well, that was something.

She wondered who 'J' was, and the other people she was supposed to meet in the lobby, and then she put the sheet of paper down and got out of bed. She had a lot of time. Why was she getting up at 6:30 a.m.? Maybe she swam every morning. That would make sense. She pressed a button and the curtains slid open with a low whirr to reveal a view of water and skyscrapers and the white dome of the O2 arena. She had never seen this precise view from this precise angle before. London. Canary Wharf. About twenty storeys up.

She went to the bathroom – beige tiles, large shower cubicle, fluffy white towels – and realised she didn't feel as bad as she usually did in the morning. There was a mirror filling half the opposing wall. She gasped at her appearance. And then she laughed. She looked so ridiculously healthy. And strong. And in this life had terrible taste in nightwear (pyjamas, mustard-and-green, plaid).

The bathroom was quite large. Large enough to get down on and do some push-ups. Ten full ones in a row – no knees – without even getting out of breath.

Then she held a plank. And tried it with one hand. Then the other hand, with hardly a tremor. Then she did some burpees.

No problem at all.

Wow.

She stood up and patted her rock-hard stomach. Remembered how wheezy she had been in her root life, walking up the high street, technically only yesterday.

She hadn't felt this fit since she was a teenager. In fact, this might be the fittest she had *ever* felt. Stronger, certainly.

Searching Facebook for 'Isabel Hirsh', she found out that her former best friend was alive and still living in Australia and this made Nora happy. She didn't even care that they weren't social media friends, as it was highly probable that in this life Nora hadn't gone to Bristol University. And even if she had, she wouldn't have been doing the same course. It was a *bit* humbling to realise that, even though *this* Isabel Hirsh might never have met Nora Seed, she was still doing the same thing she was doing in Nora's root life.

She also checked in on Dan. He was (seemingly) happily married to a spin-class instructor called Gina. 'Gina Lord (née Sharpe)'. They'd had a wedding in Sicily.

Nora then googled 'Nora Seed'.

Her Wikipedia page (she had a Wikipedia page!) informed her that she had indeed made it to the Olympics. Twice. And that she specialised in freestyle. She had won a gold medal for 800m free-style, with a ridiculous time of eight minutes and five seconds, and had a silver for 400m.

This had been when she was twenty-two years old. She had won another silver medal when she was twenty-six, for her participation in a 4 x 100m relay. It got even *more* ridiculous when she read that she had briefly been the world record-holder for women's 400m freestyle at the World Aquatic Championships. She had then retired from international competition.

She had retired at twenty-eight.

She apparently now worked for the BBC during their coverage

of swimming events, had appeared on the TV show *A Question of Sport*, had written an autobiography called *Sink or Swim*, was an occasional assistant coach at British Swimming GB, and still swam for two hours every day.

She gave a lot of money to charitable causes – namely to Marie Curie Cancer Care – and she had organised a fundraising charity swimathon around Brighton Pier for the Marine Conservation Society. Since retiring from professional sport, she had swum the Channel twice.

There was a link to a TED talk she had given about the value of stamina in sport, and training, and life. It had over a million views. As she began to watch it, Nora felt as though she was watching someone else. This woman was confident, commanded the stage, had great posture, smiled naturally as she spoke, and managed to make the crowd smile and laugh and clap and nod their heads at all the right moments.

She had never imagined she could be like this, and tried to memorise what this other Nora was doing, but realised there was no way she would be able to.

'People with stamina aren't made any differently to anyone else,' she was saying. 'The only difference is they have a clear goal in mind, and a determination to get there. Stamina is essential to stay focused in a life filled with distraction. It is the ability to stick to a task when your body and mind are at their limit, the ability to keep your head down, swimming in your lane, without looking around, worrying who might overtake you . . .'

Who the hell *was* this person?

She skipped a little further into the video, and this other Nora was still talking with the confidence of a self-help Joan of Arc.

'If you aim to be something you are not, you will always fail. Aim to be you. Aim to look and act and think like you. Aim to be the truest version of you. Embrace that you-ness. Endorse it. Love it. Work hard at it. And don't give a second thought when people mock it or ridicule it. Most gossip is envy in disguise. Keep your head down. Keep your stamina. Keep swimming . . .'

'Keep swimming,' Nora mumbled, echoing this other self and wondering if the hotel had a pool.

The video disappeared and a second later her phone started to buzz.

A name appeared. 'Nadia'.

She didn't know any Nadias in her original life. She had no idea if seeing the name would have inspired this version of her with happy anticipation or sinking dread.

There was only one way to find out.

'Hello?'

'Sweetheart,' came a voice she didn't recognise. A voice that was close but not entirely warm. She had an accent. Maybe Russian. 'I hope you are okay.'

'Hi Nadia. Thanks. I'm fine. I'm just here in the hotel. Getting ready for a conference.' She tried to sound jolly.

'Oh yeah, the conference. Fifteen thousand pounds for a talk. Sounds good.'

It sounded ridiculous. But she also wondered how Nadia – whoever Nadia was – knew this.

'Oh yeah.'

'Joe told us.'

'Joe?'

'Yeah. Well, listen, I need to talk to you at some point about your father's birthday.'

'What?'

'I know he'd love it if you could come up and see us.'

Her whole body went cold and weak, as if she had seen a ghost.

She remembered her father's funeral, hugging her brother as they cried on each other's shoulders.

'My dad?'

My dad. My dead dad.

'He's just come in from the garden. Do you want a word with him?'

This was so remarkable, so world-shattering, it was totally out of synch with her tone of voice. She said it casually, almost as if it was nothing at all.

'What?'

'Do you want a word with Dad?'

It took her a moment. She felt suddenly off-balance.

'I—'

She could hardly speak. Or breathe. She didn't know what to say. Everything felt unreal. It was like time travel. As though she had fallen through two decades.

It was too late to respond because the next thing she heard was Nadia saying: 'Here he is . . .'

Nora nearly hung up the phone. Maybe she should have. But she didn't. Now she knew it was a possibility, she needed to hear his voice again.

His breath first.

Then: 'Hi Nora, how are you?'

Just that. Casual, non-specific, everyday. It was him. His voice. His strong voice that had always been so clipped. But a little thinner, maybe, a little weaker. A voice fifteen years older than it was meant to be.

'Dad,' she said. Her voice was a stunned whisper. 'It's you.'

'You all right, Nora? Is this a bad line? Do you want to FaceTime?'

FaceTime. To see his face. No. That would be too much. This was already too much. Just the idea that there was a version of her dad alive at a time after FaceTime was invented. Her dad belonged in a world of landlines. When he died, he was only just warming to radical concepts like emails and text messages.

'No,' she said. 'It was me. I was just thinking of something. I'm a bit distant. Sorry. How are you?'

'Fine. We took Sally to the vets yesterday.'

She assumed Sally was a dog. Her parents had never had a dog, or any pet. Nora had begged for a dog or a cat when she was little but her dad had always said they tied you down.

'What was wrong with her?' Nora asked, trying to sound natural now.

'Just her ears again. That infection keeps coming back.'

'Oh right,' she said, as though she knew Sally and her problematic ears. 'Poor Sally. I . . . I love you, Dad. And I just want to say that—'

'Are you all right, Nora? You're sounding a bit . . . emotional.'

'I just didn't . . . *don't* tell you that enough. I just want you to know I love you. You are a good father. And in another life – the life where I quit swimming – I am full of regret over that.'

'Nora?'

She felt awkward asking him anything, but she had to know. The questions started to burst out of her like water from a geyser.

'Are you okay, Dad?'

'Why wouldn't I be?'

'Just. You know . . . You used to worry about chest pains.'

'Haven't had them since I got healthy again. That was years ago. You remember. My health kick? Hanging around Olympians does that to you. Got me back to rugby-fit. Coming up to sixteen years off the drink too. Cholesterol and blood pressure low, the doc says.'

'Yes, of course . . . I remember the health kick.' And then another question came to her. But she had no idea how to ask it. So she did it directly.

'How long have you been with Nadia now again?'

'Are you having memory problems or something?'

'No. Well, yes, maybe. I have just been thinking a lot about life recently.'

'Are you a philosopher now?'

'Well, I studied it.'

'When?'

'Never mind. I just can't remember how you and Nadia met.'

She heard an awkward sigh down the phone. He sounded terse. 'You know how we met . . . Why are you bringing all this up? Is this something that therapist is opening up? Because you know my feelings on that.'

I have a therapist.

'Sorry, Dad.'

'That's all right.'

'I just want to know that you're happy.'

''Course I am. I've got an Olympic champion for a daughter and have finally found the love of my life. And you're getting back on your feet again. Mentally, I mean. After Portugal.'

Nora wanted to know what had happened in Portugal but she had another question to ask first.

'What about Mum? Wasn't she the love of your life?'

'Once upon a time she was. But things change, Nora. Come on, you're a grown-up.'

'I . . .'

Nora put her dad on speaker. Clicked back to her own Wikipedia page. Sure enough, her parents had divorced after her father had an affair with Nadia Vanko, mother of a Ukrainian male swimmer, Yegor Vanko. And in this timeline her mother had died way back in 2011.

And all this because Nora had never sat in that car park in Bedford and told her dad that she didn't want to be a competitive swimmer.

She felt that feeling again. Like she was fading away. That she had worked out that this life wasn't for her and was disappearing back to the library. But she stayed where she was. She said goodbye to her dad, ended the phone call and continued to read up on herself.

She was single, though had been in a relationship with the American Olympic medal-winning diver Scott Richards for three years, and briefly lived with him in California, where they resided in La Jolla, San Diego. She now lived in West London.

Having read the entire page she put the phone down and decided to go find out if there was a pool. She wanted to do what she would be doing in this life, and what she would be doing was swimming. And maybe the water would help her think of what she could say.

It was an exceptional swim, even if it gave her little creative inspiration, and it calmed her after the experience of having a conversation with her dead father. She had the pool to herself and glided through length after length of breaststroke without having to think about it. It felt so empowering, to be that fit and strong and to have such mastery of the water, that she momentarily stopped worrying about her father and having to give a speech she really wasn't prepared for.

But as she swam her mood changed. She thought of those years her dad had gained and her mother had lost, and as she thought she became angrier and angrier at her father, which fuelled her to swim even faster. She had always imagined her parents were too proud to get divorced, so instead let their resentments fester inside, projecting them onto their children, and Nora in particular. And swimming had been her only ticket to approval.

Here, in this life she was in now, she had pursued a career to keep him happy, while sacrificing her own relationships, her own love of music, her own dreams beyond anything that didn't involve a medal, her own *life*. And her father had paid this back by having an affair with this Nadia person and leaving her mother and he still got terse with her. After all that.

Screw him. Or at least this version of him.

As she switched to freestyle she realised it wasn't her fault that her parents had never been able to love her the way parents were meant to: without condition. It wasn't her fault her mother focused on her every flaw, starting with the asymmetry of her ears. No. It went back even earlier than that. The first problem had been that Nora had dared, somehow, to arrive into existence at a time when her parents' marriage was relatively fragile. Her mother fell into depression and her father turned to tumblers of single malt.

She did thirty more lengths, and her mind calmed and she started to feel free, just her and the water.

But when she eventually got out of the pool and went back to her room she dressed in the only clean clothes in her hotel room (smart navy trouser suit) and stared at the inside of her suitcase. She felt the profound loneliness emanating from it. There was a copy of her own book. She was staring out from the cover with steely-eyed determination and wearing a Team GB swimsuit. She picked it up and saw, in small print, that it was 'co-written with Amanda Sands'.

Amanda Sands, the internet told her, was 'ghost-writer to a whole host of sporting celebrities'.

Then she looked at her watch. It was time to head to the lobby.

Standing waiting for her were two smartly dressed people she didn't recognise and one she most definitely did. He was wearing a suit and was clean-shaven in this life, his hair side-parted and business-like, but he was the same Joe. His dark eyebrows as bushy as ever – 'That's the Italian in you,' as their mother used to say.

'Joe?'

What's more, he was smiling at her. A big, brotherly, uncomplicated smile.

'Morning, sis,' he said, surprised by and a little awkward from the length of the hug she was giving him.

When the hug was over, he introduced the other two people he was standing with.

'This is Priya from Gulliver Research, the people organising the conference obviously, and this is Rory, obviously, from Celebrity Speakers.'

'Hi Priya!' said Nora. 'Hi Rory. So nice to meet you.'

'Yes, it is,' said Priya, smiling. 'We're so pleased to have you.'

'You say that like we've never met before!' said Rory, with a booming laugh.

Nora backtracked. 'Yes, I know *we've* met, Rory. Just my little joke. You know my sense of humour.'

'You have a sense of humour?'

'Good one, Rory!'

'Okay,' her brother said, looking at her and smiling. 'Do you want to see the space?'

She couldn't stop smiling. Here was her brother. Her brother, whom she hadn't seen in two years and hadn't had any semblance of a good relationship with in far longer, looking healthy and happy and like he actually *liked* her. 'The space?'

'Yeah. The hall. Where you're doing the talk.'

'It's all set up,' Priya added, helpfully.

'Bloody big room,' said Rory approvingly, as he cradled a paper cup of coffee.

So, Nora agreed and was led into a vast blue conference room with a wide stage and around a thousand empty chairs. A technician in black came up and asked her: 'What do you fancy? Lapel or headset or handheld?'

'Sorry?'

'What kind of mic will you want up there?'

'Oh!'

'Headset,' her brother interjected on Nora's behalf.

'Yeah. Headset,' said Nora.

'I was just thinking,' her brother said, 'after that nightmare we had with the microphone in Cardiff.'

'Yeah, totally. What a nightmare.'

Priya was smiling at her, wanting to ask something. 'Am I right in thinking you've got no multimedia stuff? No slides or anything?'

'Um, I—'

Her brother and Rory were looking at her, a little concerned.

This was clearly a question she should know the answer to and didn't.

'Yes,' she said, then saw her brother's expression, 'I . . . don't. Yes, I don't. I don't have any multimedia stuff.'

And they all looked at her like she was not quite right but she smiled through it.

Peppermint Tea

Ten minutes later she was sitting on her own with her brother in something called the 'VIP Business Lounge', which was just a small, airless room with some chairs and a table offering a selection of today's newspapers. A couple of middle-aged men in suits were typing things into laptops.

By this point she had worked out that her brother was her manager. And that he'd been her manager for seven years, since she'd given up professional swimming.

'Are you okay about all this?' her brother asked, having just got two drinks from the coffee machine. He tore a sachet to release a teabag. Peppermint. He placed it into the cup of hot water he'd taken from the coffee machine.

Then he handed it to Nora.

She had never drunk peppermint tea in her life. 'That's for me?'

'Well, yeah. It was the only herbal they had.'

He had a coffee for himself that Nora secretly craved. Maybe in this life she didn't drink caffeine.

Are you okay about all this?

'Okay about all what?' Nora wondered.

'The talk, today.'

'Oh, um, yeah. How long is it again?'

'Forty minutes.'

'Sure.'

'It's a lot of money. I upped it from ten.'

'That's very good of you.'

'Well, I still get my twenty per cent. Hardly a sacrifice.'

Nora tried to think how she could unlock their shared history. How she could find out why, in this life, they were sitting together and getting along. It might have been money, but her brother had never been particularly money-motivated. And yes, sure, he'd obviously been upset when Nora walked away from the deal with the record company but that had been because he wanted to play guitar in The Labyrinths for the rest of his life and be a rock star.

After dipping it a few times Nora let the teabag free in the water. 'Do you ever think of how our lives could have been different? You know, like if I had never stuck with swimming?'

'Not really.'

'I mean, what do you think you'd be doing if you weren't my manager?'

'I manage other people too, you know.'

'Well, yeah, of course I know that. Obviously.'

'I suppose I probably wouldn't be managing anyone without you. I mean, you were the first. And you introduced me to Kai and then Natalie. And then Eli, so . . .'

She nodded, as if she had any idea who Kai and Natalie and Eli were. 'True, but maybe you'd have found some other way.'

'Who knows? Or maybe I'd still be in Manchester, I don't know.'

'Manchester?'

'Yeah. You remember how much I loved it up there. At uni.'

It was really hard not to look surprised at any of this, at the fact that this brother she was getting on with, and working with, was also someone who went to university. In her root life her brother did A-levels and applied to go to Manchester to do History, but he never got the grades he needed, probably because he was too busy getting stoned with Ravi every night. And then decided he didn't want to go to uni at all.

They chatted a bit more.

At one point he became distracted by his phone.

Nora noticed his screensaver was of a radiant, handsome, smiling man she had never seen before. She noticed her brother's wedding ring and feigned a neutral expression.

'So, how's married life?'

Joe smiled. It was a genuinely happy smile. She hadn't seen him smile like that for years. In her root life, Joe had always been unlucky in love. Although she had known her brother was gay since he was a teenager, he hadn't officially come out until he was twenty-two. And he'd never had a happy or long-term relationship. She felt guilt, that her life had the power to shape her brother's life in such meaningful ways.

'Oh, you know Ewan. Ewan's Ewan.'

Nora smiled back as if she knew who Ewan was and exactly what he was like. 'Yeah. He's great. I'm so happy for you both.'

He laughed. 'We've been married five years now. You're talking as if me and him have just got together.'

'No, I'm just, you know, I sometimes think that you're lucky. So in love. And happy.'

'He wants a dog.' He smiled. 'That's our current debate. I mean, I wouldn't mind a dog. But I'd want a rescue. And I wouldn't want a bloody Maltipoo or a Bichon. I'd want a wolf. You know, a proper dog.'

Nora thought of Voltaire. 'Animals are good company . . .'

'Yeah. You still want a dog?'

'I do. Or a cat.'

'Cats are too disobedient,' he said, sounding like the brother she remembered. 'Dogs know their place.'

'Disobedience is the true foundation of liberty. The obedient must be slaves.'

He looked perplexed. 'Where did *that* come from? Is that a quote?'

'Yeah. Henry David Thoreau. You know, my fave philosopher.'

'Since when were you into philosophy?'

Of course. In this life she'd never have done a Philosophy

degree. While her root self had been reading the works of Thoreau and Lao Tzu and Sartre in a stinky student flat in Bristol, her current self had been standing on Olympic podiums in Beijing. Weirdly, she felt just as sad for the version of her who had never fallen in love with the simple beauty of Thoreau's *Walden*, or the stoical Meditations of Marcus Aurelius, as she had felt sympathy for the version of her who never fulfilled her Olympic potential.

'Oh, I don't know . . . I just came across some of his stuff on the internet.'

'Ah. Cool. Will check him out. You could drop some of that into your speech.'

Nora felt herself go pale. 'Um, I'm thinking of maybe doing something a little different today. I might, um, improvise a little.'

Improvising was, after all, a skill she'd been practising.

'I saw this great documentary about Greenland the other night. Made me remember when you were obsessed with the Arctic and you cut out all those pictures of polar bears and stuff.'

'Yeah. Mrs Elm said the best way to be an arctic explorer was to be a glaciologist. So that's what I wanted to be.'

'Mrs Elm,' he whispered. 'That rings a bell.'

'School librarian.'

'That was it. You used to live in that library, didn't you?'

'Pretty much.'

'Just think, if you hadn't stuck with swimming, you'd be in Greenland right now.'

'Svalbard,' she said.

'Sorry?'

'It's a Norwegian archipelago. Way up in the Arctic Ocean.'

'Okay, Norway then. You'd be there.'

'Maybe. Or maybe I'd just still be in Bedford. Moping around. Unemployed. Struggling to pay the rent.'

'Don't be daft. You'd have always done something big.'

She smiled at her elder brother's innocence. 'In some lives me and you might not even get on.'

'Nonsense.'

'I hope so.'

Joe seemed a bit uncomfortable, and clearly wanted to change the topic.

'Hey, guess who I saw the other day?'

Nora shrugged, hoping it was going to be someone she'd heard of.

'Ravi. Do you remember Ravi?'

She thought of Ravi, telling her off in the newsagent's only yesterday. 'Oh yeah. Ravi.'

'Well, I bumped into him.'

'In Bedford?'

'Ha! God, no. Haven't been there for years. No. It was at Blackfriars station. Totally random. Like, I haven't seen him in over a decade. At *least*. He wanted to go to the pub. So, I explained I was teetotal now, and then I got into having to explain I'd been an alcoholic. And all of that. That I hadn't had a glass of wine or a puff on a joint in years.' Nora nodded as if this wasn't a bombshell. 'Since I got into a mess after Mum died. I think he was like, "Who is this guy?" But he was fine. He was cool. He's working as a cameraman now. Still doing some music on the side. Not rock stuff. DJ-ing apparently. Remember that band me and him had, years ago. The Labyrinths?'

It was becoming easier to fake vagueness. 'Oh yeah. The Labyrinths. Course. That's a blast from the past.'

'Yeah. Got the sense he pines for those days. Even though we were crap and I couldn't sing.'

'What about you? Do you ever think about what could have been if The Labyrinths had made it big?'

He laughed, a little sadly. 'I don't know if anything *could have been*.'

'Maybe you needed an extra person. I used to play those keyboards Mum and Dad got you.'

'Did you? When did you have time for that?'

A life without music. A life without reading the books she had loved.

But also: a life where she got on with her brother. A life where she hadn't had to let him down.

'Anyway, Ravi wanted to say hi. And wanted a catch-up. He only works one tube stop away. So he's going to try and come to the talk.'

'What? Oh. That's . . . I wish he wouldn't.'

'Why?'

'I just never really liked him.'

Joe frowned. 'Really? I can't remember you saying that . . . He's okay. A good guy. Bit of a waster, maybe, back in the day, but he seems to have got his act together a bit . . .'

Nora was unsettled. 'Joe?'

'Yeah.'

'You know when Mum died?'

'Yeah.'

'Where was I?'

'What do you mean? Are you okay today, sis? Are the new tablets working?'

'Tablets?'

She checked in her bag and started to rummage. Saw a small box of anti-depressants in her bag. Her heart sank.

'I just wanted to know. Did I see much of Mum before she died?'

Joe frowned. He was still the same Joe. Still unable to read his sister. Still wanting to escape reality. 'You know we weren't there. It happened so fast. She didn't tell us how ill she was. To protect us. Or maybe because she didn't want us to tell her to stop drinking.'

'Drinking? Mum was drinking?'

Joe's worry increased. 'Sis, have you got amnesia? She was on a bottle of gin every day since Nadia came onto the scene.'

'Yeah. Course. I remember.'

'Plus you had the European Championships coming up and she didn't want to interfere with that . . .'

'Jesus. I should have been there. One of us should have been there, Joe. We both—'

His expression frosted suddenly. 'You were never that close to Mum, were you? Why this sudden—'

'I got closer to her. I mean, I would have. I—'

'You're freaking me out. You're acting not quite yourself.'

Nora nodded. 'Yes, I . . . I just . . . yes, I think you're right . . . I think it's just the tablets . . .'

She remembered her mother, in her final months, saying: 'I don't know what I would have done without you.' She'd probably said it to Joe too. But in this life, she'd had neither of them.

Then Priya arrived into the room. Grinning, clutching her phone and some kind of a clipboard.

'It's time,' she said.

The Tree That Is Our Life

Five minutes later Nora was back in the hotel's vast conference room. At least a thousand people were watching the first speaker conclude her presentation. The author of *Zero to Hero*. The book Dan had beside his bed in another life. But Nora wasn't really listening, as she sat in her reserved seat in the front row. She was too upset about her mother, too nervous about the speech, so she just picked up the odd word or phrase that floated into her mind like croutons in minestrone. 'Little-known fact', 'ambition', 'what you may be surprised to hear is that', 'if I can do it', 'hard knocks'.

It was hard to breathe in this room. It smelled of musky perfume and new carpet.

She tried to stay calm.

Leaning into her brother, she whispered, 'I don't think I can do this.'

'What?'

'I think I'm having a panic attack.'

He looked at her, smiling, but with a toughness in his eyes she remembered from a different life, when she'd had a panic attack before one of their early gigs with The Labyrinths at a pub in Bedford. 'You'll be fine.'

'I don't know if I can do this. I've gone blank.'

'You're overthinking it.'

'I have anxiety. I have no other type of thinking available.'

'Come on. Don't let us down.'

Don't let us down.

'But—'

She tried to think of music.

Thinking of music had always calmed her down.

A tune came to her. She was slightly embarrassed, even within herself, to realise the song in her head was 'Beautiful Sky'. A happy, hopeful song that she hadn't sung in a long time. *The sky grows dark / The black over blue / Yet the stars still dare / To shine for—*

But then the person Nora was sitting next to – a smartly dressed business woman in her fifties, and the source of the musky perfume smell – leaned in and whispered, 'I'm so sorry about what happened to you. You know, the stuff in Portugal . . .'

'What stuff?'

The woman's reply was drowned out as the audience erupted into applause at that moment.

'What?' she asked again.

But it was too late. Nora was being beckoned towards the stage and her brother was elbowing her.

Her brother's voice, bellowing almost: 'They want you. Off you go.'

She headed tentatively towards the lectern on the stage, towards her own huge face smiling out triumphantly, golden medal around her neck, projected on the screen behind her.

She had always hated being watched.

'Hello,' she said nervously, into the microphone. 'It is very nice to be here today . . .'

A thousand or so faces stared, waiting.

She had never spoken to so many people simultaneously. Even when she had been in The Labyrinths, they had never played a gig for more than a hundred people, and back then she kept the talking between the songs as minimal as possible. Working at String Theory, although she was perfectly okay talking with customers, she rarely spoke up in staff meetings, even though there had never been more than five people in the room. Back at university, while Izzy always breezed through presentations Nora would worry about them for weeks in advance.

Joe and Rory were staring at her with baffled expressions.

The Nora she had seen in the TED talk was not this Nora, and she doubted she could ever become that person. Not without having done all that she had done.

'Hello. My name is Nora Seed.'

She hadn't meant it to be funny but the whole room laughed at this. There had clearly been no need to introduce herself.

'Life is strange,' she said. 'How we live it all at once. In a straight line. But really that's not the whole picture. Because life isn't simply made of the things we do, but the things we don't do too. And every moment of our life is a . . . kind of turning.'

Still nothing.

'Think about it. Think about how we start off . . . as this set thing. Like the seed of a tree planted in the ground. And then we . . . we grow . . . we grow . . . and at first we are a trunk . . .'

Absolutely nothing.

'But then the tree – the tree that is our life – develops branches. And think of all those branches, departing from the trunk at different heights. And think of all those branches, branching off again, heading in often opposing directions. Think of those branches becoming other branches, and those becoming twigs. And think of the end of each of those twigs, all in different places, having started from the same one. A life is like that, but on a bigger scale. New branches are formed every second of every day. And from our perspective – from everyone's perspective – it feels like a . . . like a continuum. Each twig has travelled only one journey. But there are still other twigs. And there are also other todays. Other lives that would have been different if you'd taken different directions earlier in your life. This is a tree of life. Lots of religions and mythologies have talked about the tree of life. It's there in Buddhism, Judaism and Christianity. Lots of philosophers and writers have talked about tree metaphors too. For Sylvia Plath, existence was a fig tree and each possible life she could live – the happily-married one, the successful-poet one – was this sweet juicy fig, but she couldn't get to taste the sweet juicy figs and so they just rotted right in front of her. It can drive you insane, thinking of all the other lives we don't live.

'For instance, in most of my lives I am not standing at this podium talking to you about success . . . In most lives I am not an Olympic gold medallist.' She remembered something Mrs Elm had told her in the Midnight Library. 'You see, doing one thing differently is very often the same as doing everything differently. Actions can't be reversed within a lifetime, however much we try . . .'

People were listening now. They clearly needed a Mrs Elm in their lives.

'The only way to learn is to live.'

And she went on in this manner for another twenty minutes, remembering as much as possible of what Mrs Elm had told her, and then she looked down at her hands, glowing white from the light of the lectern.

As she absorbed the sight of a raised, thin pink line of flesh, she knew the scar was self-inflicted, and it put her off her flow. Or rather, put her into a new one.

'And . . . and the thing is . . . the thing is . . . what we consider to be the most successful route for us to take, actually isn't. Because too often our view of success is about some external bullshit idea of achievement – an Olympic medal, the ideal husband, a good salary. And we have all these metrics that we try and reach. When really success isn't something you measure, and life isn't a race you can win. It's all . . . bollocks, actually . . .'

The audience definitely looked uncomfortable now. Clearly this was not the speech they were expecting. She scanned the crowd and saw a single face smiling up at her. It took a second, given the fact that he was smartly dressed in a blue cotton shirt and with hair far shorter than it was in his Bedford life, for her to realise it was Ravi. This Ravi looked friendly, but she couldn't shake the knowledge of the other Ravi, the one who had stormed out of the newsagent's, sulking about not being able to afford a magazine and blaming her for it.

'You see, I know that you were expecting my TED talk on the path to success. But the truth is that success is a delusion. It's all a delusion. I mean, yes, there are things we can overcome. For instance, I am someone who gets stage fright and yet, here I am, on a stage. Look at me . . . on a stage! And someone told me recently, they told me that my problem isn't actually stage fright. My problem is *life fright*. And you know what? They're fucking right. Because life is frightening, and it is frightening for a reason, and the reason is that it doesn't matter which branch of a life we get to live, we are always the same rotten tree. I wanted to be many things in my life. All kinds of things. But if your life is rotten, it will be rotten no matter what you do. The damp rots the whole useless thing . . .'

Joe was desperately slicing his hand in the air around his neck, making a 'cut it' gesture.

'Anyway, just be kind and . . . Just be kind. I have a feeling I am about to go, so I would just like to say I love my brother Joe. I love you, brother, and I love everyone in this room, and it was very nice to be here.'

And the moment she had said it was nice to be there, was also the moment she wasn't there at all.

System Error

She arrived back in the Midnight Library.

But this time she was a little away from the bookshelves. This was the loosely defined office area she had glimpsed earlier, in one of the broader corridors. The desk was covered with administrative trays barely containing scattered piles of papers and boxes, and the computer.

The computer was a really old-fashioned-looking, cream-coloured boxy one on the desk by the papers. The kind that Mrs Elm would once have had in her school library. She was at the keyboard now, typing with urgency, staring at the monitor as Nora stood behind her.

The lights above – the same bare light bulbs hanging down from wires – were flickering wildly.

'My dad was alive because of me. But he'd also had an affair, and my mum died earlier, and I got on with my brother because I had never let him down, but he was still the same brother, really, and he was only really okay with me in that life because I was helping him make money and . . . and . . . it wasn't the Olympic dream I imagined. It was the same me. And something had happened in Portugal. I'd probably tried to kill myself or something . . . Are there any other lives at all or is it just the furnishings that change?'

But Mrs Elm wasn't listening. Nora noticed something on the desk. An old plastic orange fountain pen. The exact same kind that Nora had once owned at school.

'Hello? Mrs Elm, can you hear me?'

Something was wrong.

The librarian's face was tight with worry. She read from the screen, to herself. 'System error.'

'Mrs Elm? Hello? Yoo-hoo! Can you see me?'

She tapped her shoulder. That seemed to do it.

Mrs Elm's face broke out in massive relief as she turned away from the computer. 'Oh Nora, you got here?'

'Were you expecting me not to? Did you think that life would be the one I wanted to live?'

She shook her head without really moving it. If that was possible. 'No. It's not that. It's just that it looked fragile.'

'What looked fragile?'

'The transfer.'

'Transfer?'

'From the book to here. The *life you chose* to here. It seems there is a problem. A problem with the whole system. Something beyond my immediate control. Something *external*.'

'You mean, in my actual life?'

She stared back at the screen. 'Yes. You see, the Midnight Library only exists because you do. In your root life.'

'So, I'm dying?'

Mrs Elm looked exasperated. 'It's a possibility. That is to say, it's a possibility that we are reaching the end of possibility.'

Nora thought of how good it had felt, swimming in the pool. How vital and alive. And then something happened inside her. A strange feeling. A pull in her stomach. A physical *shift*. A change in her. The idea of death suddenly troubled her. At that same time the lights stopped flickering overhead and shone brightly.

Mrs Elm clapped her hands as she absorbed new information on the computer screen.

'Oh, it's back. That's good. The glitch is gone. We are running again. Thanks, I believe, to *you*.'

'What?'

'Well, the computer says the root cause within the host has been temporarily fixed. And you are the root cause. You are the host.' She smiled. Nora blinked, and when she opened her eyes both she and Mrs Elm were standing in a different part of the library. Between stacks of bookshelves again. Standing, stiffly, awkwardly, facing each other.

'Right. Now, settle,' said Mrs Elm, before releasing a deep and meaningful exhale. She was clearly talking to herself.

'My mum died on different dates in different lives. I'd like a life where she is still here. Does that life exist?'

Mrs Elm's attention switched to Nora.

'Maybe it does.'

'Great.'

'But you can't get there.'

'Why not?'

'Because this library is about *your* decisions. There was no choice you could have made that led to her being alive beyond yesterday. I'm sorry.'

A light bulb flickered above Nora's head. But the rest of the library stayed as it was.

'You need to think about something else, Nora. What was good about the last life?'

Nora nodded. 'Swimming. I liked swimming. But I don't think I was happy in that life. I don't know if I am truly happy in any life.'

'Is happiness the aim?'

'I don't know. I suppose I want my life to mean something. I want to do something good.'

'You once wanted to be a glaciologist,' Mrs Elm appeared to remember.

'Yeah.'

'You used to talk about it. You said you were interested in the Arctic, so I suggested you become a glaciologist.'

'I remember. I liked the sound of it straight away. My mum and dad never liked the idea, though.'

'Why?'

'I don't really know. They encouraged swimming. Well, Dad did. But anything that involved academic work, they were funny about.'

Nora felt a deep sadness, down in her stomach. From her arrival into life, she was considered by her parents in a different way to her brother.

'Other than swimming, Joe was the one expected to pursue things,' she told Mrs Elm. 'My mum put me off anything that could take me away. Unlike Dad, she didn't even push me to swim. But surely there must be a life where I didn't listen to my mum and where I am now an Arctic researcher. Far away from everything. With a purpose. Helping the planet. Researching the impact of climate change. On the front line.'

'So, you want me to find that life for you?'

Nora sighed. She still had no idea what she wanted. But at least the Arctic Circle would be different.

'All right. Yes.'

Svalbard

She woke in a small bed in a little cabin on a boat. She knew it was a boat because it was rocking, and indeed the rocking, gentle as it was, had woken her up. The cabin was spare and basic. She was wearing a thick fleece sweater and long johns. Pulling back the blanket, she noticed that she had a headache. Her mouth was so dry her cheeks felt sucked-in against her teeth. She coughed a deep, chesty cough and felt a million pool-lengths away from the body of an Olympian. Her fingers smelt of tobacco. She sat up to see a pale-blonde, robust, hard-weathered woman sitting on another bed staring at her.

'God morgen, Nora.'

She smiled. And hoped that in this life she wasn't fluent in whichever Scandinavian language this woman spoke.

'Good morning.'

She noticed a half-empty bottle of vodka and a mug on the floor beside the woman's bed. A dog calendar (April: Springer Spaniel) was propped up on the chest between the beds. The three books on top of it were all in English. The one nearest to the woman said *Principles of Glacier Mechanics.* Two on Nora's: *A Naturalist's Guide to the Arctic* and a Penguin Classic edition of *The Saga of the Volsungs: The Norse Epic of Sigurd the Dragon Slayer.* She noticed something else. It was cold. Properly cold. The cold that almost burns, that hurts your fingers and toes and stiffens your cheeks. Even inside. With layers of thermal underwear. With a sweater on. With the bars of two electric heaters glowing orange. Every exhale made a cloud.

'Why are you here, Nora?' the woman asked, in heavily accented English.

A tricky question, when you didn't know where 'here' was.

'Bit early in the morning, isn't it, for philosophy?' Nora laughed, nervously.

She saw a wall of ice outside the porthole, rising out of the sea. She was either very far north or very far south. She was very far somewhere.

The woman was still staring at her. Nora had no idea if they were friends or not. The woman seemed tough, direct, earthy, but probably an interesting form of company.

'I don't mean philosophy. I don't even mean what got you into glaciological research. Although, it might be the same thing. I mean, why did you choose to go as far away from civilisation as possible? You've never told me.'

'I don't know,' she said. 'I like the cold.'

'No one likes *this* cold. Unless they are a sado-masochist.'

She had a point. Nora reached for the sweater at the end of her bed and put it on, over the sweater she was already wearing. As she did she saw, beside the vodka bottle, a laminated lanyard lying on the floor.

Ingrid Skirbekk
Professor of Geoscience
International Polar Research Institute

'I don't know, Ingrid. I just like glaciers, I suppose. I want to understand them. Why they are . . . melting.'

She wasn't sounding like a glacier expert, judging from Ingrid's raised eyebrows.

'What about you?' she asked, hopefully.

Ingrid sighed. Rubbed her palm with a thumb. 'After Per died, I couldn't stand to be in Oslo any more. All those people that weren't him, you know? There was this coffee shop we used to go to, at the university. We'd just sit together, together but silent. Happy silent. Reading newspapers, drinking coffee. It was hard to avoid places like that. We used to walk around everywhere. His troublesome soul lingered on every street . . . I kept telling his memory to piss the fuck off but it wouldn't. Grief is a bastard. If I'd have stayed any longer, I'd have hated humanity. So, when a research position came up in Svalbard I was like, yes, this has come to save me . . . I wanted to be somewhere he had never been. I wanted somewhere where I didn't have to feel his ghost. But the truth is, it only half-works, you know? Places are places and memories are memories and life is fucking life.'

Nora took all this in. Ingrid was clearly telling this to someone she thought she knew reasonably well, and yet Nora was a stranger. It felt odd. Wrong. This must be the hardest bit about being a spy, she thought. The emotion people store in you, like a bad investment. You feel like you are robbing people of something.

Ingrid smiled, breaking the thought. 'Anyway, thanks for last night . . . That was a good chat. There are a lot of dickheads on this boat and you are not a dickhead.'

'Oh. Thanks. Neither are you.'

And it was then that Nora noticed the gun, a large rifle with a hefty brown handle, leaning against the wall at the far end of the room, under the coat hooks.

The sight made her feel happy, somehow. Made her feel like her eleven-year-old self would have been proud. She was, it seemed, *having an adventure.*

Hugo Lefèvre

Nora walked with her headache and obvious hangover through an undecorated wooden passageway to a small dining hall that smelled of pickled herring, and where a few research scientists were having breakfast.

She got herself a black coffee and some stale, dry rye bread and sat down.

Around her, outside the window, was the most eerily beautiful sight she had ever seen. Islands of ice, like rocks rendered clean and pure white, were visible amid the fog. There were seventeen other people in the dining hall, Nora counted. Eleven men, six women. Nora sat by herself but within five minutes a man with short hair and stubble two days away from a full beard sat down at her table. He was wearing a parka, like most of the room, but he seemed ill-suited to it, as if he would be more at home on the Riviera wearing designer shorts and a pink polo shirt. He smiled at Nora. She tried to translate the smile, to understand the kind of relationship they had. He watched her for a little while, then shuffled his chair along to sit opposite her. She looked for a lanyard, but he wasn't wearing one. She wondered if she should know his name.

'I'm Hugo,' he said, to her relief. 'Hugo Lefèvre. You are Nora, yes?'

'Yes.'

'I saw you around, in Svalbard, at the research centre, but we never said hello. Anyway, I just wanted to say I read your paper on pulsating glaciers and it blew my mind.'

'Really?'

'Yes. I mean, it's always fascinated me, why they do that here and nowhere else. It's such a strange phenomenon.'

'Life is full of strange phenomena.'

Conversation was tempting, but dangerous. Nora smiled a small, polite smile and then looked out of the window. The islands of ice turned into actual islands. Little snow-streaked pointed hills, like the tips of mountains, or flatter, craggy plates of land. And beyond them, the glacier Nora had seen from the cabin porthole. She could get a better measure of it now, although its top portion was concealed under a visor of cloud. Other parts of it were entirely free from fog. It was incredible.

You see a picture of a glacier on TV or in a magazine and you see a smooth lump of white. But this was as textured as a mountain. Black-brown and white. And there were infinite varieties of that white, a whole visual smorgasbord of variation – white-white, blue-white, turquoise-white, gold-white, silver-white, translucent-white – rendered glaringly alive and impressive. Certainly more impressive than the breakfast.

'Depressing, isn't it?' Hugo said.

'What?'

'The fact that the day never ends.'

Nora felt uneasy with this observation. 'In what sense?'

He waited a second before responding.

'The never-ending light,' he said, before taking a bite of a dry cracker. 'From April on. It's like living one interminable day . . . I hate that feeling.'

'Tell me about it.'

'You'd think they'd give the portholes curtains. Hardly slept since I've been on this boat.'

Nora nodded. 'How long is that again?'

He laughed. It was a nice laugh. Close-mouthed. Civilised. Hardly a laugh at all.

'I drank a lot with Ingrid last night. Vodka has stolen my memory.'

'Are you sure it's the vodka?'

'What else would it be?'

His eyes were inquisitive, and made Nora feel automatically guilty.

She looked over at Ingrid, who was drinking her coffee and typing on her laptop. She wished she had sat with her now.

'Well, that was our third night,' Hugo said. 'We have been meandering around the archipelago since Sunday. Yeah, Sunday. That's when we left Longyearbyen.'

Nora made a face as if to say she knew all this. 'Sunday seems for ever away.'

The boat felt like it was turning. Nora was forced to lean a little in her seat.

'Twenty years ago there was hardly any open water in Svalbard in April. Look at it now. It's like cruising the Mediterranean.'

Nora tried to make her smile seem relaxed. 'Not quite.'

'Anyway, I heard you got the short straw today?'

Nora tried to look blank, which wasn't hard. 'Really?'

'You're the spotter, aren't you?'

She had no idea what he was talking about, but feared the twinkle in his eye.

'Yes,' she answered. 'Yes, I am. I am the spotter.'

Hugo's eyes widened with shock. Or mock-shock. It was hard to tell the difference with him.

'The *spotter*?'

'Yes?'

Nora desperately wanted to know what the spotter actually did, but couldn't ask.

'Well, bonne chance,' said Hugo, with a testing gaze.

'Merci,' said Nora, staring out at the crisp Arctic light and a landscape she had only ever seen in magazines. 'I'm ready for a challenge.'

Walking in Circles

An hour later and Nora was on an expanse of snow-covered rock. More of a skerry than an island. A place so small and uninhabitable it had no name, though a larger island – ominously titled Bear Island – was visible across the ice-cold water. She stood next to a boat. Not the *Lance*, the large boat she'd had breakfast on – that was moored safely out at sea – but the small motor-dinghy that had been dragged up out of the water almost single-handedly by a big boulder of a man called Rune, who, despite his Scandinavian name, spoke in languid west-coast American.

At her feet was a fluorescent yellow rucksack. And lying on the ground was the Winchester rifle that had been leaning against the wall in the cabin. This was *her* gun. In this life, she owned a firearm. Next to the gun was a saucepan with a ladle inside it. In her hands was another, less deadly, gun – a signal pistol ready to fire a flare.

She had discovered what kind of 'spotting' she was doing. While nine of the scientists conducted a climate-tracking fieldwork on this tiny island, she was the lookout for polar bears. Apparently this was a very real prospect. And if she saw one, the very first thing she had to do was fire the flare. This would serve the dual purpose of a) frightening the bear away and b) warning the others.

It was not foolproof. Humans were tasty protein sources and the bears were not known for their fear, especially in recent years as the loss of habitat and food sources had made them ever more vulnerable and forced them to be more reckless.

'Soon as you've fired the flare,' said the eldest of the group, a beardless, sharp-featured man called Peter who was the field leader, and who spoke in a state of permanent fortissimo, 'bang the pan with the ladle. Bang it like mad and scream. They have sensitive hearing. They're like cats. Nine times out of ten, the noise scares them off.'

'And the other time out of ten?'

He nodded down at the rifle. 'You kill it. Before it kills you.'

Nora wasn't the only one with a gun. They all had guns. They were armed scientists. Anyway, Peter laughed and Ingrid patted her back.

'I truly hope,' said Ingrid, laughing raspily, 'you don't get eaten. I would miss you. So long as you aren't menstruating, you should be okay.'

'Jesus. What?'

'They can smell the blood from a mile away.'

Another person – someone who was so thoroughly wrapped up it was impossible to tell who they were even if she had known them – wished her 'good luck' in a muffled far-away voice.

'We'll be back in five hours . . .' Peter told her. He laughed again, and Nora hoped that meant it was a joke. 'Walk in circles to keep warm.'

And then they left her, walking off over the rocky ground and disappearing into the fog.

For an hour, nothing happened. Nora walked in circles. She hopped from left foot to right foot. The fog thinned a little and she stared out at the landscape. She wondered why she was not back in the library. After all, this was definitely a bit *shit*. There were surely lives where she was sitting beside a swimming pool in the sunshine right now. Lives where she was playing music, or lying in a warm lavender-scented bath, or having incredible third-date sex, or reading on a beach in Mexico, or eating in a Michelin-starred restaurant, or strolling the streets of Paris, or getting lost in Rome, or tranquilly gazing at a temple near Kyoto, or feeling the warm cocoon of a happy relationship.

In most lives, she would have at least been physically *comfortable*. And yet, she was feeling something new here. Or something old that she had long buried. The glacial landscape reminded her that she was, first and foremost, a human living on a planet. Almost everything she had done in her life, she realised – almost everything she had bought and worked for and consumed – had taken her further away from understanding that she and all humans were really just one of nine million species.

'If one advances confidently,' Thoreau had written in *Walden*, 'in the direction of his dreams, and endeavours to live the life which he has imagined, he will meet with a success unexpected in common hours.' He'd also observed that part of this success was the product of being alone. 'I never found the companion that was so companionable as solitude.'

And Nora felt similarly, in that moment. Although she had only been left alone for an hour at this point, she had never experienced this level of solitude before, amid such unpopulated nature.

She had thought, in her nocturnal and suicidal hours, that solitude was the problem. But that was because it hadn't been true solitude. The lonely mind in the busy city yearns for connection because it thinks human-to-human connection is the point of everything. But amid pure nature (or the 'tonic of wildness' as Thoreau called it) solitude took on a different character. It became in itself a kind of connection. A connection between herself and the world. And between her and herself.

She remembered a conversation she'd had with Ash. Tall and slightly awkward and cute and forever in need of a new songbook for his guitar.

The chat hadn't been in the shop but in the hospital, when her mother was ill. Shortly after discovering she had ovarian cancer, she had needed surgery. Nora had taken her mum to see all the consultants at Bedford General Hospital, and she had held her mum's hand more in those few weeks than in all the rest of their relationship put together.

While her mum was undergoing surgery, Nora had waited in the hospital canteen. And Ash – in his scrubs, and recognising her as the person he'd chatted to on many occasions in String Theory – saw she looked worried and popped in to say hi.

He worked at the hospital as a general surgeon, and she'd ended up asking him lots of questions about the sort of stuff he did (on that particular day he'd removed an appendix and a bile duct). She also asked about normal post-surgery recovery time and procedure times, and he had been very reassuring. They'd ended up talking for a very long time about all sorts of things, which he seemed to sense she'd been in need of. He'd said something about not over-googling health symptoms. And that had led to them talking about social media – he believed that the more people were connected on social media, the lonelier society became.

'That's why everyone hates each other nowadays,' he reckoned. 'Because they are overloaded with non-friend friends. Ever heard about Dunbar's number?'

And then he had told her about a man called Roger Dunbar at Oxford University, who had discovered that human beings were wired to know only a hundred and fifty people, as that was the average size of hunter-gatherer communities.

'And the Domesday Book,' Ash had told her, under the stark lighting of the hospital canteen, 'if you look at the Domesday Book, the average size of an English community at that time was a hundred and fifty people. Except in Kent. Where it was a hundred people. I'm from Kent. We have anti-social DNA.'

'I've been to Kent,' Nora had countered. 'I noticed that. But I like that theory. I can meet that many people on Instagram in an hour.'

'Exactly. Not healthy! Our brains can't handle it. Which is why we crave face-to-face communication more than ever. And . . . which is why I would never buy my Simon & Garfunkel guitar chord songbooks online!'

She smiled at the memory, then was brought back to the reality of the Arctic landscape by the sound of a loud splash.

A few metres away from her, between the rocky skerry she was standing on and Bear Island, there was another little rock, or collection of rocks, sticking out of the water. Something was emerging from the sea froth. Something heavy, slapping against the stone with a great wet weight. Her whole body shaking, she got ready to fire the flare, but it wasn't a polar bear. It was a walrus. The fat, brown wrinkled beast shuffled over the ice, then stopped to stare at her. She (or he) looked old, even for a walrus. The walrus knew no shame, and could hold a stare for an indefinite amount of time. Nora felt scared. She only knew two things about walruses: that they could be vicious, and that they were never alone for very long.

There were probably other walruses about to haul out of the water.

She wondered if she should fire the flare.

The walrus stayed where it was, like a ghost of itself in the grainy light, but slowly disappeared behind a veil of fog. Minutes went by. Nora had seven layers of clothing on, but her eyelids felt like they were stiffening and could freeze shut if she closed them for too long. She heard the voices of the others occasionally drift over to her and, for a while, her colleagues returned close enough for her to see some of them. Silhouettes in the fog, hunched over the ground, reading ice samples with equipment she wouldn't have understood. But then they disappeared again. She ate one of the protein bars in her rucksack. It was cold and hard as toffee. She checked her phone but there was no signal.

It was very quiet.

The quiet made her realise how much noise there was elsewhere in the world. Here, noise had meaning. You heard something and you had to pay attention.

As she was chewing there came another splashing sound, but this time from a different direction. The combination of fog and weak light made it hard to see. But it wasn't a walrus. That became clear when she realised the silhouette moving towards her was big. Bigger than a walrus, and much bigger than any human.

A Moment of Extreme Crisis
in the Middle of Nowhere

'Oh *fuck*,' whispered Nora, into the cold.

The Frustration of Not Finding a
Library When You Really Need One

The fog cleared to reveal a huge white bear, standing upright. It dropped down to all fours and continued moving toward her with surprising velocity and a heavy and terrifying grace. Nora did nothing. Her mind was jammed with panic. She was as still as the permafrost she stood on.

Fuck.

Fuck fuck.

Fuck fuck fucking fuck.

Fuck fuck fuck fuck fuck.

Eventually a survival impulse kicked in and Nora raised the signal pistol and fired it, and the flare shot out like a tiny comet and disappeared into the water, the glow fading along with her hope. The creature was still coming towards her. She fell to her knees and started clanging the ladle against the saucepan and shouted at the top of her lungs.

'BEAR! BEAR! BEAR!'

The bear stopped, momentarily.

'BEAR! BEAR! BEAR!'

It was now walking forward again.

The banging wasn't working. The bear was close. She wondered if she could reach the rifle, lying on the ice, just slightly too far away. She could see the bear's vast pawed feet, armed with claws, pressing into the snow-dusted rock. Its head was low and its black eyes were looking directly at her.

'LIBRARY!' Nora screamed. 'MRS ELM! PLEASE SEND ME BACK! THIS IS THE WRONG LIFE! IT IS REALLY, REALLY,

REALLY WRONG! TAKE ME BACK! I DON'T WANT ADVENTURE! WHERE'S THE LIBRARY?! I WANT THE LIBRARY!'

There was no hatred in the polar bear's stare. Nora was just food. Meat. And that was a humbling kind of terror. Her heart pounded like a drummer reaching the crescendo. The end of the song. And it became astoundingly clear to her, finally, in that moment:

She didn't want to die.

And that was the problem. In the face of death, life seemed more attractive, and as life seemed more attractive, how could she get back to the Midnight Library? She had to be disappointed in a life, not just scared of it, in order to try again with another book.

There was death. Violent, oblivious death, in bear form, staring at her with its black eyes. And she knew then, more than she'd known anything, that she wasn't ready to die. This knowledge grew bigger than fear itself as she stood there, face to face with a polar bear, itself hungry and desperate to exist, and banged the ladle against the saucepan. Harder. A fast, staccato bang bang bang.

I'm. Not. Scared.

I'm. Not. Scared.

I'm. Not. Scared.

I'm. Not. Scared.

I'm. Not. Scared.

I'm. Not. Scared.

The bear stood and stared, the way the walrus had. She glanced at the rifle. Yes. It was too far away. By the time she could grab it and work out how to fire it, it would already be too late. She doubted she'd be able to kill a polar bear anyway. So she banged the ladle.

Nora closed her eyes, wishing for the library as she carried on making noise. When she opened them, the bear was slipping headfirst into the water. She kept banging the saucepan even after the creature had disappeared. About a minute later, she heard the humans calling her name through the fog.

Island

She was in shock. But it was a slightly different kind of shock than the others on the dinghy assumed. It wasn't the shock of having been close to death. It was the shock of realising she actually wanted to live.

They passed a small island, teeming with nature. Green lichens spread over rocks. Birds – little auks and puffins clustered together – huddled against the Arctic wind. Life surviving against the odds.

Nora sipped the coffee that Hugo handed her, fresh from his flask. Holding it with cold hands even under three pairs of gloves.

To be part of nature was to be part of the will to live.

When you stay too long in a place, you forget just how big an expanse the world is. You get no sense of the length of those longitudes and latitudes. Just as, she supposed, it is hard to have a sense of the vastness inside any one person.

But once you sense that vastness, once something reveals it, hope emerges, whether you want it to or not, and it clings to you as stubbornly as lichen clings to rock.

Permafrost

The surface air temperatures in Svalbard were warming at twice the global rate. Climate change was happening faster here than almost anywhere on Earth.

One woman, wearing a purple woollen hat pulled down over her eyebrows, talked about witnessing one of the icebergs doing a somersault – something that happened apparently because the warming waters had dissolved it from beneath, causing it to become top heavy.

Another problem was that the permafrost on the land was thawing, softening the ground, leading to landslides and avalanches that could destroy the wooden houses of Longyearbyen, the largest town in Svalbard. There was also a risk of bodies surfacing in the local cemetery.

It was inspiring, being among these scientists who were trying to discover precisely what was happening to the planet, trying to observe glacial and climatic activity, and in so doing to inform, and to protect life on Earth.

Back on the main boat, Nora sat quietly in the dining area as everyone offered sympathy for the bear encounter. She felt unable to tell them she was grateful for the experience. She just smiled politely and did her best to avoid conversation.

This life was an intense one, without compromise. It was currently minus seventeen degrees, and she had nearly been eaten by a polar bear, and yet maybe the problem with her root life had partly been its blandness.

She had come to imagine mediocrity and disappointment were her destiny.

Indeed, Nora had always had the sense that she came from a long line of regrets and crushed hopes that seemed to echo in every generation.

For instance, her grandfather on her mother's side was called Lorenzo Conte. He had left Puglia – the handsome heel in the boot of Italy – to come to Swinging London in the 1960s.

Like other men in the desolate port town of Brindisi, he'd emigrated to Britain, exchanging life on the Adriatic for a job at the London Brick Company. Lorenzo, in his naivety, had imagined having a wonderful life – making bricks all day, and then of an evening he would rub shoulders with The Beatles and walk arm-in-arm down Carnaby Street with Jean Shrimpton or Marianne Faithful. The only problem was that, despite its name, the London Brick Company wasn't actually in London. It was based sixty miles north in Bedford, which, for all its modest charms, turned out not as swinging as Lorenzo would have liked. But he made a compromise with his dreams and settled there. The work may not have been glamorous, but it paid.

Lorenzo married a local English woman called Patricia Brown, who was also getting used to life's disappointments, having exchanged her dream of being an actress for the mundane, daily theatre of the suburban housewife, and whose culinary skills were forever under the ghostly shadow of her dead Puglian mother-in-law and her legendary spaghetti dishes, which, in Lorenzo's eyes, could never be surpassed.

They had a baby girl within a year of getting married – Nora's mother – and they called her Donna.

Donna grew up with her parents arguing almost continually, and had consequently believed marriage was something that was not only inevitable, but also inevitably miserable. She became a secretary at a law firm, and then a communications officer for Bedford council, but then she'd had an experience which was never really discussed, at least not with Nora. She'd experienced some kind of breakdown – the first of several – that caused her to stay at home, and, although she recovered, she never went back to work.

There was an invisible baton of failure her mother had passed down, and Nora had held it for a long time. Maybe that was why she had given up on so many things. Because she had it written in her DNA that she had to fail.

Nora thought of this as the boat chugged through the Arctic waters and gulls – black-legged kittiwakes, according to Ingrid – flew overhead.

On both sides of her family there had been an unspoken belief that life was meant to fuck you over. Nora's dad, Geoff, had certainly lived a life that seemed to miss its target.

He had grown up with only a mother, as his dad had died of a heart attack when he was two, cruelly hiding somewhere behind his first memories. Nora's paternal grandmother had been born in rural Ireland but emigrated to England to become a school cleaner, struggling to bring in enough money for food, let alone anything approaching *fun*.

Geoff had been bullied early on in life but had grown big and broad enough to easily put those bullies in their place. He worked hard and proved good at football and the shot put and, in particular, rugby. He played for the Bedford Blues youth team, becoming their best player, and had a shot at the big time before a collateral ligament injury stopped him in his tracks. He then became a PE teacher and simmered with quiet resentment at the universe. He forever dreamed of travel, but never did much of it beyond a subscription to *National Geographic* and the occasional holiday to somewhere in the Cyclades – Nora remembered him in Naxos, snapping a picture of the Temple of Apollo at sunset.

Maybe that's what all lives were, though. Maybe even the most seemingly perfectly intense or worthwhile lives ultimately felt the same. Acres of disappointment and monotony and hurts and rivalries but with flashes of wonder and beauty. Maybe that was the only meaning that mattered. To be the world, witnessing itself. Maybe it wasn't the lack of achievements that had made her and her brother's parents unhappy, maybe it was the expectation to achieve in the first place. She had no idea about any of it, really. But on that boat she realised something. She had loved her parents more than she ever knew, and right then, she forgave them completely.

One Night in Longyearbyen

It took two hours to get back to the tiny port at Longyearbyen. It was Norway's – and the world's – most northern town, with a population of around two thousand people.

Nora knew these basic things from her root life. She had, after all, been fascinated by this part of the world since she was eleven, but her knowledge didn't stretch far beyond the magazine articles she had read and she was still nervous of talking.

But the boat trip back had been okay, because her inability to discuss the rock and ice and plant samples they had taken, or to understand phrases such as 'striated basalt bedrock' and 'post-glacial isotopes', was put down to the shock of her polar bear encounter.

And she *was* in a kind of shock, it was true. But it was not the shock her colleagues were imagining. The shock hadn't been that she'd thought she'd been about to die. She had been about to die ever since she first entered the Midnight Library. No, the shock was that she felt like she was about to *live*. Or at least, that she could imagine wanting to be alive again. And she wanted to do something good with that life.

The life of a human, according to the Scottish philosopher David Hume, was of no greater importance to the universe than that of an oyster.

But if it was important enough for David Hume to write that thought down, then maybe it was important enough to aim to do something good. To help preserve life, in all its forms.

As Nora understood it, the work this other Nora and her fellow scientists had been doing was something to do with determining the speed at which the ice and glaciers had been melting in the region, to gauge the acceleration rate of climate change. There was more to it than that, but that was at the core of it, as far as Nora could see.

So, in this life, she was doing her bit to save the planet. Or at least to monitor the steady devastation of the planet in order to alert people to the facts of environmental crisis. That was potentially depressing but also a good and ultimately fulfilling thing to do, she imagined. There was purpose. There was meaning.

They were impressed too. The others. With the polar bear story. Nora was a hero of sorts – not in an Olympic-swimming-champion way, but in another equally fulfilling kind of fashion.

Ingrid had her arm around her. 'You are the saucepan warrior. And I think we need to mark your fearlessness, and our potentially groundbreaking findings, with a meal. A nice meal. And some vodka. What do you say, Peter?'

'A nice meal? In Longyearbyen? Do they have them?'

As it turned out: they did.

Back on dry land they went to a smart wooden shack of a place called Gruvelageret perched off a lonely road in an austere, snow-crisp valley. She drank Arctic ale and surprised her colleagues by eating the only vegan option on a menu that included reindeer steak and moose burger. Nora must have looked tired because quite a few of her colleagues told her that she did, but maybe it was just that there weren't many places in the conversation that she could enter with confidence. She felt like a learner driver at a busy junction, nervously waiting for a clear and safe patch of road.

Hugo was there. He still looked to her like he would rather be in Antibes or St Tropez. She felt a little uneasy as he stared at her, a little too observed.

On the hurried walk back to their land-based accommodation, which reminded Nora of a university halls of residence but on a smaller scale and more Nordic and wooden and minimal, Hugo jogged to catch her up and walk by her side.

'It is interesting,' he said.

'What is interesting?'

'How at breakfast this morning you didn't know who I was.'

'Why? You didn't know who I was either.'

'Of course I did. We were chatting for about two hours yesterday.'

Nora felt like she was inside some kind of trap. 'We were?'

'I studied you at breakfast before I came over and I could see you were different today.'

'That's creepy, Hugo. Studying women at breakfast.'

'And I noticed things.'

Nora lifted her scarf over her face. 'It's too cold. Can we talk about this tomorrow?'

'I noticed you improvising. All day you have been non-committal in everything you say.'

'Not true. I'm just shook up. You know, the bear.'

'Non. Ce n'est pas ça. I'm talking about before the bear. And after the bear. And all day.'

'I have no idea what you're—'

'There is a look. I have seen it before in other people. I'd recognise it anywhere.'

'I have no idea what you are talking about.'

'Why do glaciers pulsate?'

'What?'

'This is your area of study. It's why you're here, isn't it?'

'The science isn't entirely settled on the matter.'

'Okay. Bien. Name me one of the glaciers around here. Glaciers have names. Name one . . . Kongsbreen? Nathorstbreen? Ring any bells?'

'I don't want this conversation.'

'Because you aren't the same person you were yesterday, are you?'

141

'None of us are,' said Nora, briskly. 'Our brains change. It's called neuroplasticity. Please. Stop mansplaining glaciers to a glaciologist, Hugo.'

Hugo seemed to retreat a little and she felt a bit guilty. There was a minute of silence. Just the crunch of their feet in the snow. They were nearly back at the accommodation, the others not too far behind them.

But then, he said it.

'I am like you, Nora. I visit lives that aren't mine. I have been in this one for five days. But I have been in many others. I was given an opportunity – a rare opportunity – for this to happen. I have been sliding between lives for a long while.'

Ingrid grabbed Nora's arm.

'I still have some vodka,' she announced as they reached the door. She held her key card in her glove and tapped it against the scanner. The door opened.

'Listen,' Hugo mumbled, conspiratorially, 'if you want to know more, meet me in the communal kitchen in five minutes.'

And Nora felt her heart race, but this time she had no ladle or saucepan to bang. She didn't particularly *like* this Hugo character, but was far too intrigued not to hear what he had to say. And she also wanted to know if he could be trusted.

'Okay,' she said. 'I'll be there.'

Expectation

Nora had always had a problem accepting herself. From as far back as she could remember, she'd had the sense that she wasn't enough. Her parents, who both had their own insecurities, had encouraged that idea.

She imagined, now, what it would be like to accept herself completely. Every mistake she had ever made. Every mark on her body. Every dream she hadn't reached or pain she had felt. Every lust or longing she had suppressed.

She imagined accepting it all. The way she accepted nature. The way she accepted a glacier or a puffin or the breach of a whale.

She imagined seeing herself as just another brilliant freak of nature. Just another sentient animal, trying their best.

And in doing so, she imagined what it was like to be free.

Life and Death and the Quantum Wave Function

With Hugo, it wasn't a library.

'It's a video store,' he said, leaning against the cheap-looking cupboard where the coffee was kept. 'It looks exactly like a video store I used to go to in the outskirts of Lyon – Video Lumière – where I grew up. The Lumière brothers are heroes in Lyon and there's a lot of things named after them. They invented cinema there. Anyway, that is beside the point: the point is that every life I choose is an old VHS that I play right in the store, and the moment it starts – the moment the movie starts – is the moment I disappear.'

Nora suppressed a giggle.

'What's so funny?' Hugo wondered, a little hurt.

'Nothing. Nothing at all. It just seemed mildly amusing. A video store.'

'Oh? And a library, that is entirely sensible?'

'More sensible, yes. I mean, at least you can still use books. Who plays videos these days?'

'Interesting. I had no idea there was such a thing as between-life snobbery. You are an education.'

'Sorry, Hugo. Okay, I will ask a sensible question. Is there anyone else there? A person who helps you choose each life?'

He nodded. 'Oh yeah. It's my Uncle Philippe. He died years ago. And he never even worked in a video store. It's so illogical.'

Nora told him about Mrs Elm.

'A school librarian?' mocked Hugo. 'That's pretty funny too.'

Nora ignored him. 'Do you reckon they're ghosts? Guiding spirits? Guardian angels? What are they?'

It felt so ludicrous, in the heart of a scientific facility, to be talking like this.

'They are,' Hugo gestured, as if trying to pluck the right term from the air, 'an interpretation.'

'Interpretation?'

'I have met others like us,' Hugo said. 'You see, I have been in the in-between state for a long time. I have encountered a few other sliders. That's what I call them. Us. We are sliders. We have a root life in which we are lying somewhere, unconscious, suspended between life and death, and then we arrive in a place. And it is always something different. A library, a video store, an art gallery, a casino, a restaurant . . . What does that tell you?'

Nora shrugged. And thought. Listening to the hum of the central heating. 'That it's all bullshit? That none of this is real?'

'No. Because the template is always the same. For instance: there is always someone else there – a guide. Only ever one person. They are always someone who has helped the person at a significant time in their life. The setting is always somewhere with emotional significance. And there is usually talk of root lives or branches.'

Nora thought about being consoled by Mrs Elm when her dad died. Staying with her, comforting her. It was probably the most kindness anyone had ever shown her.

'And there is always an infinite range of choices,' Hugo went on. 'An infinite number of video tapes, or books, or paintings, or meals . . . Now, I am a scientist. And I have lived many scientific lives. In my original root life, I have a degree in Biology. I have also, in another life, been a Nobel Prize-winning chemist. I have been a marine biologist trying to protect the Great Barrier Reef. But my weakness was always physics. At first I had no idea of how to find out what was happening to me. Until I met a woman in one life who was going through what we are going through, and in her root life she was a quantum physicist. Professor Dominique Bisset at Montpellier University. She explained it all to me. The many-worlds interpretation of quantum physics. So that means we—'

A kind-faced, pink-skinned, auburn-bearded man whose name Nora didn't know came into the kitchen to rinse a coffee cup, then smiled at them.

'See you tomorrow,' he said, in a soft American (maybe Canadian) accent, before padding away in his slippers.

'Yes,' said Nora.

'See you,' said Hugo, before returning – in a more hushed tone – to his main thread. 'The universal wave function is real, Nora. That's what Professor Bisset said.'

'What?'

Hugo held up a finger. A slightly annoying, wait-a-minute kind of finger. Nora resisted a strong urge to grab it and twist it. 'Erwin Schrödinger . . .'

'He of the cat.'

'Yes. The cat guy. He said that in quantum physics every alternative possibility happens *simultaneously*. All at once. In the same place. Quantum superposition. The cat in the box is both alive and dead. You could open the box and see that it was alive or dead, that's how it goes, but in one sense, even after the box is open, the cat is still both alive and dead. Every universe exists over every other universe. Like a million pictures on tracing paper, all with slight variations within the same frame. The many-worlds interpretation of quantum physics suggests there are an infinite number of divergent parallel universes. Every moment of your life you enter a new universe. With every decision you make. And traditionally it was thought that there could be no communication or transference between those worlds, even though they happen in the same space, even though they happen literally millimetres away from us.'

'But what about us? We're doing that.'

'Exactly. I am here but I also know I am not here. I am also lying in a hospital in Paris, having an aneurysm. And I am also skydiving in Arizona. And travelling around southern India. And tasting wine in Lyon, and lying on a yacht off the Côte d'Azur.'

'I knew it!'

'Vraiment?'

He was, she decided, quite beautiful.

'You seem more suited to strolling the Croisette in Cannes than an Arctic adventure.'

He widened his right hand like a starfish. 'Five days! Five days I have been in this life. That is my record. Maybe this is the life for me . . .'

'Interesting. You're going to have a very cold life.'

'And who knows? Maybe you are too . . . I mean, if the bear didn't take you back to your library maybe nothing will.' He started to fill the kettle. 'Science tells us that the "grey zone" between life and death is a mysterious place. There is a singular point at which we are not one thing or another. Or rather we are both. Alive and dead. And in that moment between the two binaries, sometimes, just sometimes, we turn ourselves into a Schrödinger's cat who may not only be alive or dead but may be every quantum possibility that exists in line with the universal wave function, including the possibility where we are chatting in a communal kitchen in Longyearbyen at one in the morning . . .'

Nora was taking all this in. She thought of Volts, still and lifeless under the bed and lying by the side of the road.

'But sometimes the cat is just dead and dead.'

'Sorry?'

'Nothing. It's just . . . my cat died. And I tried another life and even in that one he was still dead.'

'That's sad. I had a similar situation with a Labrador. But the point is, there are others like us. I have lived so many lives, I have come across a few of them. Sometimes just to say your own truth out loud is enough to find others like you.'

'It's crazy to think that there are other people who could be . . . what did you call us?

'Sliders?'

'Yep. That.'

'Well, it's possible of course, but I think we're rare. One thing I've noticed is that the other people I've met – the dozen or so – have all been around our age. All thirties or forties or fifties. One was twenty-nine, en fait. All have had a deep desire to have done things differently. They had regrets. Some contemplated that they may be better off dead but also had a desire to live as another version of themselves.'

'Schrödinger's life. Both dead and alive in your own mind.'

'Exactement! And whatever those regrets did to our brain, whatever – how would you say? – neurochemical event happened, that confused yearning for death-and-life was somehow just enough to send us into this state of total *in-between*.'

The kettle was getting noisier, the water starting to bubble like Nora's thoughts.

'Why is it always just one person that we see? In the place. The library. Whatever.'

Hugo shrugged. 'If I was religious, I'd say it was God. And as God is probably someone we can't see or comprehend then He – or She – or whichever pronoun God is – becomes an image of someone good we have known in our lives. And if I wasn't religious – which I'm not – I would think that the human brain can't handle the complexity of an open quantum wave function and so it organises or translates this complexity into something it understands. A librarian in a library. A friendly uncle in a video store. Et cetera.'

Nora had read about multiverses and knew a bit about Gestalt psychology. About how human brains take complex information about the world and simplify it, so that when a human looks at a tree it translates the intricately complex mass of leaves and branches into this thing called 'tree'. To be a human was to continually dumb the world down into an understandable story that keeps things simple.

She knew that *everything* humans see is a simplification. A human sees the world in three dimensions. That is a simplification. Humans are fundamentally limited, generalising creatures, living on auto-pilot, who straighten out curved streets in their minds, which explains why they get lost all the time.

'It's like how humans never see the second hand of a clock mid-tick,' said Nora.

'What?'

She saw that Hugo's watch was of the analogue variety. 'Try it. You just can't. Minds can't see what they can't handle.'

Hugo nodded, as he observed his own watch.

'So,' Nora said, 'whatever exists between universes is most likely not a library, but that is the easiest way for me to understand it. That would be my hypothesis. I see a simplified version of the truth. The librarian is just a kind of mental metaphor. The whole thing is.'

'Isn't it fascinating?' said Hugo.

Nora sighed. 'In the last life I spoke to my dead dad.'

Hugo opened a jar of coffee and scooped out granules into two mugs.

'And I didn't drink coffee. I drank peppermint tea.'

'That sounds terrible.'

'It was bearable.'

'Another thing that is strange,' Hugo said. 'At any point in this conversation you or I could disappear.'

'Have you seen that happen?' Nora took the mug Hugo handed her.

'Yeah. A few times. It's freaky. But no one else would notice. They become a bit vague with their memory for the last day, but you would be surprised. If you went back to the library right now, and I was still standing here talking to you in the kitchen, you would say something like "My mind's just gone blank – what were we talking about?", and then I'd realise what had happened and I'd say we were talking about glaciers and you'd bombard me with facts about them. And your brain would fill in the gaps and make up a narrative about what just happened.'

'Yeah, but what about the polar bear? What about the meal tonight? Would I – this other me – would she remember what I ate?'

'Not necessarily. But I have seen it happen. It's amazing what the brain can fill in. And what it is fine with forgetting.'

'So, what was I like? Yesterday, I mean.'

He locked eyes. They were pretty eyes. Nora momentarily felt pulled into his orbit like a satellite to Earth.

'Exquisite, charming, intelligent, beautiful. Much like now.'

She laughed it off. 'Stop being so French.'

Awkward pause.

'How many lives have you had?' she said eventually. 'How many have you experienced?'

'Too many. Nearing three hundred.'

'Three hundred?'

'I have been so many things. On every continent on Earth. And yet I have never found the life for me. I am resigned to being this way for ever. There will never be a life that I truly want to live for ever. I get too curious. I get too much of a yearning to live another way. And you don't need to make that face. It's not sad. I am happily in limbo.'

'But what if one day there is no video store?' Nora thought about Mrs Elm, panicking at the computer, and the flickering lights in the library. 'What if one day you disappear for good? Before you have found a life to settle in?'

He shrugged. 'Then I will die. And it means I would have died anyway. In the life I lived before. I kind of like being a slider. I like imperfection. I like keeping death as an option. I like never having to settle.'

'I think my situation is different. I think my death is more imminent. If I don't find a life to live in pretty soon, I think I'll be gone for good.'

She explained the problem she'd had last time, with transferring back.

'Oh. Yeah, well, that might be bad. But it might not be. You do realise there are infinite possibilities here? I mean, the multiverse isn't about just some universes. It's not about a handful of universes. It's not even about a lot of universes. It's not about a million or a billion or a trillion universes. It's about an *infinite* number of universes. Even with you in them. You could be you in any version of the world, however unlikely that world would be. You are only limited by your imagination. You can be very creative with the regrets you want to undo. I once undid a regret about not doing something I'd contemplated as a teenager – doing aerospace engineering and becoming an astronaut – and so in one life I became an astronaut. I haven't been to space. But I became someone who had been there, for a little while. The thing you have to remember is that this is an opportunity and it is rare and we can undo any mistake we made, live any life we want. Any life. Dream big . . . You can be anything you want to be. Because in one life, you are.'

She sipped her coffee. 'I understand.'

'But you will never live if you are looking for the meaning of life,' he said, wisely.

'You're quoting Camus.'

'You got me.'

He was staring at her. Nora no longer minded his intensity, but was becoming a little concerned about her own. 'I was a Philosophy student,' she said, as blandly as she could manage, avoiding his eyes.

He was close to her now. There was something equally annoying and attractive about Hugo. He exuded an arrogant amorality that made his face something to either slap or kiss, depending on the circumstances.

'In one life we have known each other for years and are married . . .' he said.

'In most lives I don't know you at all,' she countered, now staring straight at him.

'That's so sad.'

'I don't think so.'

'Really?'

'Really.' She smiled.

'We're special, Nora. We're chosen. No one understands us.'

'No one understands anyone. We're not chosen.'

'The only reason I am still in this life is because of you . . .'

She lunged forward and kissed him.

If Something Is Happening to Me, I Want to Be There

It was a very pleasant sensation. Both the kiss, and the knowledge she could be this forward. Being aware that everything that could possibly happen happened to her somewhere, in some life, kind of absolved her a little from decisions. That was just the reality of the universal wave function. Whatever was happening could – she reasoned – be put down to quantum physics.

'I don't share a room,' he said.

She stared at him fearlessly now, as if facing down a polar bear had given her a certain capacity for dominance she'd never been aware of. 'Well, Hugo, maybe you could break the habit.'

But the sex turned out to be a disappointment. A Camus quote came to her, right in the middle of it.

I may have not been sure about what really did interest me, but I was absolutely sure about what didn't.

It probably wasn't the best sign of how their nocturnal encounter was going, that she was thinking of Existential philosophy, or that this quote in particular was the one that appeared in her mind. But hadn't Camus also said, 'If something is going to happen to me, I want to be there'?

Hugo, she concluded, was a strange person. For a man who had been so intimate and deep in his conversation, he was very detached from the moment. Maybe if you lived as many lives as he had, the only person you really had any kind of intimate relationship with was yourself. She felt like she might not have been there at all.

And in a few moments, she wasn't.

God and Other Librarians

'Who are you?'

'You know my name. I am Mrs Elm. Louise Isabel Elm.'

'Are you God?'

She smiled. 'I am who I am.'

'And who is that?'

'The librarian.'

'But you aren't a real person. You're just a . . . *mechanism*.'

'Aren't we all?'

'Not like that. You are the product of some strange interaction between my mind and the multiverse, some simplification of the quantum wave function or whatever it is.'

Mrs Elm looked perturbed by the suggestion. 'What is the matter?'

Nora thought of the polar bear as she stared down at the yellow-brown stone floor. 'I nearly died.'

'And remember, if you die in a life, there is no way back here.'

'That's not fair.'

'The library has strict rules. Books are precious. You have to treat them carefully.'

'But these are other lives. Other variants of me. Not *me* me.'

'Yes, but while *you* are experiencing them, it is *you* who has to pay the consequences.'

'Well, I think that stinks, to be perfectly honest.'

The librarian's smile curled at its edges, like a fallen leaf. 'Well, this is interesting.'

'What is interesting?'

'The fact that you have so thoroughly changed your attitude towards dying.'

'What?'

'You wanted to die and now you don't.'

It dawned on Nora that Mrs Elm might be close to having a point, although not quite the whole point. 'Well, I still think my actual life isn't worth living. In fact, this experience has just managed to confirm that.'

She shook her head. 'I don't think you think that.'

'I do think that. That's why I said it.'

'No. *The Book of Regrets* is getting lighter. There's a lot of white space in there now . . . It seems that you have spent all your life saying things that you aren't really thinking. This is one of your barriers.'

'Barriers?'

'Yes. You have a lot of them. They stop you from seeing the truth.'

'About what?'

'About yourself. And you really need to start trying. To see the truth. Because this matters.'

'I thought there were an infinite number of lives to choose from.'

'You need to pick the life you'd be most happy inside. Or soon there won't be a choice at all.'

'I met someone who has been doing this for a long time and he still hasn't found a life that he is satisfied with . . .'

'Well, Hugo's is a privilege you might not have.'

'Hugo? How do you—'

But then she remembered Mrs Elm knew a lot more than she should.

'You need to choose carefully,' continued the librarian. 'One day the library may not be here and you'll be gone for ever.'

'How many lives do I have?'

'This isn't a magic lamp and I am no genie. There is no set

number. It could be one. It could be a hundred. But you only have an infinite number of lives to choose from so long as the time in the Midnight Library stays, well, at *midnight*. Because while it stays at midnight, your life – your root life – is somewhere between life and death. If time moves here, that means something very . . .' She searched for a delicate word. '. . . *decisive* has happened. Something that razes the Midnight Library to the ground, and takes us with it. And so I would err on the side of caution. I would try to think very keenly about where you want to be. You have clearly made some progress, I can tell. You seem to realise that life could be worth living, if only you found the right one to exist inside. But you don't want that gate to close before you get a chance to go through it.'

They both were silent for a very long time, as Nora observed all the books all around her. All the possibilities. Calmly and slowly, she walked along the aisle, wondering what lay beyond the covers of each book, and wishing the green spines would offer some kind of clue.

'Now, which book do you fancy?' came Mrs Elm's words behind her.

Nora remembered Hugo's words in the kitchen.

Dream big.

The librarian had a penetrating gaze. 'Who *is* Nora Seed? And what does she want?'

When Nora thought of her closest access to happiness, it was music. Yes, she still played the piano and keyboard sometimes, but she had given up *creating*. She had given up singing. She thought of those happy early pub gigs playing 'Beautiful Sky'. She thought of her brother larking about on stage with her and Ravi and Ella.

So now she knew precisely which book to ask for.

Fame

She was sweating. That was the first observation. Her body was coursing with adrenaline and her clothes were clinging to her. There were people around her, a couple of whom had guitars. She could hear noise. Vast, powerful human noise – a roar of life slowly finding rhythm and shape. Becoming a chant.

There was a woman in front of her, towelling her face.

'Thanks,' Nora said, smiling.

The woman looked startled, as if she'd just been spoken to by a god.

She recognised a man holding drumsticks. It was Ravi. His hair was dyed white-blonde and he was dressed in a sharp-cut indigo suit with a bare chest where his shirt should have been. He looked an entirely different person to the one who had been looking at the music magazines in the newsagent's in Bedford only yesterday, or the corporate-looking guy in the blue shirt who had sat watching her do her catastrophic talk in the InterContinental Hotel.

'Ravi,' she said, 'you look amazing!'

'What?'

He hadn't heard her over the noise, but now she had a different question.

'Where is Joe?' she asked, almost as a shout.

Ravi looked momentarily confused, or scared, and Nora braced herself for some terrible truth. But none came.

'The usual, I reckon. Schmoozing it up with the foreign press.'

Nora had no idea what was going on. He seemed to be still part of the band, but also not in the band enough to be performing on stage with them. And if he *wasn't* in the band, then whatever had caused him to leave the band hadn't caused him to disappear completely. From what Ravi said, and the way he said it, Joe was still very much part of the team. Ella wasn't there, though. On bass was a large muscly man with a shaved head and tattoos. She wanted to know more, but now was clearly not the time.

Ravi swept his hand through the air, gesturing towards what Nora could now see was a very large stage.

She was overwhelmed. She didn't know what to feel.

'Encore time,' said Ravi.

Nora tried to think. It had been a long time since she had performed *anything*. And even then it was only in front of a crowd of about twelve uninterested people in a pub basement.

Ravi leaned in. 'You okay, Nora?'

It seemed a bit brittle. The way he said her name seemed to contain the same kind of resentment she'd heard when she'd bumped into him yesterday, in that very different life.

'Yes,' she said, full shouting now. 'Of course. It's just . . . I have no idea what we should do for the encore.'

Ravi shrugged. 'Same as always.'

'Hmm. Yeah. Right.' Nora tried to think. She looked out at the stage. She saw a giant video screen with the words THE LABYRINTHS flashing and rotating out to the roaring crowd. *Wow*, she thought. *We're big.* Proper, stadium-level big. She saw a keyboard and the stool she had been sitting at. Her bandmates whose names she didn't know were about to walk back on stage.

'Where are we again?' she asked, above the crowd noise. 'I've gone blank.'

The big shaven-headed guy holding the bass told her: 'São Paulo.'

'We're in Brazil?'

They looked at her as if she was mad.

'Where have you been the last four days?'

'"Beautiful Sky"', said Nora, realising she could probably still remember most of the words. 'Let's do that.'

'*Again?*' Ravi laughed, his face shining with sweat. 'We did it ten minutes ago.'

'Okay. Listen,' said Nora, her voice now a shout over the crowd demanding an encore. 'I was thinking we do something different. Mix it up. I wondered if we could do a different song to usual.'

'We have to do "Howl"', said the other band member. A turquoise lead guitar strapped around her. 'We always do "Howl".'

Nora had never heard of 'Howl' in her life.

'Yeah, I know,' she bluffed, 'but let's mix it up. Let's do something they aren't expecting. Let's surprise them.'

'You're overthinking this, Nora,' said Ravi.

'I have no other type of thinking available.'

Ravi shrugged. 'So, what should we do?'

Nora struggled to think. She thought of Ash – with his Simon & Garfunkel guitar songbook. 'Let's do "Bridge Over Troubled Water".'

Ravi was incredulous. 'What?'

'I think we should do that. It will surprise people.'

'I love that song,' said the female bandmate. 'And I know it.'

'Everyone knows it, Imani,' Ravi said, dismissively.

'Exactly,' Nora said, trying her hardest to sound like a rock star, 'let's do it.'

Milky Way

Nora walked onto the stage.

At first she couldn't see the faces, because the lights were pointing towards her, and beyond that glare everything seemed like darkness. Except for a mesmerising milky way of camera flashes and phone torches.

She could hear them, though.

Human beings when there's enough of them together acting in total unison become something else. The collective roar made her think of another kind of animal entirely. It was at first kind of threatening, as if she was Hercules facing the many-headed Hydra who wanted to kill him, but this was a roar of total support, and the power of it gave her a kind of strength.

She realised, in that moment, that she was capable of a lot more than she had known.

Wild and Free

She reached the keyboard, sat down on the stool and brought the microphone a little closer.

'Thank you, São Paulo,' she said. 'We love you.'

And Brazil roared back.

This, it seemed, was power. The power of fame. Like those pop icons she had seen on social media, who could say a single word and get a million likes and shares. Total fame was when you reached the point where looking like a hero, or genius, or god, required minimal effort. But the flipside was that it was precarious. It could be equally easy to fall and look like a devil or a villain, or just an arse.

Her heart raced, as if she were about to set foot on a tight-rope.

She could see some of the faces in the crowd now, thousands of them, emerging from the dark. Tiny and strange, the clothed bodies almost invisible. She was staring out at twenty thousand disembodied heads.

Her mouth was dry. She could hardly speak, so wondered how she was going to sing. She remembered Dan mock-wincing as she'd sung for him.

The noise of the crowd subsided.

It was time.

'Right,' she said. 'Here is a song you might have heard before.'

This was a stupid thing to say, she realised. They had all paid tickets for this concert presumably because they had heard a lot of these songs before.

'It's a song that means a lot to me and my brother.'

Already the place was erupting. They screamed and roared and clapped and chanted. The response was phenomenal. She felt, momentarily, like Cleopatra. An utterly terrified Cleopatra.

Adjusting her hands into position for E-flat major, she was momentarily distracted by a tattoo on her weirdly hairless forearm, written in beautifully angled calligraphic letters. It was a quote from Henry David Thoreau. *All good things are wild and free.* She closed her eyes and vowed not to open them until she had finished the song.

She understood why Chopin had liked playing in the dark so much. It was so much easier that way.

Wild, she thought to herself. *Free.*

As she sang, she felt alive. Even more alive than she had felt swimming in her Olympic-champion body.

She wondered why she had been so scared of this, of singing to a crowd. It was a great feeling.

Ravi came over to her at the end of the song, while they were still on stage. 'That was fucking special, man,' he shouted in her ear.

'Oh good,' she said.

'Now let's kill this and do "Howl".'

She shook her head, then spoke into the microphone, hurriedly, before anyone else had a chance to. 'Thank you for coming, every-body! I really hope you all had a nice evening. Get home safely.'

'Get home safely?' Ravi said in the coach on the way back to the hotel. She hadn't remembered him being such an arse. He seemed unhappy.

'What was wrong with that?' she wondered out loud.

'Hardly your normal style.'

'Wasn't it?'

'Well, bit of a contrast to Chicago.'

'Why? What did I do in Chicago?'

Ravi laughed. 'Have you been lobotomised?'

She looked at her phone. In this life she had the latest model. A message from Izzy.

It was the same message she'd had in her life with Dan, in the pub. Not a message at all but a photo of a whale. Actually, it might have been a slightly different photo of a whale. That was interesting. Why was she still friends with Izzy in this life and not in her root life? After all, she was pretty sure she wasn't married to Dan in this life. She checked her hand and was relieved to see a totally naked ring finger.

Nora supposed it was because she had already been super-famous with The Labyrinths *before* Izzy decided to go to Australia, so Nora's decision not to go may have been more understandable. Or maybe Izzy just liked the idea of a famous friend.

Izzy wrote something under the picture of the whale.

All good things are wild and free.

She must have known about the tattoo.

Another message came through now from her.

'Hope Brazil was a blast. Am sure you rocked it! And thanks ten million for sorting out the tix for Brisbane. Am totally stoked. As we Gold Coasters say.'

There were a few emojis of whales and hearts and thanking hands and a microphone and some musical notes.

Nora checked her Instagram. In this life she had 11.3 million followers.

And *bloody hell*, she looked amazing. Her naturally black hair had a kind of white stripe in it. Vampiric make-up. And a lip piercing. She did look tired but she supposed that was just a result of living on tour. It was a glamorous kind of tired. Like Billie Eilish's cool aunt.

She took a selfie and saw that while she didn't look exactly like the excessively styled and filtered photos on her feed, which had been for magazine shoots, she did look cooler than she ever imagined she could look. As with her Australian life, she also put poems up online. The difference with this life, though, was that each poem had about half a million likes. One of the poems was even called 'Fire' but it was different to the other one.

She had a fire inside her.
She wondered if the fire was to warm her or destroy her.
Then she realised.
A fire had no motive.
Only she could have that.
The power was hers.

A woman sat next to her. This woman wasn't in the band, but she exuded importance. She was about fifty years old. Maybe she was the manager. Maybe she worked for the record company. She had the air of a strict mum about her. But she began with a smile.

'Stroke of genius,' she said. 'The Simon & Garfunkel thing. You're trending across South America.'

'Cool.'

'Have posted about it from your accounts.'

She'd said this like it was a perfectly normal thing. 'Oh. Right. Okay.'

'There's a couple of last-minute press things tonight at the hotel. Then tomorrow it's an early start . . . We fly to Rio first thing, then eight hours of press. All at the hotel.'

'Rio?'

'You're up to speed with this week's tour schedule, right?'

'Um, kind of. Could you just remind me again?'

She sighed, with good humour, as if Nora not knowing the tour schedule was totally in character. 'Sure. Rio tomorrow. Two nights. Then the final night in Brazil – Porto Alegre – then Santiago, Chile, Buenos Aires, then Lima. And that's the last leg of South America.

Then next week it's the start of the Asia leg – Japan, Hong Kong, the Philippines, Taiwan.'

'Peru? We're famous in Peru?'

'Nora, you've been to Peru before, remember? Last year. They went out of their minds. All fifteen thousand of them. It's at the same place. The racecourse.'

'The racecourse. Sure. Yeah. I remember. Was a good night. Really . . . good.'

That's what this life probably felt like, she realised. One big racecourse. But she had no idea if she was the horse or the jockey in that analogy.

Ravi tapped the woman on the shoulder. 'Joanna, what time's that podcast tomorrow?'

'Oh damn. Actually, it's tonight now. Timings. Sorry. Forgot to say. But they only really have to speak to Nora. So you can get an early night if you want.'

Ravi shrugged, dejected. 'Sure. Yeah.'

Joanna sighed. 'Don't shoot the messenger. Though it's never stopped you before.'

Nora wondered again where her brother was, but the tension between Joanna and Ravi made it feel wrong to ask something she should so obviously know. So she stared out of the window as the coach drove along the four-lane highway. The glowing tail-lights of cars and lorries and motorbikes in the dark, like red and watching eyes. Distant skyscrapers with a few tiny squares of light against a humid backdrop of dark sky and darker clouds. A shadowy army of trees lined the sides and middle of the highway, splitting the traffic into two directions.

If she was still in this life tomorrow evening, she would be expected to perform an entire concert's worth of songs, most of which she didn't actually know. She wondered how quickly she could learn the set list.

Her phone rang. A video call. The caller was 'Ryan'.

Joanna saw the name and smirked a little. 'You'd better get that.'

So she did, even though she had no idea who this Ryan was, and the image on the screen seemed too blurry to recognise.

But then he was there. A face she had seen, in movies and imaginings, many times.

'Hey, babe. Just checking in with a friend. We're still friends, right?'

She knew the voice too.

American, rugged, charming. Famous.

She heard Joanna whispering to someone else on the coach: 'She's on the phone to Ryan Bailey.'

Ryan Bailey

Ryan Bailey.

As in *the* Ryan Bailey. As in the Ryan Bailey of her fantasies, where they talked about Plato and Heidegger through a veil of steam in his West Hollywood hot tub.

'Nora? You there? You look scared.'

'Um, yeah. I'm . . . yeah . . . I'm . . . I've just . . . I'm here . . . On a bus . . . A big . . . touring . . . yeah . . . Hi.'

'Guess where I am?'

She had no idea what to say. 'Hot tub' seemed entirely inappropriate as an answer. 'I honestly don't know.'

He panned the phone around a vast and opulent-looking villa, complete with bright furnishings and terracotta tiles and a four-poster double bed veiled in a mosquito net.

'Nayarit, Mexico.' He pronounced Mexico in a parody of Spanish, with the x as an h. He looked and sounded slightly different to the Ryan Bailey in the movies. A bit puffier. A bit more slurred. Drunker, perhaps. 'On location. They got me shooting *Saloon 2.*'

'*Last Chance Saloon 2*? Oh, I so want to see the first one.'

He laughed as if she had told the most hilarious joke.

'Still dry as ever, Nono.'

Nono?

'Staying at the Casa de Míta,' he went on. 'Remember? The weekend we had there? They've put me in the exact same villa. You remember? I'm having a mezcal margarita in your honour. Where are you?'

'Brazil. We were just doing a concert in São Paulo.'

'Wow. Same landmass. That's cool. That's, yeah, cool.'

'It was really good,' she said.

'You're sounding very formal.'

Nora was aware half of the bus was listening in. Ravi was staring at her as he drank a bottle of beer.

'I'm just . . . you know . . . on the bus . . . There are people around.'

'People,' he sighed, as if it was a swear word. 'There are always people. That's the fucking problem. But hey, I've been thinking a lot recently. About what you said on Jimmy Fallon . . .'

Nora tried to act as if every sentence he said wasn't an animal running into the road.

'What did I say?'

'You know, about how it just ran its course. Me and you. How there were no hard feelings. I just want to thank you for saying that. Because I know I am a difficult fucking person. I know that. But I'm getting work for that. The therapist I'm seeing is really fucking good.'

'That's . . . great.'

'I miss you, Nora. We had great times. But there is more to life than fantastic sex.'

'Yes,' said Nora, trying to keep her imagination in check. 'Absolutely.'

'We had all kinds of great. But you were right to finish it. You did the right thing, in the cosmic order of things. There is no *rejection,* there is only *redirection.* You know, I've been thinking a lot. About the cosmos. I've been tuning in. And the cosmos has been telling me I need to get my shit together. It's balance, man. What we had was too intense and our lives are too intense and it's like Darwin's third law of motion. About an action leading to a reaction. Something had to give. And you were the one who saw that and now we are just particles floating in the universe that may reconnect one day at the Chateau Marmont . . .'

She had no idea what to say. 'I think that was Newton.'

'What?'

'The third law of motion.'

He tilted his head, like a confused dog. 'What?'

'Never mind. It doesn't matter.'

He sighed.

'Anyway, I'm going to finish this margarita. Because I've got an early training session. Mezcal, you see. Not tequila. Got to keep pure. Got this new trainer. This MMA guy. He's intense.'

'Okay.'

'And Nono . . .'

'Yeah?'

'Can you just call me your special name for me again?'

'Um—'

'You know the one.'

'Obviously. Yeah. Course.' She tried to think what it could be. *Ry-ry? Rye bread? Plato?*

'I can't.'

'People?'

She made a show of looking around. 'Exactly. People. And you know, now that we've moved on with our lives, it seems a bit . . . inappropriate.'

He smiled a melancholy smile. 'Listen. I'll be there for the final LA show. Front row. Staples Center. You won't be able to stop me, got it?'

'That's so sweet.'

'Friends for ever?'

'Friends for ever.'

Sensing they were nearing the end of the conversation, Nora suddenly had something to ask.

'Were you really into philosophy?'

He burped. It was strange how shocking it was to realise that Ryan Bailey was a human being in a human body that generated gas.

'What?'

'Philosophy. Years ago, when you were playing Plato in *The Athenians* you gave an interview and you said you read a lot of philosophy.'

'I read *life*. And life is a philosophy.'

Nora had no idea what he meant, but deep down she was proud of this other version of her for dumping an A-list movie star.

'I think you said at the time you read Martin Heidegger.'

'Who is Martin Hot Dog? Oh, it was probably just press bullshit. You know, you say all sorts of shit.'

'Yeah. Of course.'

'Adios, amiga.'

'Adios, Ryan.'

And then he was gone and Joanna was smiling at her, saying nothing.

There was something teacherly and comforting about Joanna. She imagined that this version of herself liked Joanna. But then she remembered she was supposed to do a podcast on behalf of a band where she didn't know the names of fifty per cent of its members. Or the title of their last album. Or *any* of their albums.

The coach pulled up at a grand-looking hotel outside of town. Fancy cars with darkened windows. Palm trees wrapped in fairy lights. Architecture from another planet.

'A former palace,' Joanna told her. 'Designed by a top Brazilian architect. I forget his name.' She looked it up. 'Oscar Niemeyer,' she said after a moment. 'Modernist. But this is meant to be more opulent than his usual stuff. Best hotel in Brazil . . .'

And then Nora saw a small crowd of people holding out their phones with outstretched arms, as if beggars with bowls, filming her arrival.

You can have everything and feel nothing.
@NoraLabyrinth, 74.8K Retweets, 485.3K Likes

A Silver Tray of Honey Cakes

It was wild to think of this life co-existing with her others in the multiverse, like just another note in a chord.

Nora found it almost impossible to believe that while in one life she was struggling to pay the rent, in another she was causing such excitement among people all over the world.

The handful of fans who had filmed the tour bus arrive at the hotel were now waiting for autographs. They didn't seem too bothered about the other band members but they did seem desperate to interact with Nora.

She looked at one, as she crunched over the gravel towards them. The girl had tattoos and was wearing an outfit that made her look like a flapper girl who had somehow got caught up in a cyberpunk version of a post-apocalyptic war. Her hair was styled exactly like Nora's, complete with matching white stripe.

'Nora! Noraaaah! Hi! We love you, queen! Thank you for coming to Brazil! You rock!' And then a chant started: 'Nora! Nora! Nora!'

While she was signing autographs in an illegible scribble, a man in his early twenties took off his T-shirt and asked her to sign his shoulder.

'It's for a tattoo,' he said.

'Really?' she asked, writing her name onto the man's body.

'This is the highlight of my life,' he gushed. 'My name is Francisco.'

Nora wondered how her writing on his skin with a Sharpie could be a highlight of his existence.

'You saved my life. "Beautiful Sky" saved my life. That song. It's so powerful.'

'Oh. Oh wow. "Beautiful Sky"? You know "Beautiful Sky"?'

The fan burst into hysterics. 'You're so funny! This is why you are my idol! I love you so much! Do I know "Beautiful Sky"? That's brilliant!'

Nora didn't know what to say. That little song she had written when she was nineteen years old at university in Bristol had changed the life of a person in Brazil. It was overwhelming.

This, clearly, was the life she was destined for. She doubted that she would ever have to go back to the library. She could cope with being adored. It was better than being in Bedford, sitting on the number 77 bus, humming sad tunes to the window.

She posed for selfies.

One young woman looked close to tears. She had a large photo of Nora kissing Ryan Bailey.

'I was so sad when you broke up with him!'

'I know, yeah, it was sad. But, you know, things happen. It's a . . . learning curve.'

Joanna appeared at her arm and gently guided her away, towards the hotel.

When she reached the elegant, jasmine-scented lobby (marble, chandeliers, floral displays) she saw that the rest of the band were already in the bar. But where was her brother? Maybe he'd been schmoozing the press somewhere else.

As she started to move towards the bar, she realised that everyone – concierge, receptionists, guests – was looking at her.

Nora was about to finally seize the opportunity to ask about her brother's whereabouts when Joanna beckoned over a man who was wearing a T-shirt with THE LABYRINTHS printed on it in a retro sci-fi movie font. The guy was probably in his forties, with a greying beard and thinning hair, but he seemed intimidated by Nora's presence. He did a tiny bow when he shook Nora's hand.

'I'm Marcelo,' he said. 'Thanks for agreeing to the interview.'

Nora noticed another man behind Marcelo – younger, with piercings, tattoos and a big smile – holding recording equipment.

'We'd reserved a quiet space in the bar,' Joanna said. 'But there's . . . people. I think we had better do this in Nora's suite.'

'Great,' said Marcelo. 'Great, great.'

As they walked over to the lift, Nora glanced back at the bar and saw the other band members. 'You know, maybe you'd like to speak to the others too?' she said to Marcelo. 'They remember things I don't. A lot of things.'

Marcelo smiled and shook his head and delicately said, 'It works better this way, I feel . . .'

'Oh, okay,' she said.

Every eye was on them as they waited for the lift to arrive. Joanna leaned into Nora.

'Are you okay?'

'Of course. Yeah. Why?'

'I don't know. It's just, you seem different tonight.'

'Different how?'

'Just . . . different.'

As they got in the lift Joanna asked another woman, one Nora recognised from the coach, to bring some drinks from the bar – two beers for the podcasters, a sparkling mineral water for Nora and a caipirinha for herself.

'And bring them up to the suite, Maya.'

Maybe I am teetotal in this life, thought Nora, as she walked out of the lift and along the plush salmon-pink carpet to her suite.

And then, as she entered it, she tried to act like this was all perfectly normal. This gigantic room, leading to another gigantic room, leading to a gigantic bathroom. There was a vast bouquet of flowers for her, with a note signed by the hotel's manager.

Wow, she resisted saying, as she gazed around at the lavish furnishings, the sweeping floor-to-ceiling curtains, the pristine white bed the size of an acre, the TV the size of a small cinema, the champagne on ice, the silver tray full of 'Brazilian honey cakes' as the card informed them.

'Don't suppose you'll be having any of these,' said Joanna, taking one of the little delicacies from the tray. 'Now you're on that new plan. Harley said I had to keep an eye on you.'

Nora watched Joanna bite into one of the cakes and wondered how good any plan could be if it didn't involve eating something so clearly delicious as a Brazilian honey cake. She had no idea who Harley was, but she knew she didn't like them.

'Also . . . just so you know, the fires are still going on in LA and they're evacuating half of Calabasas now, but hopefully it won't get as high as your place . . .'

Nora didn't know whether to be pleased at the idea of having a house in LA, or worried that it was about to go on fire.

The two Brazilian podcast guys took a few moments to set up their equipment. And Nora sunk herself into the vast sofa in the living area as Joanna – attending to a few rogue crumbs around her mouth with a heavily manicured finger – explained that their music podcast, *O Som*, was the most popular in Brazil.

'Great demographics,' Joanna enthused. 'And the numbers are stratospheric. It's totally worth doing.'

And she stayed there, watching like a hawk mother, as the podcast began.

The Podcast of Revelations

'So, it has been a crazy year for you,' Marcelo began, in his very good English.

'Oh yeah. It has been quite a ride,' said Nora, trying to sound like a rock star.

'Now, if I may ask about the album . . . *Pottersville*. You wrote all the lyrics, yes?'

'Mostly, yes,' Nora guessed, staring at the small, familiar mole on her left hand.

'She wrote all of them,' interjected Joanna.

Marcelo nodded while the other guy, still smiling toothily, fiddled about with sound levels via a laptop.

'I think "Feathers" is my favourite track,' said Marcelo, as the drinks arrived.

'I'm glad you like it.'

Nora tried to think of a way she could get out of this interview. A headache? A bad stomach?

'But the one I'd like to talk about first is the first one you decided to release. "Stay Out Of My Life". It seemed such a personal statement.'

Nora forced a smile. 'The lyrics say it all really.'

'Obviously there has been some speculation about whether it refers to the . . . how do you say it in English?'

'Restraining order?' offered Joanna, helpfully.

'Yes! The restraining order.'

'Um,' said Nora, taken aback. 'Well. I prefer to get it all out in the song. I find that stuff difficult to talk about.'

'Yes, I understand. It is just that in your recent *Rolling Stone* interview you talked a little about your former boyfriend, Dan Lord, and mentioned how difficult it was to get the . . . the . . . the restraining order against him, after he stalked you . . . Didn't he try to break into your house? Then tell reporters that he wrote the lyrics for "Beautiful Sky"?'

'Jesus.'

She hovered at the intersection of tears and laughter, and managed, somehow, to give neither.

'I wrote it when I was still with him. But he didn't like it. He didn't like me being in this band. He hated it. He hated my brother. He hated Ravi. He hated Ella, who was one of the original members. Anyway, Dan was very jealous.'

This was so surreal. In one life, the life he'd supposedly wanted, Dan was so bored in his marriage to Nora he was having an affair, while in *this* life he was breaking into her house because he couldn't stand her success.

'He's a dick,' said Nora. 'I don't know the Portuguese swear word for a terrible person.'

'Cabrão. It means someone's a dick.'

'Or an asshole,' the younger guy added, stone-faced.

'Yeah, well, he's a cabrão. He turned out to be someone else entirely. It's weird. The way when your life changes people act in different ways. The price of fame, I suppose.'

'And you wrote a song called "Henry David Thoreau". You don't get many songs named after philosophers . . .'

'I know. Well, when I studied Philosophy at university, he was my favourite. Hence my tattoo. And it made a marginally better song title than "Immanuel Kant".'

She was getting into the swing of it now. It wasn't too hard to act a life when it was the one she was destined for.

'And "Howl", obviously. Such a powerful song. Number one in twenty-two countries. Grammy award-winning video with a Hollywood A-list cast. I suppose you are done talking about it?'

'I suppose, yes.'

Joanna went to get herself another honey cake.

Marcelo smiled, gently, as he pressed on. 'For me it seemed so primal. The song, I mean. Like you were letting everything out. And then I discovered you wrote it on the very night you fired your last manager. Before Joanna. After you found out he'd been ripping you off . . .'

'Yeah. That wasn't good,' she improvised. 'It was such a betrayal.'

'I was a big Labyrinths fan before "Howl". But that was the one for me. That and "Lighthouse Girl". "Howl" was where I was like, *Nora Seed is a genius.* The lyrics are pretty abstract, but the way you just let out that rage was so soft and soulful and powerful all at once. It's like early Cure fused with Frank Ocean via The Carpenters and Tame Impala.'

Nora tried, and failed, to imagine what that could possibly sound like.

He started to sing, to everyone's surprise: '"Silence the music to improve the tune / Stop the fake smiles and howl at the moon".'

Nora smiled and nodded, as if she knew these lyrics. 'Yeah. Yeah. I was just . . . howling.'

Marcelo's face became serious. He seemed genuinely concerned for her. 'You've had so much shit to deal with these last few years. Stalkers, bad managers, the fake feuds, the court case, the copyright issues, the messy break-up with Ryan Bailey, the reception of the last album, rehab, that incident in Toronto . . . that time you collapsed from exhaustion in Paris, personal tragedy, drama drama drama. And all that media intrusion. Why do you think the press hate you so much?'

Nora began to feel a bit queasy. Was this what fame was like? Like a permanent bittersweet cocktail of worship and assault? It was no wonder so many famous people went off the rails when the rails veered in every direction. It was like being slapped and kissed at the same time.

'I . . . I don't know . . . it's pretty crackers . . .'

'I mean, do you ever wonder what your life would have been like if you had decided to take a different path?'

Nora listened to this as she stared at the bubbles rising in her mineral water.

'I think it is easy to imagine there are easier paths,' she said, realising something for the first time. 'But maybe there are no easy paths. There are just paths. In one life, I might be married. In another, I might be working in a shop. I might have said yes to this cute guy who asked me out for a coffee. In another I might be researching glaciers in the Arctic Circle. In another, I might be an Olympic swimming champion. Who knows? Every second of every day we are entering a new universe. And we spend so much time wishing our lives were different, comparing ourselves to other people and to other versions of ourselves, when really most lives contain degrees of good and degrees of bad.'

Marcelo and Joanna and the other Brazilian guy were staring at her wide-eyed, but she was on a roll now. Freewheeling.

'There are patterns to life . . . Rhythms. It is so easy, while trapped in just the one life, to imagine that times of sadness or tragedy or failure or fear are a result of that particular existence. That it is a by-product of living a certain way, rather than simply *living*. I mean, it would have made things a lot easier if we understood there was no way of living that can immunise you against sadness. And that sadness is intrinsically part of the fabric of happiness. You can't have one without the other. Of course, they come in different degrees and quantities. But there is no life where you can be in a state of sheer happiness for ever. And imagining there is just breeds more unhappiness in the life you're in.'

'That is a great answer,' Marcelo said, after he was sure she was finished. 'But tonight I would say, at the concert, you seemed happy. When you played "Bridge Over Troubled Water" instead of "Howl", that was such a powerful statement. It was saying: *I am strong*. It felt like you were telling us, your fans, that you were okay. And so, how is touring going?'

'Well, it's great. And yes, I just thought I'd send a message that, you know, I am out here living my best life. But I miss home after a while.'

'Which one?' asked Marcelo, with a quietly cheeky smile. 'I mean, do you feel more at home in London, or LA, or on the Amalfi Coast?'

It seemed this was the life where her carbon footprint was the highest.

'I don't know. I suppose I would say London.'

Marcelo took a sharp intake of breath, as if the next question was something he had to swim under. He scratched his beard. 'Okay, but I suppose it must be hard for you, as I know you shared that flat with your brother?'

'Why would it be hard?'

Joanna gave her a curious glance from above her cocktail.

Marcelo looked at her with sentimental fondness. His eyes seemed glazed. 'I mean,' he went on, after a delicate sip of beer, 'your brother was such a big part of your life, such a big part of the band . . .'

Was.

So much dread in such a small word. Like a stone falling through water.

She remembered asking Ravi about her brother before the encore. She remembered the crowd's reaction when she had mentioned her brother on stage.

'He's still around. He was here tonight.'

'She means she feels him,' said Joanna. 'They all feel him. He was such a strong spirit. Troubled, but strong . . . It was a tragedy how the drink and drugs and the whole life got to him in the end . . .'

'What are you talking about?' Nora asked. She was no longer acting a life. She genuinely needed to know.

Marcelo looked sad for her. 'You know, it's only been two years since his death . . . his overdose . . .'

Nora gasped.

She didn't arrive back in the library instantly because she hadn't absorbed it. She stood up, dazed, and staggered out of the suite.

'Nora?' laughed Joanna, nervously. 'Nora?'

She got in the lift and went down to the bar. To Ravi.

'You said Joe was schmoozing the media.'

'What?'

'You said. I asked you what Joe was doing and you said, "schmoozing the media".'

He put his beer down and stared at her like a riddle. 'And I was right. She was schmoozing the media.'

'She?'

He pointed over to Joanna, who was looking aghast as she headed over from the lifts in the lobby.

'Yeah. Jo. She was with the press.'

And Nora felt the sadness like a punch.

'Oh no,' she said. 'Oh Joe . . . oh Joe . . . oh . . .'

And the grand hotel bar disappeared. The table, the drinks, Joanna, Marcelo, the sound guy, the hotel guests, Ravi, the others, the marble floor, the barman, the waiters, the chandeliers, the flowers, all became nothing at all.

'Howl'

To the winter forest
And nowhere to go
This girl runs
From all she knows

The pressure rises to the top
The pressure rises (it won't stop)

They want your body
They want your soul
They want fake smiles
That's rock and roll
The wolves surround you
A fever dream
The wolves surround you
So start the scream

Howl, into the night,
Howl, until the light,
Howl, your turn to fight,
Howl, just make it right

Howl howl howl howl

(Motherfucker)

You can't fight for ever
You have to comply
If your life isn't working
You have to ask why

(Spoken)
Remember
When we were young enough
Not to fear tomorrow
Or mourn yesterday
And we were just
Us
And time was just
Now
And we were in
Life
Not rising through
Like arms in a sleeve
Because we had time
We had time to breathe

The bad times are here
The bad times have come
But life can't be over
When it hasn't begun
The lake shines and the water's cold
All that glitters can turn to gold
Silence the music to improve the tune
Stop the fake smiles and howl at the moon

Howl, into the night,
Howl, until the light,
Howl, your turn to fight,

Howl, just make it right

Howl howl howl howl

(Repeat to fade)

Love and Pain

'I hate this . . . process,' Nora told Mrs Elm, with real force in her voice. 'I want it to STOP!'

'Please be quiet,' said Mrs Elm, with a white knight in her hand, concentrating on her move. 'This is a library.'

'We're the only two people here!'

'That's not the point. It is still a library. If you are in a cathedral, you are quiet because you are in a cathedral, not because other people are there. It's the same with a library.'

'Okay,' Nora said, in a lower voice. 'I don't like this. I want it to stop. I want to cancel my membership of the library. I would like to hand in my library card.'

'You *are* the library card.'

Nora returned to her original point. 'I want it to stop.'

'No you don't.'

'Yes I do.'

'Then why are you still here?'

'Because I have no choice.'

'Trust me, Nora. If you really didn't want to be here, you wouldn't be here. I told you this right at the start.'

'I don't like it.'

'Why?'

'Because it is too painful.'

'Why is it painful?'

'Because it's real. In one life, my brother is dead.'

The librarian's face became stern again. 'And in one life – one of his lives – you are dead. Will that be painful for him?'

'I doubt it. He doesn't want anything to do with me these days. He has his own life and he blames me that it is unfulfilled.'

'So, this is all about your brother?'

'No. It's about everything. It seems impossible to live without hurting people.'

'That's because it is.'

'So why live at all?'

'Well, in fairness, dying hurts people too. Now, what life do you want to choose next?'

'I don't.'

'What?'

'I don't want another book. I don't want another life.'

Mrs Elm's face went pale, like it had done all those years ago when she'd got the call about Nora's dad.

Nora felt a trembling beneath her feet. A minor earthquake. She and Mrs Elm held onto the shelves as books fell to the floor. The lights flickered and then went dark completely. The chessboard and table tipped over.

'Oh no,' said Mrs Elm. 'Not again.'

'What's the matter?'

'You know what the matter is. This whole place exists because of you. You are the power source. When there is a severe disruption in that power source the library is in jeopardy. It's you, Nora. You are giving up at the worst possible moment. You can't give up, Nora. You have more to offer. More opportunities to have. There are so many versions of you out there. Remember how you felt after the polar bear. Remember how much you wanted life.'

The polar bear.

The polar bear.

'Even these bad experiences are serving a purpose, don't you see?'

She saw. The regrets she had been living with most of her life were wasted ones.

'Yes.'

The minor earthquake subsided.

But there were books scattered everywhere, all over the floor.

The lights had come back on, but still flickered.

'I'm sorry,' said Nora. She started trying to pick up the books and put them back in place.

'No,' snapped Mrs Elm. 'Don't touch them. Put them down.'

'Sorry.'

'And stop saying sorry. Now, you can help me with this. This is safer.'

She helped Mrs Elm pick up the chess pieces and set up the board for a new game, putting the table back in place too.

'What about all the books on the floor? Are we just going to leave them?'

'Why do you care? I thought you wanted them to disappear completely?'

Mrs Elm may well have just been a mechanism that existed in order to simplify the intricate complexity of the quantum universe, but right now – sitting down between the half-empty bookshelves near her chessboard, set up for a new game – she looked sad and wise and infinitely human.

'I didn't mean to be so harsh,' Mrs Elm managed, eventually.

'That's okay.'

'I remember when we started playing chess in the school library, you used to lose your best players straight away,' she said. 'You'd go and get the queen or the rooks right out there, and they'd be gone. And then you would act like the game was lost because you were just left with pawns and a knight or two.'

'Why are you mentioning this now?'

Mrs Elm saw a loose thread on her cardigan and tucked it inside her sleeve, then decided against it and let it loose again.

'You need to realise something if you are ever to succeed at chess,' she said, as if Nora had nothing bigger to think about. 'And the thing you need to realise is this: the game is never over until it is over. It isn't over if there is a single pawn still on the board. If one side is down to a pawn and a king, and the other side has every player, there is still a game. And even if you were a pawn – maybe we all are – then you should remember that a pawn is the most magical piece of all. It might look small and ordinary but it isn't. Because a pawn is never just a pawn. A pawn is a queen-in-waiting. All you need to do is find a way to keep moving forward. One square after another. And you can get to the other side and unlock all kinds of power.'

Nora stared at the books around her. 'So, are you saying I only have pawns to play with?'

'I am saying that the thing that looks the most ordinary might end up being the thing that leads you to victory. You have to keep going. Like that day in the river. Do you remember?'

Of course she remembered.

How old had she been? Must have been seventeen, as she was no longer swimming in competitions. It was a fraught period in which her dad was cross with her all the time and her mum was going through one of her near-mute depression patches. Her brother was back from art college for the weekend with Ravi. Showing his friend the sights of glorious Bedford. Joe had arranged an impromptu party by the river, with music and beer and a ton of weed and girls who were frustrated Joe wasn't interested in them. Nora had been invited and drank too much and somehow got talking to Ravi about swimming.

'So, could you swim the river?' he asked her.

'Sure.'

'No you couldn't,' someone else had said.

And so, in a moment of idiocy, she had decided to prove them wrong. And by the time her stoned and heavily inebriated older brother realised what she was doing, it was too late. The swim was well under way.

As she remembered this, the corridor at the end of the aisle in the library turned from stone to flowing water. And even as the shelves around her stayed where they were, the tiles beneath her feet now sprouted grass and the ceiling above her became sky. But unlike when she disappeared into another version of the present, Mrs Elm and the books remained. She was half in the library and half inside the memory.

She was staring at someone in the corridor-river. It was her younger self in the water, as the last of the summer light dissolved towards dark.

Equidistance

The river was cold, and the current strong.

She remembered, as she watched herself, the aches in her shoulders and arms. The stiff heaviness of them, as if she'd been wearing armour. She remembered not understanding why, for all that effort, the silhouette of the sycamore trees stubbornly stayed the same size, just as the bank stayed exactly the same distance away. She remembered swallowing some of the dirty water. And looking around at the other bank, the bank from where she had come and the place where she was kind of now standing, watching, along with that younger version of her brother and his friends, beside her, oblivious to her present self, and to the bookshelves on either side of them.

She remembered how, in her delirium, she had thought of the word 'equidistant'. A word that belonged in the clinical safety of a classroom. Equidistant. Such a neutral, mathematical kind of word, and one that became a stuck thought, repeating itself like a manic meditation as she used the last of her strength to stay almost exactly where she was. Equidistant. Equidistant. Equidistant. Not aligned to one bank or the other.

That was how she had felt most of her life.

Caught in the middle. Struggling, flailing, just trying to survive while not knowing which way to go. Which path to commit to without regret.

She looked at the bank on the other side – now with added bookshelves, but still with the large silhouette of a sycamore tree leaning over the water like a worried parent, the wind shushing through its leaves.

'But you did commit,' said Mrs Elm, evidently having heard Nora's thoughts. 'And you survived.'

Someone Else's Dream

'Life is always an act,' Mrs Elm said, as they watched her brother being pulled back from the water's edge by his friends. As he then watched a girl whose name she'd long forgotten make an emergency call. 'And you acted when it counted. You swam to that bank. You clawed yourself out. You coughed your guts out and had hypothermia but you crossed the river, against incredible odds. You found something inside you.'

'Yes. Bacteria. I was ill for weeks. I swallowed so much of that shitty water.'

'But you lived. You had hope.'

'Yeah, well, I was losing it by the day.'

She stared down, to see the grass shrink back into the stone, and looked back to catch the last sight of the water before it shimmered away and the sycamore tree dissolved into air along with her brother and his friends and her own young self.

The library looked exactly like the library again. But now the books were all back on the shelves and the lights had stopped flickering.

'I was so stupid, doing that swim, just trying to impress people. I always thought Joe was better than me. I wanted him to like me.'

'Why did you think he was better than you? Because your parents did?'

Nora felt angry at Mrs Elm's directness. But maybe she had a point. 'I always had to do what they wanted me to do in order to impress them. Joe had his issues, obviously. And I didn't really understand those issues until I knew he was gay, but they say sibling rivalry isn't about siblings but parents, and I always felt my parents just encouraged his dreams a bit more.'

'Like music?'

'Yeah.'

'When he and Ravi decided they wanted to be rock stars, Mum and Dad bought Joe a guitar and then an electric piano.'

'How did that go?'

'The guitar bit went well. He could play "Smoke On The Water" within a week of getting it, but he wasn't into the piano and decided he didn't want it cluttering up his room.'

'And that's when you got it.' Mrs Elm said this as a statement rather than a question. She *knew*. Of course she knew.

'Yeah.'

'It was moved into your room, and you welcomed it like a friend, and started learning to play it with steadfast determination. You spent your pocket money on piano-teaching guides and *Mozart for Beginners* and *The Beatles for Piano*. Because you liked it. But also because you wanted to impress your older brother.'

'I never told you all this.'

A wry smile. 'Don't worry. I read the book.'

'Right. Course. Yeah. Got you.'

'You might need to stop worrying about other people's approval, Nora,' Mrs Elm said in a whisper, for added power and intimacy. 'You don't need a permission slip to be your—'

'Yes. I get it.'

And she did get it.

Every life she had tried so far since entering the library had really been someone else's dream. The married life in the pub had been Dan's dream. The trip to Australia had been Izzy's dream, and her regret about not going had been a guilt for her best friend more than a sorrow for herself. The dream of her becoming a swimming champion belonged to her father. And okay, so it was true that she had been interested in the Arctic and being a glaciologist when she was younger, but that had been steered quite significantly by her chats with Mrs Elm herself, back in the school library. And The Labyrinths, well, that had always been her brother's dream.

Maybe there was no perfect life for her, but somewhere, surely, there was a life worth living. And if she was to find a life truly worth living, she realised she would have to cast a wider net.

Mrs Elm was right. The game wasn't over. No player should give up if there were pieces still left on the board.

She straightened her back and stood up tall.

'You need to choose more lives from the bottom or top shelves. You have been seeking to undo your most obvious regrets. The books on the higher and lower shelves are the lives a little bit further removed. Lives you are still living in one universe or another but not ones you have been imagining or mourning or thinking about. They are lives you could live but never dreamed of.'

'So they're unhappy lives?'

'Some will be, some won't be. It's just they are not the most *obvious* lives. They are ones which might require a little imagination to reach. But I am sure you can get there . . .'

'Can't you guide me?'

Mrs Elm smiled. 'I could read you a poem. Librarians like poems.' And then she quoted Robert Frost. 'Two roads diverged in a wood, and I – / I took the one less travelled by, / And that has made all the difference . . .'

'What if there are more than two roads diverging in the wood? What if there are more roads than trees? What if there is no end to the choices you could make? What would Robert Frost do then?'

She remembered studying Aristotle as a first-year Philosophy student. And being a bit depressed by his idea that excellence was never an accident. That excellent outcomes were the result of 'the wise choice of many alternatives'. And here she was, in the privileged position of being able to sample these many alternatives. It was a shortcut to wisdom and maybe a shortcut to happiness too. She saw it now not as a burden but a gift to be cherished.

'Look at that chessboard we put back in place,' said Mrs Elm, softly. 'Look at how ordered and safe and peaceful it looks now, before a game starts. It's a beautiful thing. But it is boring. It is dead. And yet the moment you make a move on that board, things change. Things begin to get more chaotic. And that chaos builds with every single move you make.'

She took a seat at the chess table, opposite Mrs Elm. She stared down at the board and moved a pawn two spaces forward.

Mrs Elm mirrored the move on her side of the board.

'It's an easy game to play,' she told Nora. 'But a hard one to master. Every move you make opens a whole new world of possibility.'

Nora moved one of her knights. They progressed like this for a little while.

Mrs Elm provided a commentary. 'At the beginning of a game, there are no variations. There is only one way to set up a board. There are nine million variations after the first six moves. And after eight moves there are two hundred and eighty-eight billion different positions. And those possibilities keep growing. There are more possible ways to play a game of chess than the amount of atoms in the observable universe. So it gets very messy. And there is no right way to play; there are many ways. In chess, as in life, possibility is the basis of everything. Every hope, every dream, every regret, every moment of living.'

Eventually, Nora won the game. She had a sneaky suspicion that Mrs Elm had *let* her, but still she was feeling a bit better.

'Okey-dokey,' said Mrs Elm. 'Now, time for a book, I reckon. What do you say?'

Nora gazed along the bookshelves. If only they had more specific titles. If only there was one that said *Perfect Life Right Here.*

Her initial instinct had been to ignore Mrs Elm's question. But where there were books, there was always the temptation to open them. And she realised it was the same with lives.

Mrs Elm repeated something she said earlier.

'Never underestimate the big importance of small things.'

This was useful, as it turned out.

'I want,' she said, 'a gentle life. The life where I worked with animals. Where I chose the animal shelter job – where I did my work experience at school – over the one at String Theory. Yes. Give me that one, please.'

A Gentle Life

It turned out that this particular existence was quite easy to slip into.

Sleep was good in this life, and she didn't wake up until the alarm went off at a quarter to eight. She drove to work in a tatty old Hyundai that smelled of dogs and biscuits and was decorated with crumbs, passing the hospital and the sports centre, and pulling up in the small car park outside the modern, grey-bricked, single-storey rescue centre.

She spent the morning feeding and walking the dogs. The reason it was quite easy to blend into this life was at least partly because she had been greeted by an affable, down-to-earth woman with brown curly hair and a Yorkshire accent. The woman, Pauline, said Nora was to start work in the dog shelter, rather than the cat shelter, and so Nora had a legitimate excuse to ask what to do and look confused. Also, the issue of knowing people's names was solved by the fact that all the workers had name badges.

Nora had walked a bullmastiff, a new arrival, around the field behind the shelter. Pauline told her that the bullmastiff had been horribly treated by its owner. She pointed out a few small round scars.

'Cigarette burns.'

Nora wanted to live in a world where no cruelty existed, but the only worlds she had available to her were worlds with humans in them. The bullmastiff was called Sally. She was scared of everything. Her shadow. Bushes. Other dogs. Nora's legs. Grass. Air. Though she clearly took a liking to Nora, and even succumbed to a (very quick) tummy rub.

Later, Nora helped clean out some of the little dog huts. She imagined they called them huts because it sounded better than cages, which was really a more apt name for them. There was a three-legged Alsatian called Diesel, who had been there a while apparently. When they played catch, Nora discovered his reflexes were good, his mouth catching the ball almost every time. She liked this life – or more precisely, she liked the version of herself in this life. She could tell the kind of person she was from the way people spoke to her. It felt nice – comforting, solidifying – to be a good person.

Her mind felt different here. She thought a lot in this life, but her thoughts were gentle.

'Compassion is the basis of morality,' the philosopher Arthur Schopenhauer had written, in one of his softer moments. Maybe it was the basis of life too.

There was one man who worked there called Dylan, who had a natural way with all the dogs. He was about her age, maybe younger. He had a kind, gentle, sad look about him. His long surf-dude hair golden as a retriever. He came and sat next to Nora on a bench at lunch, overlooking the field.

'What are you having today?' he asked, sweetly, nodding to Nora's lunchbox.

She honestly didn't know – she had found it already prepared when she'd opened her magnet- and calendar-cluttered fridge that morning. She peeled off the lid to find a cheese and Marmite sandwich and a packet of salt and vinegar crisps. The sky darkened and the wind picked up.

'Oh crap,' Nora said. 'It's going to rain.'

'Maybe, but the dogs are all still in their cages.'

'Sorry?'

'Dogs can smell when rain is coming, so they often head indoors if they think it's going to happen. Isn't that cool? That they can predict the future with their *nose*?'

'Yes,' said Nora. 'Way cool.'

Nora bit into her cheese sandwich. And then Dylan put his arm around her.

Nora jumped up.

'—the hell?' she said.

Dylan looked deeply apologetic. And a little horrified at himself. 'I'm sorry. Did I hurt your shoulder?'

'No . . . I just . . . I . . . No. No. It's fine.'

She discovered that Dylan was her boyfriend and that he had gone to the same secondary school as her. Hazeldene Comp. And that he was two years younger.

Nora could remember the day her dad died, when she was in the school library staring as a blond boy from a couple of years below ran past outside the rain-speckled window. *Either chasing someone or being chased.* That had been him. She had vaguely liked him, from a distance, but without really knowing him or thinking about him at all.

'You all right, Norster?' Dylan asked.

Norster?

'Yeah. I was just . . . Yeah. I'm fine.'

Nora sat down again but left a bit more bench between them. There was nothing overtly wrong with Dylan. He was sweet. And she was sure that in this life she genuinely liked him. Maybe even loved him. But entering a life wasn't the same as entering an emotion.

'By the way, did you book Gino's?'

Gino's. The Italian. Nora had gone there as a teenager. She was surprised it was still going.

'What?'

'Gino's? The pizza place? For tonight? You said you kind of know the manager there.'

'My dad used to, yeah.'

'So, did you manage to call?'

'Yes,' she lied. 'But actually, it is fully booked.'

'On a weeknight? Weird. That's a shame. I love pizza. And pasta. And lasagne. And—'

'Right,' said Nora. 'Yes. I get it. I completely get it. I know it was strange. But they had a couple of big bookings.'

Dylan already had his phone out. He was eager. 'I'll try La Cantina. You know. The Mexican. Tons of vegan options. I love a Mexican, don't you?'

Nora couldn't think of a legitimate reason for her not to do this, aside from Dylan's not-entirely-riveting conversation, and compared to the sandwich she was currently eating and the state of the rest of her fridge, Mexican food sounded promising.

So, Dylan booked them a table. And they carried on talking as dogs barked in the building behind them. It emerged during the conversation that they were thinking of moving in together.

'We could watch *Last Chance Saloon*,' he said.

She wasn't really listening. 'What's that?'

He was shy, she realised. Bad with eye contact. Quite endearing. 'You know, that Ryan Bailey film you wanted to watch. We saw the trailer for it. You said it's meant to be funny and I did some research and it has an eighty-six per cent on Rotten Tomatoes and it's on Netflix so . . .'

She wondered if Dylan would believe her if she told him that in one life she was a lead singer of an internationally successful pop-rock band and global icon who had actually dated and voluntarily *broken up with* Ryan Bailey.

'Sounds good,' she said, as she stared at an empty crisp packet floating across the sparse grass.

Dylan rushed off the bench to grab the packet and dropped it into the bin next to the bench.

He flopped back to Nora, smiling. Nora understood what this other Nora saw in him. There was something pure about him. Like a dog himself.

Why Want Another Universe
If This One Has Dogs?

The restaurant was on Castle Road, around the corner from String Theory, and they had to walk past the shop to get there. The familiarity of it felt strange. When she reached the shop she saw that something wasn't right. There were no guitars in the window. There was nothing in the window, except a faded piece of A4 paper stuck on the inside of the glass.

She recognised Neil's handwriting.

Alas, String Theory is no longer able to trade in these premises. Due to an increase in rent we simply couldn't afford to go on. Thanks to all our loyal customers. Don't Think Twice, It's All Right. You Can Go Your Own Way. God Only Knows What We'll Be Without You.

Dylan was amused. 'I see what they did there.' Then a moment later. 'I was named after Bob Dylan. Did I ever tell you that?'

'I can't remember.'

'You know, the musician.'

'Yes. I have heard of Bob Dylan, Dylan.'

'My older sister is called Suzanne. After the Leonard Cohen song.'

Nora smiled. 'My parents loved Leonard Cohen.'

'Ever been in there?' Dylan asked her. 'Looked like a great shop.'

'Once or twice.'

'Thought you would have been, what with you being musical. You used to play the piano, didn't you?'

Used to.

'Yeah. Keyboards. A little.'

Nora saw the notice looked old. She remembered what Neil had said to her. *I can't pay you to put off customers with your face looking like a wet weekend.*

Well, Neil, maybe it wasn't my face after all.

They carried on walking.

'Dylan, do you believe in parallel universes?'

He shrugged. 'I think so.'

'What do you think you are doing in another life? Do you think this is a good universe? Or would you rather be in a universe where you left Bedford?'

'Not really. I am happy here. Why want another universe if this one has dogs? Dogs are the same here as they are in London. I had a place, you know. I'd got into Glasgow University to do Veterinary Medicine. And I went for a week but I missed my dogs too much. Then my dad lost his job and couldn't really afford for me to go. So yeah, I never got to be a vet. And I *really* wanted to be a vet. But I don't regret it. I have a good life. I've got some good friends. I've got my dogs.'

Nora smiled. She liked Dylan, even if she doubted she could be as attracted to him as this other Nora. He was a good person, and good people were rare.

As they reached the restaurant, they saw a tall dark-haired man in running gear jogging towards them. It took a disorientating moment for Nora to realise it was Ash – the Ash who had been a surgeon, the Ash who had been a customer at String Theory and who had asked her out for coffee, the Ash who had comforted her in the hospital and who had knocked on her door, in another world, last night, to tell her that Voltaire was dead. It seemed so recent, that memory, and yet it was hers alone. He was obviously doing some training for the half-marathon on Sunday. There was no reason to believe that the Ash in this life was any different from the one in her root life, except the chances were that he probably hadn't found a dead Voltaire last night. Or maybe he had, though Voltaire wouldn't have been called Voltaire.

'Hi,' she said, forgetting which timeline she was in.

And Ash smiled back at her, but it was a confused smile. Confused, but kind, which somehow made Nora feel even more cringey. Because of course in this life there had not been the knock on her door, there had never even been the asking for a coffee, or the purchase of a Simon & Garfunkel songbook.

'Who was that?' Dylan asked.

'Oh, just someone I knew in another life.'

Dylan was confused but shook it away like rain.

And then they were there.

Dinner with Dylan

La Cantina had hardly changed in years.

Nora had a flashback to the evening she had taken Dan there years ago, on his first visit to Bedford. They'd sat at a table in a corner and had too many margaritas and talked about their joint future. It was the first time that Dan had expressed his dream of living in a pub in the country. They had been on the verge of moving in together, just as Nora and Dylan apparently were in this life. Now she remembered it, Dan had been pretty rude to the waiter, and Nora had overcompensated with excessive smiles. It was one of life's rules – *Never trust someone who is willingly rude to low-paid service staff* – and Dan had failed at that one, and many of the others. Although Nora had to admit, La Cantina would not have been her top choice to return to.

'I love this place,' Dylan said now, looking around at the busy, garish red-and-yellow décor. Nora wondered, quietly, if there was any place Dylan didn't or wouldn't love. He seemed like he would be able to sit in a field near Chernobyl and marvel at the beautiful scenery.

Over black bean tacos, they talked about dogs and school. Dylan had been two years below Nora and remembered her primarily as 'the girl who was good at swimming'. He even remembered the school assembly – which Nora had long tried to repress – where she had been called on stage and given a certificate for being an exceptional representative of Hazeldene Comp. Now she thought about it, that was possibly the moment Nora had begun to go off swimming. The moment she found it harder being with her friends, the moment she slunk away into the margins of school life.

'I used to see you in the library during breaks,' he said, smiling at the memory. 'I remember seeing you playing chess with that librarian we used to have . . . what was her name?'

'Mrs Elm,' Nora said.

'That's it! Mrs Elm!' And then he said something even more startling. 'I saw her the other day.'

'Did you?'

'Yeah. She was on Shakespeare Road. With someone dressed in a uniform. Like a nurse's outfit. I think she was heading into the care home after a walk. She looked very frail. Very old.'

For some reason, Nora had assumed Mrs Elm had died years ago, and that the version of Mrs Elm she always saw in the library had made that idea more likely, as that version was always the exact version she had been at school, preserved in Nora's memory like a mosquito in amber.

'Oh no. Poor Mrs Elm. I loved her.'

Last Chance Saloon

After the meal Nora went back to Dylan's house to watch the Ryan Bailey movie. They had a half-drunk bottle of wine that the restaurant let them take home. Her self-justification regarding going to Dylan's was that he was sweet and open and would reveal a lot about their life without having to pry too deep.

He lived in a small terraced house on Huxley Avenue that he had inherited from his mum. The house was made even smaller by the amount of dogs there. There were five that Nora could see, though there may have been more lurking upstairs. Nora had always imagined she liked the smell of dog, but she suddenly realised there was a limit to this fondness.

Sitting down on the sofa she felt something hard beneath her – a plastic ring for the dogs to gnaw on. She put it on the carpet amid the other chew toys. The toy bone. The foam yellow ball with chunks bitten out of it. A half-massacred soft toy.

A Chihuahua with cataracts tried to have sex with her right leg.

'Stop that, Pedro,' said Dylan, laughing, as he pulled the little creature away from her.

Another dog, a giant, meaty, chestnut-coloured Newfoundland, was sitting next to her on the sofa, licking Nora's ear with a tongue the size of a slipper, meaning that Dylan had to sit on the floor.

'Do you want the sofa?'

'No. I'm fine on the floor.'

Nora didn't push it. In fact, she was quite relieved. It made it easier to watch *Last Chance Saloon* without any further awkwardness. And the Newfoundland stopped licking her ear and rested its head on her knee and Nora felt – well, not happy exactly, but not depressed either.

And yet, as she watched Ryan Bailey tell his on-screen love interest that 'Life is for living, cupcake' while simultaneously being informed by Dylan that he was thinking of letting *another* dog sleep in his bed ('He cries all night. He wants his daddy'), Nora realised she wasn't too enamoured with this life.

And also, Dylan deserved the other Nora. The one who had managed to fall in love with him. This was a new feeling – as if she was taking someone's place.

Realising she had a high tolerance for alcohol in this life, she poured herself some more wine. It was a pretty ropey Zinfandel from California. She stared at the label on the back. There was for some reason a mini co-autobiography of a woman and a man, Janine and Terence Thornton, who owned the vineyard which had made the wine. She read the last sentence: *When we were first married we always dreamed of opening our own vineyard one day. And now we have made that dream a reality. Here at Dry Creek Valley, our life tastes as good as a glass of Zinfandel.*

She stroked the large dog who'd been licking her and whispered a 'goodbye' into the Newfoundland's wide, warm brow as she left Dylan and his dogs behind.

Buena Vista Vineyard

In the next visit to the Midnight Library, Mrs Elm helped Nora find the life she could have lived that was closest to the life depicted on the label of that bottle of wine from the restaurant. So, she gave Nora a book that sent her to America.

In this life Nora was called Nora Martìnez and she was married to a twinkle-eyed Mexican-American man in his early forties called Eduardo, who she had met during the gap year she'd regretted never having after leaving university. After his parents had died in a boating accident (she had learned, from a profile piece on them in *The Wine Enthusiast* magazine, which they had framed in their oak-panelled tasting room), Eduardo had been left a modest inheritance and they bought a tiny vineyard in California. Within three years they had done so well – particularly with their Syrah varietals – that they were able to buy the neighbouring vineyard when it came up for sale. Their winery was called the Buena Vista vineyard, situated in the foothills of the Santa Cruz Mountains, and they had a child called Alejandro, who was at boarding school near Monterey Bay.

Much of their business came from wine-trail tourists. Coachloads of people arrived at hourly intervals. It was quite easy to improvise, as the tourists were genuinely quite gullible. It went like this: Eduardo would decide which wines to put out in the glasses before each coach load arrived, and hand Nora the bottles – 'Woah, Nora, despacio, un poco too much' he reprimanded in his good-humoured Spanglish, when she was a bit too liberal with the measures – and then when the tourists came Nora would inhale the wines as they sipped and swilled them, and try to echo Eduardo and say the right things.

'There is a woodiness to the bouquet with this one' or 'You'll note the vegetal aromas here – the bright robust blackberries and fragrant nectarine, perfectly balanced with the echoes of charcoal'.

Each life she had experienced had a different feeling, like different movements in a symphony, and this one felt quite bold and uplifting. Eduardo was incredibly sweet-natured, and their marriage seemed to be a successful one. Maybe even one to rival the life of the couple on the wine label of the bottle of ropey wine she'd drank with Dylan, while being licked by his astronomically large dog. She even remembered their names. Janine and Terence Thornton. She felt like she too was now living in a label on a bottle. She also looked like it. Perfect Californian hair and expensive-looking teeth, tanned and healthy despite the presumably quite substantial consumption of Syrah. She had the kind of flat, hard stomach that suggested hours of Pilates every week.

However, it wasn't just easy to fake wine knowledge in this life. It was easy to fake *everything*, which could have been a sign that the key to her apparently successful union with Eduardo was that he wasn't really paying attention.

After the last of the tourists left, Eduardo and Nora sat out under the stars with a glass of their own wine in their hands.

'The fires have died out in LA now,' he told her.

Nora wondered who lived in the Los Angeles home she had in her pop star life. 'That's a relief.'

'Yeah.'

'Isn't it beautiful?' she asked him, staring up at that clear sky full of constellations.

'What?'

'The galaxy.'

'Yes.'

He was on his phone and didn't say very much. And then he put his phone down and still didn't say much.

She had known three types of silence in relationships. There was passive-aggressive silence, obviously, there was the we-no-longer-have-anything-to-say silence, and then there was the silence that Eduardo and she seemed to have cultivated. The silence of not *needing* to talk. Of just being together, of *together-being*. The way you could be happily silent with yourself.

But still, she wanted to talk.

'We're happy, aren't we?'

'Why the question?'

'Oh, I know we are happy. I just like to hear you say it sometimes.'

'We're happy, Nora.'

She sipped her wine and looked at her husband. He was wearing a sweater even though it was perfectly mild. They stayed there a while and then he went to bed before her.

'I'm just going to stay out here for a while.'

Eduardo seemed fine with that, and sloped off after planting a small kiss on the top of her head.

She stepped out with her glass of wine and walked among the moonlit vines.

She stared at the clear sky full of stars.

There was absolutely nothing wrong with this life, but she felt inside her a craving for other things, other lives, other possibilities. She felt like she was still in the air, not ready to land. Maybe she was more like Hugo Lefèvre than she had realised. Maybe she could flick through lives as easily as flicking pages.

She gulped the rest of the wine, knowing there would be no hangover. 'Earth and wood,' she said to herself. She closed her eyes.

It wasn't long now.

Not long at all.

She just stood there and waited to disappear.

The Many Lives of Nora Seed

Nora came to understand something. Something Hugo had never fully explained to her in that kitchen in Svalbard. You didn't have to enjoy every aspect of each life to keep having the option of experiencing them. You just had to never give up on the idea that there would be a life somewhere that could be enjoyed. Equally, enjoying a life didn't mean you stayed in that life. You only stayed in a life for ever if you couldn't imagine a better one, and yet, paradoxically, the more lives you tried the easier it became to think of something better, as the imagination broadened a bit more with every new life she sampled.

So, in time, and with Mrs Elm's assistance, Nora took lots of books from the shelves, and ended up having a taste of lots of different lives in her search for the right one. She learned that undoing regrets was really a way of making wishes come true. There was almost *any* life she was living in one universe, after all.

In one life she had quite a solitary time in Paris, and taught English at a college in Montparnasse and cycled by the Seine and read lots of books on park benches. In another, she was a yoga teacher with the neck mobility of an owl.

In one life she had kept up swimming but had never tried to pursue the Olympics. She just did it for fun. In that life she was a lifeguard in the beach resort of Sitges, near Barcelona, was fluent in both Catalan and Spanish, and had a hilarious best friend called Gabriela who taught her how to surf, and who she shared an apartment with, five minutes from the beach.

There was one existence where Nora had kept up the fiction

writing she had occasionally toyed with at university and was now a published author. Her novel *The Shape of Regret* received rave reviews and was shortlisted for a major literary award. In that life she had lunch in a disappointingly banal Soho members' club with two affable, easy-going producers from Magic Lantern Productions, who wanted to option it for film. She ended up choking on a piece of flatbread and knocking her red wine over one of the producer's trousers and messing up the whole meeting.

In one life she had a teenage son called Henry, who she never met properly because he kept slamming doors in her face.

In one life she was a concert pianist, currently on tour in Scandinavia, playing night after night to besotted crowds (and fading into the Midnight Library during one disastrous rendition of Chopin's Piano Concerto No. 2 at the Finlandia Hall in Helsinki).

In one life she only ate toast.

In one life she went to Oxford and became a lecturer in Philosophy at St Catherine's College and lived by herself in a fine Georgian townhouse in a genteel row, amid an environment of respectable calm.

In another life Nora was a sea of emotion. She felt everything deeply and directly. Every joy and every sorrow. A single moment could contain both intense pleasure and intense pain, as if both were dependent on each other, like a pendulum in motion. A simple walk outside and she could feel a heavy sadness simply because the sun had slipped behind a cloud. Yet, conversely, meeting a dog who was clearly grateful for her attention caused her to feel so exultant that she felt she could melt into the pavement with sheer bliss. In that life she had a book of Emily Dickinson poems beside her bed and she had a playlist called 'Extreme States of Euphoria' and another one called 'The Glue to Fix Me When I Am Broken'.

In one life she was a travel vlogger who had 1,750,000 YouTube subscribers and almost as many people following her on Instagram, and her most popular video was one where she fell off a gondola in Venice. She also had one about Rome called 'A Roma Therapy'.

In one life she was a single parent to a baby that literally wouldn't sleep.

In one life she ran the showbiz column in a tabloid newspaper and did stories about Ryan Bailey's relationships.

In one life she was the picture editor at the *National Geographic.*

In one life she was a successful eco-architect who lived a carbon-neutral existence in a self-designed bungalow that harvested rainwater and ran on solar power.

In one life she was an aid worker in Botswana.

In one life a cat-sitter.

In one life a volunteer in a homeless shelter.

In one life she was sleeping on her only friend's sofa.

In one life she taught music in Montreal.

In one life she spent all day arguing with people she didn't know on Twitter and ended a fair proportion of her tweets by saying 'Do better' while secretly realising she was telling herself to do that.

In one life she had no social media accounts.

In one life she'd never drunk alcohol.

In one life she was a chess champion and currently visiting Ukraine for a tournament.

In one life she was married to a minor Royal and hated every minute.

In one life her Facebook and Instagram only contained quotes from Rumi and Lao Tzu.

In one life she was on to her third husband and already bored.

In one life she was a vegan power-lifter.

In one life she was travelling around South America and caught up in an earthquake in Chile.

In one life she had a friend called Becky, who said 'Oh what larks!' whenever anything good was happening.

In one life she met Hugo yet again, diving off the Corsican coast, and they talked quantum mechanics and got drunk together at a beachside bar until Hugo slipped away, out of that life, mid-sentence, so Nora was left talking to a blank Hugo who was trying to remember her name.

In some lives Nora attracted a lot of attention. In some lives she attracted none. In some lives she was rich. In some lives she was poor. In some lives she was healthy. In some lives she couldn't climb the stairs without getting out of breath. In some lives she was in a relationship, in others she was solo, in many she was somewhere in between. In some lives she was a mother, but in most she wasn't.

She had been a rock star, an Olympian, a music teacher, a primary school teacher, a professor, a CEO, a PA, a chef, a glaciologist, a climatologist, an acrobat, a tree-planter, an audit manager, a hair-dresser, a professional dog walker, an office clerk, a software developer, a receptionist, a hotel cleaner, a politician, a lawyer, a shoplifter, the head of an ocean protection charity, a shop worker (again), a wait-ress, a first-line supervisor, a glass-blower and a thousand other things. She'd had horrendous commutes in cars, on buses, in trains, on ferries, on bike, on foot. She'd had emails and emails and emails. She'd had a fifty-three-year-old boss with halitosis touch her leg under a table and text her a photo of his penis. She'd had colleagues who lied about her, and colleagues who loved her, and (mainly) colleagues who were entirely indifferent. In many lives she chose not to work and in some she didn't choose not to work but still couldn't find any. In some lives she smashed through the glass ceiling and in some she just polished it. She had been excessively over- and under-qualified. She had slept brilliantly and terribly. In some lives she was on anti-depressants and in others she didn't even take ibuprofen for a headache. In some lives she was a physically healthy hypochondriac and in some a seriously ill hypochondriac and in most she wasn't a hypochondriac at all. There was a life where she had chronic fatigue, a life where she had cancer, a life where she'd suffered a herniated disc and broken her ribs in a car accident.

There had, in short, been a lot of lives.

And among those lives she had laughed and cried and felt calm and terrified and everything in between.

And between these lives she always saw Mrs Elm in the library.

And at first it seemed that the more lives she experienced, the fewer problems there seemed to be with the transfer. The library never felt like it was on the brink of crumbling or falling apart or at risk of disappearing completely. The lights didn't even flicker through many of the changeovers. It was as though she had reached some state of acceptance about life – that if there was a bad experience, there wouldn't *only* be bad experiences. She realised that she hadn't tried to end her life because she was miserable, but because she had managed to convince herself that there was no way out of her misery.

That, she supposed, was the basis of depression as well as the difference between fear and despair. Fear was when you wandered into a cellar and worried that the door would close shut. Despair was when the door closed and locked behind you.

But with every life she saw that metaphorical door widen a little further as she grew better at using her imagination. Sometimes she was in a life for less than a minute, while in others she was there for days or weeks. It seemed the more lives she lived, the harder it was to feel at home anywhere.

The trouble was that eventually Nora began to lose any sense of who she was. Like a whispered word passed around from ear to ear, even her name began to sound like just a noise, signifying nothing.

'It's not working,' she told Hugo, in her last proper conversation with him, in that beach bar in Corsica. 'It's not fun any more. I am not you. I need somewhere to stay. But the ground is never stable.'

'The fun is in the jumping, mon amie.'

'But what if it's in the landing?'

And that was the moment he had returned to his purgatorial video store.

'I'm sorry,' his other self said, as he sipped his wine and the sun set behind him, 'I've forgotten who you are.'

'Don't worry,' she said. 'So have I.'

As she too faded away like the sun that had just been swallowed by the horizon.

Lost in the Library

'Mrs Elm?'

'Yes, Nora, what's the matter?'

'It's dark.'

'I had noticed.'

'That's not a good sign, is it?'

'No,' said Mrs Elm, sounding flustered. 'You know perfectly well it's not a good sign.'

'I can't go on.'

'You always say that.'

'I have run out of lives. I have been everything. And yet I always end up back here. There is always something that stops my enjoyment. Always. I feel ungrateful.'

'Well, you shouldn't. And you haven't run out of anything.' Mrs Elm paused to sigh. 'Did you know that every time you choose a book it never returns to the shelves?'

'Yes.'

'Which is why you can never go back into a life you have tried. There always needs to be some . . . variation on a theme. In the Midnight Library, you can't take the same book out twice.'

'I don't follow.'

'Well, even in the dark you know these shelves are as full as the last time you looked. Feel them, if you like.'

Nora didn't feel them. 'Yeah. I know they are.'

'They're exactly as full as they were when you first arrived here, aren't they?'

'I don't—'

'That means there are still as many possible lives out there for you as there ever were. An infinite number, in fact. You can never run out of possibilities.'

'But you can run out of wanting them.'

'Oh Nora.'

'Oh what?'

There was a pause, in the darkness. Nora pressed the small light on her watch, just to check.

00:00:00

'I think,' Mrs Elm said eventually, 'if I may say so without being rude – I think you might have lost your way a little bit.'

'Isn't that why I came to the Midnight Library in the first place? Because I had lost my way?'

'Well, *yes*. But now you are lost *within your lostness*. Which is to say, very lost indeed. You are not going to find the way you want to live like this.'

'What if there was never a way? What if I am . . . trapped?'

'So long as there are still books on the shelves, you are never trapped. Every book is a potential escape.'

'I just don't understand life,' sulked Nora.

'You don't have to *understand* life. You just have to *live* it.'

Nora shook her head. This was a bit too much for a Philosophy graduate to take.

'But I don't want to be like this,' Nora told her. 'I don't want to be like Hugo. I don't want to keep flicking between lives for ever.'

'All right. Then you need to listen carefully to me. Now, do you want my advice or don't you?'

'Well, yeah. Of course. It feels a little late, but yes, Mrs Elm, I would be very grateful for your advice on this.'

'Right. Well. I think you have reached a point where you can't see the wood for the trees.'

'I'm not quite sure what you mean.'

'You are right to think of these lives like a piano where you're playing tunes that aren't really you. You are forgetting who you are. In becoming everyone, you are becoming no one. You are forgetting your root life. You are forgetting what worked for you and what didn't. You are forgetting your regrets.'

'I've been through my regrets.'

'No. Not all of them.'

'Well, not every single minor one. No, obviously.'

'You need to look at *The Book of Regrets* again.'

'How can I do that in the pitch dark?'

'Because you already know the whole book. Because it's inside you. Just as . . . just as I am.'

She remembered Dylan telling her he had seen Mrs Elm near the care home. She thought about telling her this but decided against it. 'Right.'

'We only know what we perceive. Everything we experience is ultimately just our perception of it. "It's not what you look at that matters, it's what you see."'

'You know Thoreau?'

'Of course. If you do.'

'The thing is, I don't know what I regret any more.'

'Okay, well, let's see. You say that I am just a perception. Then why did you perceive me? Why am I – Mrs Elm – the person you see?'

'I don't know. Because you were someone I trusted. You were kind to me.'

'Kindness is a strong force.'

'And rare.'

'You might be looking in the wrong places.'

'Maybe.'

The dark was punctured by the slow rising glow of the light bulbs all around the library.

'So where else in your root life have you felt that? Kindness?'

Nora remembered the night Ash knocked on her door. Maybe

lifting a dead cat off the road and carrying it in the rain around to her flat's tiny back garden and then burying it on her behalf because she was sobbing drunkenly with grief wasn't the most archetypally romantic thing in the world. But it certainly qualified as kind, to take forty minutes out of your run and help someone in need while only accepting a glass of water in return.

She hadn't really been able to appreciate that kindness at the time. Her grief and despair had been too strong. But now she thought about it, it had really been quite remarkable.

'I think I know,' she said. 'It was right there in front of me, the night before I tried to kill myself.'

'Yesterday evening, you mean?'

'I suppose. Yes. Ash. The surgeon. The one who found Volts. Who once asked me out for coffee. Years ago. When I was with Dan. I'd said no, well, because I was with Dan. But what if I hadn't been? What if I had broken up with Dan and gone on that coffee date and had dared, on a Saturday, with all the shop watching, to say yes to a coffee? Because there must be a life in which I was single in that moment and where I said what I wanted to say. Where I said, "Yes, I would like to go for a coffee sometime, Ash, that would be lovely." Where I picked Ash. I'd like to have a go at that life. Where would that have taken me?'

And in the dark she heard the familiar sound of the shelves beginning to move, slowly, with a creak, then faster, smoother, until Mrs Elm spotted the book, the life, in question.

'Right *there*.'

A Pearl in the Shell

She opened her eyes from a shallow sleep and the first thing she noticed was that she was incredibly tired. She could see a picture on the wall, in the dark. She could just about make out that the picture was a mildly abstract interpretation of a tree. Not a tall and spindly tree. Something short and wide and flowery.

There was a man next to her, asleep. It was impossible to tell, as he was turned away from her, in the dark, and given that he was largely hidden under the duvet, whether this man was Ash.

Somehow this felt weirder than usual. Of course, to be in bed with a man who she hadn't done anything more with than bury a cat and have a few interesting conversations from behind the counter of a music shop should have felt slightly strange in the normal run of things. But since entering the Midnight Library Nora had slowly got used to the peculiar.

And just because it was possible that the man was Ash, it was also possible that it wasn't. There was no predicting every future outcome after a single decision. Going for a coffee with Ash might have led, for instance, to Nora falling in love with the person serving the coffee. That was simply the unpredictable nature of quantum physics.

She felt her ring finger.

Two rings.

The man turned over.

An arm landed across her in the dark and she gently raised it and placed it back on the duvet. Then she took herself out of bed. Her plan was to go downstairs and maybe lie on a sofa and, as usual, do some research about herself on her phone.

It was a curious fact that no matter how many lives she had experienced, and no matter how different those lives were, she almost always had her phone by the bed. And in this life, it was no different, so she grabbed it and sneaked out of the room quietly. Whoever the man was, he was a deep sleeper and didn't stir.

She stared at him.

'Nora?' he mumbled, half-asleep.

It was him. She was almost sure of it. Ash.

'I'm just going to the loo,' she said.

He mumbled something close to an 'okay' and fell back asleep.

And she trod gently across the floorboards. But the moment she opened the door and stepped out of the room, she nearly jumped out of her skin.

For there, in front of her in the half-light of the landing, was another human. A small one. Child-size.

'Mummy, I had a nightmare.'

By the soft light of the dimmed bulb in the hallway she could see the girl's face, her fine hair wild from sleep, strands sticking to her clammy forehead.

Nora said nothing. This was her daughter.

How could she say anything?

The now familiar question raised itself: how could she just join in to a life that she was years late for? Nora closed her eyes. The other lives in which she'd had children had only lasted a couple of minutes or so. This one was already leading into unknown territory.

Her body shook with whatever she was trying to keep inside. She didn't want to see her. Not just for herself but for the girl as well. It seemed a betrayal. Nora was her mother, but also, in another, more important way: she was not her mother. She was just a strange woman in a strange house looking at a strange child.

'Mummy? Can you hear me? I had a nightmare.'

She heard the man move in his bed somewhere in the room

behind her. This would only become more awkward if he woke up, properly. So, Nora decided to speak to the child.

'Oh, oh that's a shame,' she whispered. 'It's not real, though. It was just a dream.'

'It was about bears.'

Nora closed the door behind her. 'Bears?'

'Because of that story.'

'Right. Yes. The story. Come on, get back in your bed . . .' This sounded harsh, she realised. 'Sweetheart,' she added, wondering what she – her daughter in this universe – was called. 'There are no bears here.'

'Only teddy bears.'

'Yes, only—'

The girl became a little more awake. Her eyes brightened. She saw her mother, so for a second Nora felt like that. Like her mother. She felt the strangeness of being connected to the world through someone else. 'Mummy, what were you doing?'

She was speaking loudly. She was deeply serious in the way that only four-year-olds (she couldn't have been much older) could be.

'Ssh,' Nora said. She really needed to know the girl's name. Names had power. If you didn't know your own daughter's name, you had no control whatsoever. 'Listen,' Nora whispered, 'I'm just going to go downstairs and do something. You go back to bed.'

'But the bears.'

'There aren't any bears.'

'There are in my dreams.'

Nora remembered the polar bear speeding towards her in the fog. Remembered that fear. That desire, in that sudden moment, to live. 'There won't be this time. I promise.'

'Mummy, why are you speaking like that?'

'Like what?'

'Like that.'

'Whispering?'

'No.'

Nora had no idea what the girl thought she was speaking like. What the gap was, between her now and her, the mother. Did motherhood affect the way you spoke?

'Like you are scared,' the girl clarified.

'I'm not scared.'

'I want someone to hold my hand.'

'What?'

'I want someone to hold my hand.'

'Right.'

'Silly Mummy!'

'Yes. Yes, I'm silly.'

'I'm really scared.'

She said this quietly, matter-of-fact. And it was then that Nora looked at her. Really, properly looked at her. The girl seemed wholly alien and wholly familiar all at once. Nora felt a swell of something inside her, something powerful and worrying.

The girl was staring at her in a way no one had stared at her before. It was scary, the emotion. She had Nora's mouth. And that slightly lost look that people had sometimes attributed to her. She was beautiful and she was hers – or kind of hers – and she felt a swell of irrational love, a surge of it, and knew – if the library wasn't coming for her right now (and it wasn't) – that she had to get away.

'Mummy, will you hold my hand . . .?'

'I . . .'

The girl put her hand in Nora's. It felt so small and warm and it made her feel sad, the way it relaxed into her, as natural as a pearl in a shell. She pulled Nora towards the adjacent room – the girl's bedroom. Nora closed the door nearly-shut behind her and tried to check the time on her watch, but in this life it was a classic-looking analogue watch with no light display so it took a second or two for her eyes to adjust. She double-checked the time on her phone as well. It was 2:32 a.m. So, depending when she had gone to bed in this life, this version of her body hadn't had much sleep. It certainly felt like it hadn't.

'What happens when you die, Mummy?'

It wasn't totally dark in the room. There was a sliver of light coming in from the hallway and there was a nearby streetlamp that meant a thin glow filtered through the dog-patterned curtains. She could see the squat rectangle that was Nora's bed. She could see the silhouette of a cuddly toy elephant on the floor. There were other toys too. It was a happily cluttered room.

Her eyes shone at Nora.

'I don't know,' Nora said. 'I don't think anyone knows for sure.'

She frowned. This didn't satisfy her. This didn't satisfy her one bit.

'Listen,' Nora said. 'There is a chance that just before you die, you'll get a chance to live again. You can have things you didn't have before. You can choose the life you want.'

'That sounds good.'

'But you don't have to have this worry for a very long time. You are going to have a life full of exciting adventures. There will be so many happy things.'

'Like camping!'

A burst of warmth radiated through Nora as she smiled at this sweet girl. 'Yes. Like camping!'

'I love it when we go camping!'

Nora's smile was still there but she felt tears behind her eyes. This seemed a good life. A family of her own. A daughter to go on camping holidays with.

'Listen,' she said, as she realised she wasn't going to be able to escape the bedroom any time soon. 'When you have worries about things you don't know about, like the future, it's a very good idea to remind yourself of things you *do* know.'

'I don't understand,' the girl said, snuggled under her duvet as Nora sat on the floor beside her.

'Well, it's like a game.'

'I like games.'

'Shall we play a game?'

'Yes,' smiled her daughter. 'Let's.'

The Game

'I ask you something we already know and you say the answer. So, if I ask "What is Mummy's name?", you would say "Nora". Get it?'

'I think so.'

'So, what is your name?'

'Molly.'

'Okay, what is Daddy's name?'

'Daddy!'

'But what is his actual name?'

'Ash!'

Well. That was a really successful coffee date.

'And where do we live?'

'Cambridge!'

Cambridge. It kind of made sense. Nora had always liked Cambridge, and it was only thirty miles from Bedford. Ash must have liked it too. And it was still commutable distance from London, if he still worked there. Briefly, after getting her First from Bristol, she had applied to do an MPhil in Philosophy and had been offered a place at Caius College.

'What part of Cambridge? Can you remember? What is our street called?'

'We live on . . . Bol . . . Bolton Road.'

'Well done! And do you have any brothers or sisters!'

'No!'

'And do Mummy and Daddy like each other?'

Molly laughed a little at that. 'Yes!'

'Do we ever shout?'

The laugh became cheeky. 'Sometimes! Especially Mummy!'

'Sorry!'

'You only shout when you are really, really, really tired and you say sorry so it is okay. Everything is okay if you say sorry. That's what you say.'

'Does Mummy go out to work?'

'Yes. Sometimes.'

'Do I still work at the shop where I met Daddy?'

'No.'

'What does Mummy do when she goes out to work?'

'Teaches people!'

'How does she – how do I teach people? What do I teach?'

'Fill-o . . . fill-o-wosso-fee . . .'

'Philosophy?'

'That's what I said!'

'And where do I teach that? At a university?'

'Yes!'

'Which university?' Then she remembered where they lived. 'At Cambridge University?'

'That's it!'

She tried to fill in the gaps. Maybe in this life she had re-applied to do a Master's, and on successfully completing that she had got into teaching there.

Either way, if she was going to bluff it in this life, she was probably going to have to read some more philosophy. But then Molly said: 'But you are stopping now.'

'Stopping? Why am I stopping?'

'To do books!'

'Books for you?'

'No, silly. To do a grown-up book.'

'I'm writing a book?'

'Yes! I just said.'

'I know. I'm just trying to get you to say some things twice.

228

Because it is doubly nice. And it makes bears even less scary. Okay?'

'Okay.'

'Does Daddy work?'

'Yes.'

'Do you know what Daddy's job is?'

'Yes. He cuts people!'

For a brief moment she forgot Ash was a surgeon and wondered if she was in the house of a serial killer. 'Cuts people?'

'Yes, he cuts people's bodies and makes them better!'

'Ah, yes. Of course.'

'He saves people!'

'Yes, he does.'

'Except when he is sad and the person died.'

'Yes, that is sad.'

'Does Daddy work in Bedford still? Or does he work in Cambridge now?'

She shrugged. 'Cambridge?'

'Does he play music?'

'Yes. Yes, he plays the music. But very very very very badly!' She giggled as she said that.

Nora laughed too. Molly's giggle was contagious. 'It's . . . Do you have any aunts and uncles?'

'Yes, I have Aunt Jaya.'

'Who is Aunt Jaya?'

'Daddy's sister.'

'Anyone else?'

'Yes, Uncle Joe and Uncle Ewan.'

Nora felt relieved her brother was alive in this timeline. And that he was with the same man he was with in her Olympic life. And he was clearly in their lives enough for Molly to know his name.

'When did we last see Uncle Joe?'

'Christmas!'

'Do you like Uncle Joe?'

'Yes! He's funny! And he gave me Panda!'

'Panda?'

'My best cuddly!'

'Pandas are bears too.'

'Nice bears.'

Molly yawned. She was getting sleepy.

'Do Mummy and Uncle Joe like each other?'

'Yes! You always talk on the phone!'

This was interesting. Nora had assumed that the only lives in which she still got on with her brother were the lives in which she had never been in The Labyrinths (unlike her decision to keep swimming, the coffee date with Ash post-dated her experience in The Labyrinths). But this was throwing that theory. Nora couldn't help but wonder if this lovely Molly herself was the missing link. Maybe this little girl in front of her had healed the rift between her and her brother.

'Do you have grandparents?'

'Only Grandma Sal.'

Nora wanted to ask more about her own parents' deaths, but this probably wasn't the time.

'Are you happy? I mean, when you aren't thinking about bears?'

'I think so.'

'Are Mummy and Daddy happy?'

'Yes,' she said, slowly. 'Sometimes. When you are not tired!'

'And do we have lots of fun times?'

She rubbed her eyes. 'Yes.'

'And do we have any pets?'

'Yes. Plato.'

'And who is Plato?'

'Our dog.'

'And what type of dog is Plato?'

But she got no answer, because Molly was asleep. And Nora lay there, on the carpet, and closed her eyes.

When she woke up, a tongue was licking her face.

A Labrador with smiling eyes and a waggy tail seemed amused or excited to see her.

'Plato?' she asked, sleepily.

That's me, Plato seemed to wag.

It was morning. Light flooded through the curtains now. Cuddly toys – including Panda, and the elephant Nora had identified earlier – littered the floor. She looked at the bed and saw it was empty. Molly wasn't in the room. And there were feet – heavier feet than Molly's – coming up the stairs.

She sat up and knew she must look terrible after sleeping on the carpet in a baggy Cure T-shirt (which she recognised) and tartan pyjama bottoms (which she didn't). She felt her face and it was creased from where she had been lying, and her hair – which was longer in this life – felt dirty and bedraggled. She tried to make herself look as presentable as it was possible to look in the two seconds before the arrival of a man she simultaneously slept with every night and also hadn't ever slept with. Schrödinger's husband, so to speak.

And then, suddenly, there he was.

The Perfect Life

Ash's gangly handsome boyishness had only been modestly dented by fatherhood. If anything, he looked healthier than he had done on her doorstep and, like then, he was wearing running gear – though here the clothes seemed a bit fancier and more expensive, and he had some kind of fitness tracker attached to his arm.

He was smiling and holding two cups of coffee, one of which was for Nora. She wondered how many coffees they had shared together, since the first.

'Oh, thank you.'

'Oh no, Nor, did you sleep in here all night?' he asked.

Nor.

'Most of it. I meant to go back to bed but Molly was in a state. I had to calm her and then I was too tired to move.'

'Oh no. I'm so sorry. I didn't hear her.' He seemed genuinely sad. 'It was probably my fault. I showed her some bears on YouTube yesterday before work.'

'No worries.'

'Anyway, I've walked Plato. I'm not in the hospital till midday today. It's going to be a late one. Are you still wanting to go into the library today?'

'Oh. You know what? I might give it a miss.'

'Okay, well, I got Mol some brekkie and will drop her off at school.'

'I can take Molly,' said Nora. 'If you've got a big day.'

'Oh, it's an okay one. A gall bladder and a pancreas so far. Easy street. Am going to get a run in.'

'Right. Yes. 'Course. For the half-marathon on Sunday.'

'What?'

'Nothing. It doesn't matter,' Nora said, 'I'm just delirious from sleeping on the floor.'

'No worries. Anyway, my sister phoned. They want her to illustrate the calendar for Kew Gardens. Lots of plants. She's really pleased.'

He smiled. He seemed happy for this sister of his who Nora had never heard of. She wanted to thank him for being so good about her dead cat, but she obviously couldn't so she just said, 'Thank you.'

'For what?'

'Just, you know, everything.'

'Oh. Right. Okay.'

'So, thank you.'

He nodded. 'That's nice. Anyway, run time.'

He drained his coffee and then disappeared. Nora scanned the room, absorbing every new piece of information. Every cuddly toy and book and plug socket, as if they were all part of the jigsaw of her life.

An hour later, Molly was being dropped off at her infant school and Nora was doing the usual. Checking her emails and social media. Her social media activity wasn't great in this life, which was always a promising sign, but she did have a *hell* of a lot of emails. From these emails she divined that she was not simply 'stopping' teaching at the moment but had officially stopped. She was on a sabbatical in order to write a book about Henry David Thoreau and his relevance for the modern-day environmentalist movement. Later in the year she planned to visit Walden Pond in Concord, Massachusetts, funded by a research grant.

This seemed pretty good.

Almost *annoyingly* good.

A good life with a good daughter and a good man in a good

house in a good town. It was an excess of good. A life where she could sit down all day reading and researching and writing about her all-time favourite philosopher.

'This is cool,' she told the dog. 'Isn't this cool?'

Plato yawned indifference.

Then she set about exploring her house, being watched by the Labrador from the comfy-looking sofa. The living room was vast. Her feet sunk into the soft rug.

White floorboards, TV, wood-burner, electric piano, two new laptops on charge, a mahogany chest on which perched an ornate chess set, nicely stacked bookshelves. A lovely guitar resting in the corner. Nora recognised the model instantly as an electro-acoustic 'Midnight Satin' Fender Malibu. She had sold one during her last week working at String Theory.

There were photos in frames dotted around the living room. Kids she didn't know with a woman who looked like Ash – presumably his sister. An old photo of her deceased parents on their wedding day, and one of her and Ash getting married. She could see her brother in the background. A photo of Plato. And one of a baby, presumably Molly.

She glanced at the books. Some yoga manuals, but not the second-hand ones she owned in her root life. Some medical books. She recognised her copy of Bertrand Russell's *History of Western Philosophy*, along with Henry David Thoreau's *Walden*, both of which she'd owned since university. A familiar *Principles of Geology* was also there. There were quite a few books on Thoreau. And copies of Plato's *Republic* and Hannah Arendt's *The Origins of Totalitarianism*, which she did own in her root life, but not in these editions. Intellectual-looking books by people like Julia Kristeva and Judith Butler and Chimamanda Ngozi Adichie. There were a lot of works on Eastern philosophy that she had never read before and she wondered if she stayed in this life, and she couldn't see why not, whether there was a

234

way to read them all before she had to do any more teaching at Cambridge.

Novels, some Dickens, *The Bell Jar,* some geeky pop-science books, a few music books, a few parenting manuals, *Nature* by Ralph Waldo Emerson and *Silent Spring* by Rachel Carson, some stuff on climate change, and a large hardback called *Arctic Dreams: Imagination and Desire in a Northern Landscape.*

She had rarely, if ever, been this consistently highbrow. This was clearly what happened when you did a Master's degree at Cambridge and then went on sabbatical to write a book on your favourite philosopher.

'You're impressed by me,' she told the dog. 'You can admit it.'

There was also a pile of music songbooks, and Nora smiled when she saw that the one on top was the Simon & Garfunkel one she had sold to Ash the day he had asked her out for a coffee. On the coffee table there was a nice glossy hardback book of photographs of Spanish scenery and on the sofa there was something called *The Encyclopedia of Plants and Flowers.*

And in the magazine rack there was the brand-new *National Geographic* with the picture of the black hole on the cover.

There was a picture on the wall. A Miró print from a museum in Barcelona.

'Have me and Ash been to Barcelona together, Plato?' She imagined them both, hand-in-hand, wandering the streets of the Gothic Quarter together, popping into a bar for tapas and Rioja.

On the wall opposite the bookshelves there was a mirror. A broad mirror with an ornate white frame. She no longer got surprised by the variations in appearance between lives. She had been every shape and size and had every haircut. In this life, she looked perfectly *pleasant.* She would have liked to be friends with this person. It wasn't an Olympian or a rock star or a Cirque du Soleil acrobat she was looking at, but it was someone who seemed to be having a good life, as far as you could tell these things. A grown-up who had a vague idea of who she was and what she was doing in life. Short hair, but not dramatically so, skin looking healthier than in her root life, either through diet, a lack of red wine, exercise, or the cleansers and moisturisers she'd seen in the bathroom, which were all more expensive than anything she owned in her root life.

'Well,' she said to Plato. 'This is a nice life, yeah?'

Plato seemed to agree.

A Spiritual Quest for a Deeper Connection with the Universe

She found the medicine drawer in the kitchen and rummaged through the plasters and ibuprofen and Calpol and multivitamins and runners' knee bandages but couldn't find any sign of any anti-depressants.

Maybe this was it. Maybe this was, finally, the life she was going to stay put in. The life she would choose. The one she would not return to the shelves.

I could be happy here.

A little later, in the shower, she scanned her body for new marks. There were no tattoos but there was a scar. Not a self-inflicted scar but a surgical-looking one – a long, delicate horizontal line below her navel. She had seen a caesarean scar before, and now she stroked her thumb along it, thinking that even if she stayed in this life she would have always turned up late for it.

Ash came back home from dropping Molly off.

She hastily dressed so he wouldn't see her naked.

They had breakfast together. They sat at their kitchen table and scrolled the day's news and ate sourdough toast and were very much like a living endorsement for marriage.

And then Ash went to the hospital and she stayed home to research Thoreau all day. She read her work-in-progress, which already had an impressive word-count of 42,729, and sat eating toast before picking Molly up from school.

Molly wanted to go to the park 'like normal' to feed the ducks, and so Nora took her, disguising the fact that she was using Google Maps to navigate her way there.

Nora pushed her on a swing till her arms ached, slid down slides with her and crawled behind her through large metallic tunnels. They then threw dry oats into the pond for the ducks, scooped from a box of porridge.

Then she sat down with Molly in front of the telly and then she fed her her dinner and read a bedtime story, all before Ash returned home.

After Ash came home, a man came to the door and tried to get in and Nora shut the door in his face.

'Nora?'

'Yes.'

'Why were you so weird to Adam?'

'What?'

'I think he was a little bit put out.'

'What do you mean?'

'You acted like he was a stranger.'

'Oh.' Nora smiled. 'Sorry.'

'He's been our neighbour for three years. We went camping with him and Hannah in the Lake District.'

'Yes. I know. Of course.'

'You looked like you weren't letting him in. Like he was an intruder or something.'

'Did I?'

'You shut the door in his face.'

'I shut the door. It wasn't in his face. I mean, yes, his face was there. Technically. But I just didn't want him to think he could barge in.'

'He was bringing the hose back.'

'Oh, right. Well, we don't need the hose. Hoses are bad for the planet.'

'Are you okay?'

'Why wouldn't I be?'

'I just worry about you . . .'

Generally, though, things turned out pretty good, and every time she wondered if she would wake up back in the library, she didn't. One day, after her yoga class, Nora sat on a bench by the River Cam and re-read some Thoreau. The day after, she watched Ryan Bailey on daytime TV being interviewed on the set of *Last Chance Saloon 2*, in which he said he was 'on a spiritual quest for a deeper connection with the universe' rather than worrying about 'settling down in a romantic context'.

She received whale photos from Izzy, and WhatsApped her to say that she had heard about a horrid car crash in Australia recently, and made Izzy promise she would always drive safely.

Nora was comforted to know she had no inclination whatsoever to see what Dan was doing with his life. Instead, she felt very grateful to be with Ash. Or rather, and more precisely: she imagined she was grateful, because he was lovely, and there were so many moments of joy and laughter and love.

Ash did long shifts but was easy to be around when he was in, even after days of blood and stress and gall bladders. He was also a bit of a nerd. He always said 'Good morning' to elderly people in the street when walking the dog and sometimes they ignored him. He sang along to the car radio. He generally didn't seem to need sleep. And was always fine doing the Molly night shift even when he was in surgery the next day.

He loved to gross Molly out with facts – a stomach gets a new lining every four days! Ear wax is a type of sweat! You have creatures called mites living in your eyelashes! – and loved to be inappropriate. He (at the duck pond, the first Saturday, within Molly's earshot) enthusiastically told a random stranger that male ducks have penises shaped like corkscrews.

On nights when he was home early enough to cook, he made a great lentil dal and a pretty good penne arrabbiata, and tended to put a whole bulb of garlic in every meal he created. But Molly had been absolutely right: his artistic talents didn't extend to musical ability. In fact, when he sang 'The Sound of Silence', accompanied by his guitar, she found herself guiltily wishing he would take the title literally.

He was, in other words, a bit of a dork – a dork who saved lives on a daily basis, but still a dork. Which was good. Nora liked dorks, and she felt one herself, and it helped make her get over the fundamental *peculiarity* of being with a husband you were only just getting to know.

This is a good life, Nora would think to herself, over and over again.

Yes, being a parent was exhausting, but Molly was easy to love, at least in daylight hours. In fact, Nora often preferred it when Molly was home from school because it added a bit of challenge to what was otherwise a rather frictionless existence. No relationship stress, no work stress, no money stress.

It was a lot to be grateful for.

There were inevitably shaky moments. She felt the familiar feeling of being in a play for which she didn't know the lines.

'Is anything wrong?' she asked Ash one night.

'It's just . . .' He looked at her with his kind smile and intense, scrutinising eyes. 'I don't know. You forgot our anniversary was coming up. You think you haven't seen films you've seen. And vice versa. You forgot you had a bike. You forget where the plates are. You've been wearing my slippers. You get into my side of the bed.'

'Jeez, Ash,' she said, a little bit too tense. 'It's like being interrogated by the three bears.'

'I just worry . . .'

'I'm fine. Just, you know, lost in research world. Lost in the woods. Thoreau's woods.'

And she felt in those moments that maybe she'd return to the Midnight Library. Sometimes she remembered the words of Mrs Elm on her first visit there. *If you really want to live a life hard enough, you don't have to worry . . . The moment you decide you want that life, really want it, then everything that exists in your head now, including this Midnight Library, will eventually be a dream. A memory so vague and intangible it will hardly be there at all.*

Which begged the question: if this was the perfect life, why hadn't she forgotten the library?

How long did it take to forget?

Occasionally she felt wisps of gentle depression float around her, for no real reason, but it wasn't comparable to how terrible she had felt in her root life, or indeed many of her other lives. It was like comparing a bit of a sniffle to pneumonia. When she thought about how bad she had felt the day she lost her job at String Theory, of the despair, of the lonely and desperate yearning to not exist, then this was *nowhere near.*

Every day she went to bed thinking she was going to wake up in this life again, because it was – on balance, and all things considered – the best she had known. Indeed, she progressed from going to bed casually assuming she'd stay in this life, to being scared to fall asleep in case she wouldn't.

And yet, night after night she would fall asleep and day after day she would wake up in the same bed. Or occasionally on the carpet, but she shared that pain with Ash, and more often than not it was a bed as Molly was getting better and better at sleeping through.

There were awkward moments, of course. Nora never knew the way to anything, or where things were in the house, and Ash sometimes wondered out loud if she should see a doctor. And at first she had avoided sex with him, but one night it happened and afterwards Nora felt guilty about the lie she was living.

They lay in the dark for a while, in post-coital silence, but she knew she had to broach the subject. Test the water.

'Ash,' she said.

'What?'

'Do you believe in the theory of parallel universes?'

She could see his face stretch into a smile. This was the kind of conversation on his wavelength. 'Yes, I think so.'

'Me too. I mean, it's science, isn't it? It's not like some geeky physicist just thought, "Hey, parallel universes are cool. Let's make a theory about them."'

'Yeah,' he agreed. 'Science distrusts anything that sounds too cool. Too sci-fi. Scientists are sceptics, as a rule.'

'Exactly, yet physicists believe in parallel universes.'

'It's just where the science leads, isn't it? Everything in quantum mechanics and string theory all points to there being multiple universes. Many, many universes.'

'Well, what would you say if I said that I have visited my other lives, and I think I have chosen this one?'

'I would think you were insane. But I'd still like you.'

'Well, I have. I have had many lives.'

He smiled. 'Great. Is there one where you kiss me again?'

'There is one where you buried my dead cat.'

He laughed. 'That's so cool, Nor. The thing I like about you is that you always make me feel normal.'

And that was it.

She realised that you could be as honest as possible in life, but people only see the truth if it is close enough to their reality. As Thoreau wrote, 'It's not what you look at that matters, it's what you see.' And Ash only saw the Nora he had fallen in love with and married, and so, in a way, that was the Nora she was becoming.

Hammersmith

During half term, while Molly was off school and on a Tuesday when Ash wasn't in the hospital, they popped on the train to London to see Nora's brother and Ewan in their flat in Hammersmith.

Joe looked well, and his husband looked the same as he had when Nora had seen him on her brother's phone in her Olympic life. Joe and Ewan met at a cross-training class at their local gym. Joe was, in this life, working as a sound engineer, while Ewan – Dr Ewan Langford, to be precise – was a consultant radiologist for the Royal Marsden Hospital, so he and Ash had a lot of hospital-related stuff to moan about together.

Joe and Ewan were lovely with Molly, asking her detailed questions about what Panda was up to. And Joe cooked them all a great garlicky pasta-and-broccoli meal.

'It's Puglian, apparently,' he told Nora. 'Getting a bit of our heritage in there.'

Nora thought of her Italian grandfather and wondered what he had felt like when he realised the London Brick Company was actually based in Bedford. Had he been truly disappointed? Or had he, actually, just decided to make the most of it? There was probably a version of their grandfather who *went* to London and on his first day got run over by a double-decker bus at Piccadilly Circus.

Joe and Ewan had a full wine rack in the kitchen and Nora noticed that one of the bottles was a Californian Syrah from the Buena Vista vineyard. Nora felt her skin prickle as she saw the two printed signatures at the bottom – Alicia and Eduardo Martìnez.

She smiled, sensing Eduardo was just as happy in this life. She wondered, momentarily, who Alicia was and what she was like. At least there were good sunsets there.

'You okay?' asked Ash, as Nora gazed absent-mindedly at the label.

'Yeah, sure. It just, um, looks like a good one.'

'That's my absolute fave,' said Ewan. 'Such a bloody good wine. Shall we get it open?'

'Well,' said Nora, 'only if you were going to have a drink anyway.'

'Well, I'm not,' said Joe. 'I've been overdoing it a bit recently. I'm in a little teetotal patch.'

'You know what your bro is like,' added Ewan, planting a kiss on Joe's cheek. 'All or nothing.'

'Oh yeah. I do.'

Ewan already had the corkscrew in his hands. 'Had one hell of a day at work. So I'm happy to guzzle the whole lot straight from the bottle if no one will join me.'

'I'm in,' said Ash.

'I'm okay,' said Nora, remembering that the last time she had seen him, in the business lounge of a hotel, her brother had confessed to being an alcoholic.

They gave Molly a picture book and Nora read it with her on the sofa.

The evening progressed. They talked news and music and movies. Joe and Ewan had quite enjoyed *Last Chance Saloon*.

A little while later, and to everyone's surprise, Nora took a left turn out of the safe environs of pop culture and cut to the chase with her brother.

'Did you ever get pissed off with me? You know, for backing out of the band?'

'That was years ago, sis. Lot of water under the bridge since then.'

'You wanted to be a rock star, though.'

'He still is a rock star,' said Ewan, laughing. 'But he's all mine.'

'I always feel like I let you down, Joe.'

'Well, don't . . . But I feel like I let you down too. Because I was such an idiot . . . I was horrid to you for a little while.'

These words felt like a tonic she had been waiting years to hear. 'Don't worry about it,' she managed.

'Before I was with Ewan, I was so dumb about mental health. I thought panic attacks were a big nothing . . . You know, mind over matter. Man up, sis. But then when Ewan started having them, I understood how real they are.'

'It wasn't just the panic attacks. It just felt wrong. I don't know . . . For what it's worth, I think you're happier in this life than the one where you're' – she nearly said *dead* – 'in the band.'

Her brother smiled and looked at Ewan. She doubted he believed it, but Nora had to accept that – as she now knew only too well – some truths were just impossible to see.

Tricycle

As the weeks went by, Nora began to feel something remarkable start to happen.

She began to remember aspects of her life that she had never actually lived.

For instance, one day someone she had never known in her root life – a friend she had apparently known while studying and teaching at the university – phoned her about meeting for lunch. And as the caller 'Lara' came up on the phone, a name came to her – 'Lara Bryan' – and she pictured her completely, and somehow knew her partner was called Mo, and that they had a baby called Aldous. And then she met her and had all these things confirmed.

This sort-of déjà-vu happened increasingly. Yes, of course there were the occasional slip-ups she made – like 'forgetting' Ash had asthma (which he tried to keep under control via running):

'How long have you had it?'

'Since I was *seven*.'

'Oh yes, of course. I thought you'd said eczema.'

'Nora, are you okay?'

'Yes. Um, fine. It's just I had some wine with Lara at lunch and I feel a bit spaced out.'

But slowly, these slip-ups became less frequent. It was as though each day was a piece fitting into a puzzle and, with each piece added, it became easier to know what the absent pieces were going to look like.

Whereas in every other life she had been continually grasping for clues and feeling like she was acting, in this one she increasingly found that the more she relaxed into it, the more things came to her.

Nora also loved spending time with Molly.

The cosy anarchy of her playing in her bedroom, or the delicate bonding that happened at story time, reading the simple magical brilliance of *The Tiger Who Came to Tea*, or hanging out in the garden.

'Watch me, Mummy,' said Molly, as she pedalled away on her tricycle one Saturday morning. 'Mummy, look! Are you watching?'

'That's very good, Molly. Good pedalling.'

'Mummy, look! Zoomy!'

'Go, Molly!'

But then the front wheel of the tricycle slipped off the lawn and down into the flowerbed. Molly fell off and knocked her head hard on a small rock. Nora rushed over and picked her up and had a look at her. Molly was clearly hurt, with a scrape on her forehead, the skin grazed and bleeding, but she didn't want to show it even as her chin wobbled.

'I'm all right,' she said slowly, in a voice as fragile as porcelain. 'I'm all right. I'm all right. I'm all right. I'm all right.' Each 'all right' got progressively closer to tears, then horse-shoed back around to calm again. For all her nocturnal fears about bears, she had a resilience to her that Nora couldn't help but admire and be inspired by. This little human being had come from her, was in some way a part of her, and if she had hidden strength then maybe Nora did too.

Nora hugged her. 'It's all right, baby . . . My brave girl. It's okay. How does it feel now, darling?'

'It's okay. It's like on holiday.'

'On holiday?'

'Yes, Mummy . . .' she said, a little upset Nora couldn't remember. 'The slide.'

'Oh yes, of course. The slide. Yes. Silly me. Silly Mummy.'

Nora felt something inside her all at once. A kind of fear, as real as the fear she had felt on the Arctic skerry, face to face with the polar bear.

A fear of what she was feeling.

Love.

You could eat in the finest restaurants, you could partake in every sensual pleasure, you could sing on stage in São Paulo to twenty thousand people, you could soak up whole thunderstorms of applause, you could travel to the ends of the Earth, you could be followed by millions on the internet, you could win Olympic medals, but this was all meaningless without love.

And when she thought of her root life, the fundamental problem with it, the thing that had left her vulnerable, really, was the absence of love. Even her brother hadn't wanted her in that life. There had been no one, once Volts had died. She had loved no one, and no one had loved her back. She had been empty, her life had been empty, walking around, faking some kind of human normality like a sentient mannequin of despair. Just the bare bones of getting through.

Yet there, right there in that garden in Cambridge, under that dull grey sky, she felt the power of it, the terrifying power of caring deeply and being cared for deeply. Okay, her parents were still dead in this life but here there was Molly, there was Ash, there was Joe. There was a net of love to break her fall.

And yet she sensed deep down that it would all come to an end, soon. She sensed that, for all the perfection here, there was something wrong amid the rightness. And the thing that was wrong couldn't be fixed because the flaw was the rightness itself. Everything was right, and yet she hadn't earned this. She had joined the movie halfway. She had taken the book from the library, but truthfully, she didn't own it. She was watching her life as if from behind a window. She was, she began to feel, a fraud. She wanted this to be *her* life. As in her real life. And it wasn't and she just wished she could forget that fact. She really did.

'Mummy, are you crying?'

'No, Molly, no. I'm fine. Mummy's fine.'

'You look like you are crying.'

'Let's just get you cleaned up . . .'

Later that same day, Molly pieced together a jigsaw of jungle animals, Nora sat on the sofa stroking Plato as his warm, weighty head rested on her lap. She stared at the ornate chess set that was sitting there on the mahogany chest.

A thought rose slowly, and she dismissed it. But then it rose again.

As soon as Ash came home, she told him she wanted to see an old friend from Bedford and wouldn't be back for a few hours.

No Longer Here

As soon as Nora entered Oak Leaf Residential Care Home, and before she'd even reached the reception, she saw a frail elderly man wearing glasses whom she recognised. He was having a slightly heated conversation with a nurse who looked exasperated. Like a sigh turned into a human.

'I really would like to go in the garden,' the old man said.

'I'm sorry, but the garden is being used today.'

'I just want to sit on the bench. And read the newspaper.'

'Maybe if you'd signed up for the gardening activity session—'

'I don't want a gardening session. I want to call Dhavak. This was all a mistake.'

Nora had heard her old neighbour talk about his son Dhavak before, when she had dropped off his medication. Apparently his son had been pushing for him to go to a care home, but Mr Banerjee had insisted on holding on to his house. 'Is there no way I can just—'

He noticed, at this point, that he was being stared at.

'Mr Banerjee?'

He stared at Nora, confused. 'Hello? Who are you?'

'I'm Nora. You know, Nora Seed.' Then, feeling too flustered to think, she added: 'I'm your neighbour. On Bancroft Avenue.'

He shook his head. 'I think you've made a mistake, dear. I haven't lived there for three years. And I am very sure you were not my neighbour.'

The nurse tilted her head at Mr Banerjee, as if he was a confused puppy. 'Maybe you've forgotten.'

'No,' said Nora quickly, realising her mistake. 'He was right. I was confused. I have memory issues sometimes. I never lived there. It was somewhere else. And someone else. I'm sorry.'

They resumed their conversation, as Nora thought about Mr Banerjee's front garden full of irises and foxgloves.

'Can I help you?'

She turned to look at the receptionist. A mild-mannered, red-haired man with glasses and blotched skin and a gentle Scottish accent.

She told him who she was and that she had phoned earlier.

He was a little confused at first.

'And you say you left a message?'

He hummed a quiet tune as he searched for her email.

'Yes, but on the phone. I was trying for ages to get through and I couldn't so I eventually left a message. I emailed as well.'

'Ah, right, I see. Well, I'm sorry about that. Are you here to see a family member?'

'No,' Nora explained. 'I am not family. I am just someone who used to know her. She'd know me, though. Her name is Mrs Elm.' Nora tried to remember the full name. 'Sorry. It's Louise Elm. If you told her my name, Nora. Nora Seed. She used to be my . . . She was the school librarian, at Hazeldene. I just thought she might like some company.'

The man stopped looking at his computer and stared up at Nora with barely suppressed surprise. At first Nora thought that she had got it wrong. Or Dylan had got it wrong, that evening at La Cantina. Or maybe the Mrs Elm in that life had experienced a different fate in this life. Though Nora didn't quite know how her own decision to work in an animal shelter would have led to a different outcome for Mrs Elm in this life. But that made no sense. As in neither life had she been in touch with the librarian since school.

'What's the matter?' Nora asked the receptionist.

'I'm ever so sorry to tell you this, but Louise Elm is no longer here.'

'Where is she?'

'She . . . actually, she died three weeks ago.'

At first she thought it must be an admin error. 'Are you sure?'

'Yes. I'm afraid I am very sure.'

'Oh,' said Nora. She didn't really know what to say, or to feel. She looked down at her tote bag that had sat beside her in the car. A bag containing the chess set she had brought to play a game with her, and to keep her company. 'I'm sorry. I didn't know. I didn't . . . You see, I haven't seen her for years. Years and years. But I heard from someone who said that she was here . . .'

'So sorry,' the receptionist said.

'No. No worries. I just wanted to thank her. For being so kind to me.'

'She died very peacefully,' he said, 'literally in her sleep.'

And Nora smiled and retreated politely away. 'That's good. Thank you. Thank you for looking after her. I'll just go now. Bye . . .'

An Incident With the Police

She stepped back out onto Shakespeare Road with her bag and her
chess set and she really didn't know what to do. There were tingles
through her body. Not quite pins and needles. More that strange,
fuzzy static feeling she had felt before when she was nearing the
end of a particular existence.

Trying to ignore the feeling in her body, she headed in the vague
direction of the car park. She passed her old garden flat at 33A
Bancroft Avenue. A man she had never seen before was taking a
box of recycling out. She thought of the lovely house in Cambridge
she now had and couldn't help but compare it to this shabby flat
on a litter-strewn street. The tingles subsided a little. She passed
Mr Banerjee's house, or what had been Mr Banerjee's house, and
saw the only owned house on the street that hadn't been divided
into flats, though now it looked very different. The small front
lawn was overgrown, and there was no sign of the clematis or busy
lizzies in pots that Nora had watered for him last summer when
he'd been recovering from his hip surgery.

On the pavement she noticed a couple of crumpled lager cans.

She saw a woman with a blonde bob and tanned skin walking
towards her on the pavement with two small children in a double
pushchair. She looked exhausted. It was the woman she had spoken
to in the newsagent's the day she had decided to die. The one who
had seemed happy and relaxed. Kerry-Anne. She hadn't noticed
Nora because one child was wailing and she was trying to pacify
the distressed, red-cheeked boy by waving a plastic dinosaur in
front of him.

Me and Jake were like rabbits but we got there. Two little terrors. But worth it, y'know? I just feel complete. I could show you some pictures . . .

Then Kerry-Anne looked up and saw Nora.

'I know you, don't I? Is it Nora?'

'Yes.'

'Hi Nora.'

'Hi Kerry-Anne.'

'You remember my name? Oh wow. I was in *awe* of you in school. You seemed to have it all. Did you ever make the Olympics?'

'Yes, actually. Kind of. One me did. But it wasn't what I wanted it to be. But then, what is? Right?'

Kerry-Anne seemed momentarily confused. And then her son threw the dinosaur onto the pavement and it landed next to one of the crumpled cans. 'Right.'

Nora picked up the dinosaur – a stegosaurus, on close inspection – and handed it to Kerry-Anne, who smiled her gratitude and headed into the house that should have belonged to Mr Banerjee, just as the boy descended into a full tantrum.

'Bye,' said Nora.

'Yeah. Bye.'

And Nora wondered what the difference had been. What had forced Mr Banerjee to go to the care home he'd been determined not to go to? She was the only difference between the two Mr Banerjees but what *was* that difference? What had she done? Set up an online shop? Picked up his prescription a few times?

Never underestimate the big importance of small things, Mrs Elm had said. *You must always remember that.*

She stared at her own window. She thought of herself in her root life, hovering between life and death in her bedroom – equidistant, as it were. And, for the first time, Nora worried about herself as if she was actually someone else. Not just another version of her, but a different actual person. As though finally, through all

254

the experiences of life she now had, she had become someone who pitied her former self. Not in self-pity, because she was a different self now.

Then someone appeared at her own window. A woman who wasn't her, holding a cat that wasn't Voltaire.

This was her hope, anyway, even as she began to feel faint and fuzzy again.

She headed into town. Walked down the high street.

Yes, she was different now. She was stronger. She had untapped things inside her. Things she might never have known about if she'd never sung in an arena or fought off a polar bear or felt so much love and fear and courage.

There was a commotion outside Boots. Two boys were being arrested by police officers as a nearby store detective spoke into a walkie-talkie.

She recognised one of the boys and went up to him.

'Leo?'

A police officer motioned for her to back away.

'Who are you?' Leo asked.

'I—' Nora realised she couldn't say 'your piano teacher'. And she realised how mad it was, given the fraught context, to say what she was about to say. But still, she said it. 'Do you have music lessons?'

Leo looked down as the handcuffs were put on him. 'I ain't done no music lessons . . .'

His voice had lost its bravado.

The police officer was frustrated now. 'Please, miss, leave this to us.'

'He's a good kid,' Nora told him. 'Please don't be too hard on him.'

'Well, this good kid just stole two hundred quid's worth from there. And has also just been found to be in possession of a concealed weapon.'

'Weapon?'

'A knife.'

'No. There must be some mix-up. He's not that sort of kid.'

'Hear that,' the police officer said to his colleague. 'Lady here thinks our friend Leo Thompson isn't the kind of kid to get into trouble.'

The other police officer laughed. 'He's always in and out of bother, this one.'

'Now, please,' the first police officer said, 'let us do our jobs here . . .'

'Of course,' said Nora, 'of course. Do everything they say, Leo . . .'

He looked at her as if she'd been sent as a practical joke.

A few years ago his mum Doreen had come into String Theory to buy her son a cheap keyboard. She'd been worried about his behaviour at school and he'd expressed an interest in music and so she wanted to get him piano lessons. Nora explained she had an electric piano, and could play, but had no formal teacher training. Doreen had explained she didn't have much money but they struck a deal, and Nora had enjoyed her Tuesday evenings teaching Leo the difference between major and minor seventh chords and thought he was a great boy, eager to learn.

Doreen had seen Leo was 'getting caught up in the wrong set', but when he got into music he started doing well in other things too. And suddenly he wasn't getting into trouble with teachers any more, and he'd play everything from Chopin through Scott Joplin to Frank Ocean and John Legend and Rex Orange County with the same care and commitment.

Something Mrs Elm had said on an early visit to the Midnight Library came to her.

Every life contains many millions of decisions. Some big, some small. But every time one decision is taken over another, the outcomes differ. An irreversible variation occurs, which in turn leads to further variations . . .

In this timeline right now, the one where she had studied a

Master's at Cambridge, and married Ash and had a baby, she hadn't been in String Theory on the day four years ago when Doreen and Leo came by. In this timeline, Doreen never found a music teacher who was cheap enough, and so Leo never persisted with music for long enough to realise he had a talent. He never sat there, side-by-side with Nora on a Tuesday evening, pursuing a passion that he extended at home, producing his own tunes.

Nora felt herself weaken. Not just tingles and fuzziness but something stronger, a sense of plunging into nothingness, accompanied by a brief darkening of her vision. A feeling of another Nora right there in the wings, ready to pick up where this one left off. Her brain ready to fill in the gaps and have a perfectly legitimate reason to be on a day trip to Bedford, and to fill in every absence as if she was here the whole time.

Worried she knew what it meant, she turned away from Leo and his friend as they were escorted away to the police car, the eyes of the whole of Bedford high street upon them, and she started to quicken her pace towards the car park.

This is a good life . . . This is a good life . . . This is a good life . . .

A New Way of Seeing

She got closer to the station, passing the garish red-and-yellow zigzags of La Cantina, like a Mexican migraine, with a waiter inside taking chairs off tables. And String Theory too, closed, with a handwritten notice on the door:

> Alas, String Theory is no longer able to trade in these premises. Due to an increase in rent we simply couldn't afford to go on. Thanks to all our loyal customers. Don't Think Twice, It's All Right. You Can Go Your Own Way. God Only Knows What We'll Be Without You.

It was the exact same note she had seen with Dylan. Judging by the date, written in small felt-tip letters from Neil's hand, it was from nearly three months ago.

She felt sad, because String Theory had meant a lot to people. Yet Nora hadn't been working at String Theory when it got into trouble.

Well. I suppose I did sell a lot of electric pianos. And some rather nice guitars too.

Growing up, she and Joe had always joked about their hometown, the way teenagers do, and used to say that HMP Bedford was the inner prison and the rest of the town was just the outer prison, and any chance you had to escape you should take it.

But the sun was out now, as she neared the station, and it seemed that she had been looking at the place wrong all these years. As she passed the statue of prison reformer John Howard in St Paul's Square, with the trees all around and the river just behind, refracting light, she marvelled at it as if she were seeing it for the first time. *It's not what you look at that matters, it's what you see.*

Driving back to Cambridge cocooned in her expensive Audi, smelling almost nauseatingly of vinyl and plastic and other synthetic materials, weaving through busy traffic, the cars sliding by like forgotten lives, she was deeply wishing she had been able to see Mrs Elm, the real one, before she had died. It would have been good to have one last game of chess with her before she passed away. And she thought of poor Leo, sat in a small windowless cell at a Bedford police station, waiting for Doreen to come and collect him.

'This is the best life,' she told herself, a little desperately now. 'This is the best life. I am staying here. This is the life for me. This is the best life. *This* is the best life.'

But she knew she didn't have long.

The Flowers Have Water

She pulled up at the house and ran inside, as Plato padded happily to greet her.

'Hello?' she asked, desperately. 'Ash? Molly?'

She needed to see them. She knew she didn't have long. She could feel the Midnight Library waiting for her.

'Outside!' said Ash, chirpily, from the back garden.

And so Nora went through to find Molly on her tricycle again, unfazed by her previous accident, while Ash was tending to a flower-bed.

'How was your trip?'

Molly climbed off her tricycle and ran over. 'Mummy! I missed you! I'm really good at biking now!'

'Are you, darling?'

She hugged her daughter close and closed her eyes and inhaled the scent of her hair and the dog and fabric conditioner and child-hood, and she hoped the wonder of it would help keep her there. 'I love you, Molly, I want you to know that. For ever and ever, do you understand?'

'Yes, Mummy. Of course.'

'And I love your daddy too. And everything will be okay because whatever happens you will always have Daddy and you will have Mummy too, it's just I might not be here in the exact same way. I'll be here, but . . .' She realised Molly needed to know nothing else except one truth. 'I love you.'

Molly looked concerned. 'You forgot Plato!'

'Well, *obviously* I love Plato . . . How could I forget Plato? Plato knows I love him, don't you, Plato? Plato, I love you.'

Nora tried to compose herself.

Whatever happens, they will be looked after. They will be loved. And they have each other and they will be happy.

Then Ash came over, with his gardening gloves on. 'You okay, Nor? You seem a bit pale. Did anything happen?'

'Oh, I'll tell you about it later. When Molly's in bed.'

'Okay. Oh, there's a shop coming any time . . . So keep an ear out for the lorry.'

'Sure. Yeah. Yeah.'

And then Molly asked if she could get the watering can out and Ash explained that as it had been raining a lot recently it wasn't necessary, because the sky had been looking after the flowers. 'They'll be okay. They're looked after. The flowers have water.' And the words echoed in Nora's mind. *They'll be okay. They're looked after . . .* And then Ash said something about going to the cinema tonight and how the babysitter was all arranged and Nora had forgotten completely but just smiled and tried really hard to hold on, to stay there, but it was happening, it was happening, she knew it from within every hidden chamber of her being, and there was absolutely nothing she could do to stop it.

Nowhere to Land

'NO!'

Unmistakably, it had happened.

She was back in the Midnight Library.

Mrs Elm was at the computer. The lights wobbled and shook and flickered overhead in fast arrhythmic blinks. 'Nora, stop. Calm down. Be a good girl. I need to sort this out.'

Dust fell in thin wisps from the ceiling, from cracks fissuring and spreading like spider webs woven at unnatural speed. There was the sound of sudden, active destruction which, in her sad fury, Nora found herself managing to ignore.

'You're not Mrs Elm. Mrs Elm is dead . . . Am I dead?'

'We've been through this. But now you mention it, maybe you're about to be . . .'

'Why aren't I still there? Why aren't I there? I could sense it was happening but I didn't want it to. You said that if I found a life I wanted to live in – that I *really* wanted to live in – then I'd stay there. You said I'd forget about this stupid place. You said I could find the life I wanted. That was the life I wanted. That was the life!'

Moments ago she had been in the garden with Ash and Nora and Plato, a garden humming with life and love, and now she was here.

'Take me back . . .'

'You know it doesn't work like that.'

'Well, take me to the closest variation. Give me the closest possible thing to that life. Please, Mrs Elm, it must be possible. There must be a life where I went for the coffee with Ash and where we had Molly and Plato, but I . . . I did something slightly different. So it was technically another life. Like I chose a different dog collar for Plato. Or . . . or . . . Or where I – I don't know – where I did Pilates instead of yoga? Or where I went to a different college at Cambridge? Or if it has to be further back, where it wasn't coffee on the date but tea? That life. Take me to the life where I did that. Come on. Please. Help me out. I'd like to try one of those lives, please . . .'

The computer started to smoke. The screen went black. The whole monitor fell to pieces.

'You don't understand,' said Mrs Elm, defeated, as she collapsed back into the office chair.

'But that's what happens, isn't it? I pick a regret. Something I wished I had done differently . . . And then you find the book, I open the book, and I *live* the book. That's how this library works, right?'

'It's not that simple.'

'Why? Is there a transference problem? You know, like what happened before?'

Mrs Elm looked at her, sadly. 'It's more than that. There was always a strong possibility that your old life would end. I told you that, didn't I? You wanted to die and maybe you would.'

'Yes, but you said I just needed somewhere to go to. "Somewhere to land", that's what you said. "Another life." Those exact words. And all I needed to do was think hard enough and choose the right life and—'

'I know. I know. But it didn't work out like that.'

The ceiling was falling down now, in pieces, as if the plaster was no more stable than the icing of a wedding cake.

Nora noticed something even more distressing. A spark flew from one of the lights and landed on a book, which consequently ignited into a glowing burst of fire. Pretty soon the fire was spreading along the entire shelf, the books burning as rapidly as if they were doused in petrol. A whole stream of hot, raging, roaring amber. Then another spark arced towards a different shelf and that too set alight. At about the same time a large chunk of dusty ceiling landed by Nora's feet.

'Under the table!' ordered Mrs Elm. 'Now!'

Nora hunched down and followed Mrs Elm – who was now on all fours – under the table, where she sat on her knees and was forced, like Mrs Elm, to keep her head down.

'Why can't you stop this?'

'It's a chain reaction now. Those sparks aren't random. The books are going to be destroyed. And then, just as inevitably, the whole place is going to collapse.'

'Why? I don't understand. I was there. I had found the life for me. The only life for me. The best one in here . . .'

'But that's the problem,' said Mrs Elm, nervously looking out from beneath the wooden legs of the table as more shelves caught on fire and as debris fell all around them. 'It still wasn't enough. Look!'

'At what?'

'At your watch. Any moment now.'

So Nora looked, and at first saw nothing untoward – but then it was happening. The watch was suddenly acting like a watch. The display was starting to move.

00:00:00

00:00:01

00:00:02

'What's happening?' Nora asked, realising that whatever it was probably wasn't good.

'Time. That's what's happening.'

'How are we going to leave this place?'

00:00:09

00:00:10

'*We're* not,' said Mrs Elm. 'There's no *we*. I can't leave the library.

When the library disappears, so do I. But there is a chance that you can get out, though you don't have long. No more than a minute . . .'

Nora had just lost one Mrs Elm, she didn't want to lose this one too. Mrs Elm could see her distress.

'Listen. I am part of the library. But this whole library is part of you. Do you understand? You don't exist because of the library; this library exists because of you. Remember what Hugo said? He told you that this is the simplest way your brain translates the strange and multifarious reality of the universe. So, this is just your brain translating something. Something significant and dangerous.'

'I gathered that.'

'But one thing is clear: you didn't want that life.'

'It was the perfect life.'

'Did you feel that? All the time?'

'Yes. I mean . . . I wanted to. I mean, I loved Molly. I might have loved Ash. But I suppose, maybe . . . it wasn't *my* life. I hadn't made it by myself. I had walked into this other version of me. I was carbon-copied into the perfect life. But it wasn't me.'

00:00:15

'I don't want to die,' said Nora, her voice suddenly raised but also fragile. She was shaking from her very core. '*I don't want to die.*'

Mrs Elm looked at her with wide eyes. Eyes shining with the small flame of an idea. 'You need to get out of here.'

'I can't! The library goes on for bloody ever. The moment I walked in it, the entrance disappeared.'

'Then you have to find it again.'

'How? There are no doors.'

'Who needs a door when you have a book?'

'The books are all on fire.'

'There's one that won't be. That's the one you need to find.'

265

'*The Book of Regrets*?'

Mrs Elm almost laughed. 'No. That is the last book you need. That will be ash by now. That will have been the first book to burn. You need to go that way!' She pointed to her left, to chaos and fire and falling plaster. 'It's the eleventh aisle that way. Third shelf from the bottom.'

'The whole place is going to fall down!'

00:00:21

00:00:22

00:00:23

'Don't you get it, Nora?'

'Get what?'

'It all makes sense. You came back here this time not because you wanted to die, but because you *want to live*. This library isn't falling down because it wants to kill you. It's falling down because it is giving you a chance to return. Something decisive has finally happened. You have decided you want to be alive. Now go on, *live*, while you still have the chance.'

'But . . . what about you? What's going to happen to you?'

'Don't worry about me,' she said. 'I promise you. I won't feel a thing.' And then she said what the real Mrs Elm had said when she had hugged Nora back at the school library on the day her dad had died. 'Things will get better, Nora. It's going to be all right.'

Mrs Elm placed a hand above the desk and hastily rummaged for something. A second later she was handing Nora an orange plastic fountain pen. The kind Nora had owned at school. The one she had noticed ages ago.

'You'll need this.'

'Why?'

'This one isn't already written. You have to start this.'

Nora took the pen.

'Bye, Mrs Elm.'

A second later, a massive chunk of ceiling slammed onto the table. A thick cloud of plaster dust clouded them, choking them.

00:00:34

00:00:35

'Go,' coughed Mrs Elm. '*Live.*'

Don't You Dare Give Up, Nora Seed!

Nora walked through the haze of dust and smoke in the direction Mrs Elm had pointed towards, as the ceiling continued to fall.

It was hard to breathe, and to see, but she had just about managed to keep count of the aisles. Sparks from the lights fell onto her head.

The dust stuck in her throat, nearly causing her to vomit. But even in the powdery fog she could see that most of the books were now ablaze. In fact, none of the shelves of books seemed intact, and the heat felt like a force. Some of the earliest shelves and books to set on fire were now nothing but ash.

Just as she reached the eleventh aisle she was hit hard by a chunk of falling debris that floored her.

Pressed under rock, she felt the pen slip out of her hand and slide away from her.

Her first attempt to free herself was unsuccessful.

This is it. I am going to die, whether I want to or not. I am going to die.

The library was a wasteland.

00:00:41

00:00:42

It was all over.

She was certain of it once more. She was going to die here, as all her possible lives were ravished all around her.

But then she saw it, amid a brief clearing in the clouds. There, on the eleventh aisle that way. Third shelf from the bottom.

A gap in the fire that was consuming every other book on the shelf.

I don't want to die.

She had to try harder. She had to want the life she always thought she didn't. Because just as this library was a part of her, so too were all the other lives. She might not have felt everything she had felt in those lives, but she had the capability. She might have missed those particular opportunities that led her to become an Olympic swimmer, or a traveller, or a vineyard owner, or a rock star, or a planet-saving glaciologist, or a Cambridge graduate, or a mother, or the million other things, but she was still in some way *all* those people. They were all her. She could have been all those amazing things, and that wasn't depressing, as she had once thought. Not at all. It was inspiring. Because now she saw the kinds of things she could do when she put herself to work. And that, actually, the life she had been living had its own logic to it. Her brother was alive. Izzy was alive. And she had helped a young boy stay out of trouble. What sometimes feels like a trap is actually just a trick of the mind. She didn't need a vineyard or a Californian sunset to be happy. She didn't even need a large house and the perfect family. She just needed potential. And she was nothing if not potential. She wondered why she had never seen it before.

She heard Mrs Elm's voice, from under the table somewhere far behind her, cutting through the noise.

'Don't give up! Don't you *dare* give up, Nora Seed!'

She didn't want to die. And she didn't want to live any other life than the one that was hers. The one that could be a messy struggle, but it was her messy struggle. A beautiful messy struggle.

00:00:52

00:00:53

As she writhed and pushed and resisted the weight on top of her, and as the seconds ticked on, she managed – with a great exertion that burned and stifled her lungs – to get back onto her feet.

She scrabbled around on the ground and found the fountain

pen, thickly coated in dust, then ran through the particles of smoke to reach the eleventh aisle.

And there it was.

The only book not burning. Still there, perfectly green.

Flinching at the heat, and with a careful index finger, she hooked the top of the spine and pulled the book from the shelf. She then did what she always did. She opened the book and tried to find the first page. But the only difficulty was that there was no first page. There were no words in the entire book. It was completely blank. Like the other books, this was the book of her future. But unlike the others, in this one that future was unwritten.

So, this was it. This was *her* life. Her root life.

And it was a blank page.

Nora stood there a moment, with her old school pen in hand. It was now nearly one minute after midnight.

The other books on the shelf had become charcoal, and the hanging light bulb flickered through the dust, vaguely illuminating the fracturing ceiling. A large piece of ceiling around the light – roughly the shape of France – was looking ready to fall and crush her.

Nora took the lid off the pen and pressed the open book against the charred stack of bookshelves.

The ceiling groaned.

There wasn't long.

She started to write. *Nora wanted to live.*

Once she'd finished the inscription she waited a moment. Frustratingly, nothing happened, and she remembered what Mrs Elm had once said. *Want is an interesting word. It means lack.* So, she crossed that out and tried again.

Nora decided to live.

Nothing. She tried again.

Nora was ready to live.

Still nothing, even when she underlined the word 'live'.

Everywhere now, there was breakage and ruination. The ceiling was falling, razing everything, smothering each of the bookshelves into piles of dust. She gaped over and saw the figure of Mrs Elm, out from under the desk where she had been sheltering Nora, standing there without any fear at all then disappearing completely as the roof caved in almost everywhere, smothering remnants of fire and shelf stacks and all else.

Nora, choking, couldn't see anything at all now.

But this part of the library was holding out, and she was still there.

Any second now, everything would be gone, she knew it.

So she stopped trying to think about what to write and, in sheer exasperation, just put down the first thing that came to her, the thing that she felt inside her like a defiant silent roar that could overpower any external destruction. The one truth she had, a truth she was now proud of and pleased with, a truth she had not only come to terms with but welcomed openly, with every fiery molecule of her being. A truth that she scribbled hastily but firmly, pressing deep into the paper with the nib, in capital letters, in the first-person present tense.

A truth that was the beginning and seed of everything possible. A former curse and a present blessing.

Three simple words containing the power and potential of a multiverse.

I AM ALIVE.

And with that, the ground shook like fury and every last remnant of the Midnight Library dissolved into dust.

Awakening

At one minute and twenty-seven seconds after midnight, Nora Seed marked her emergence back into life by vomiting all over her duvet.

Alive, but hardly.

Choking, exhausted, dehydrated, struggling, trembling, heavy, delirious, pain in her chest, even more pain in her head, this was the worst life could feel, and yet it was life, and life was precisely what she wanted.

It was hard, near impossible, to pull herself off the bed but she knew she had to get vertical.

She managed it, somehow, and grabbed her phone but it seemed too heavy and slippy to keep a grasp of and it fell onto the floor beyond view.

'Help,' she croaked, staggering out of the room.

Her hallway seemed to be tilting like it was a ship in a storm. But she reached the door without passing out, then dragged the chain lock off the latch and managed, after great effort, to open it.

'Please help me.'

She barely realised it was still raining as she stepped outside in her vomit-stained pyjamas, passing the step where Ash had stood a little over a day before to announce the news of her dead cat.

There was no one around.

No one that she could see. So she staggered towards Mr Banerjee's house in a series of dizzy stumbles and lurches, eventually managing to ring the doorbell.

A sudden square of light sprung out from the front window. The door opened.

He wasn't wearing his glasses and was confused maybe because of the state of her and the time of night.

'I'm so very sorry, Mr Banerjee. I've done something very stupid. You'd better call an ambulance . . .'

'Oh my lord. What on earth has happened?'

'Please.'

'Yes. I'll call one. Right away . . .'

00:03:48

And that is when she allowed herself to collapse, forwards and with considerable velocity, right onto Mr Banerjee's doormat.

The sky grows dark
The black over blue
Yet the stars still dare
To shine for you

The Other Side of Despair

'Life begins,' Sartre once wrote, 'on the other side of despair.'

It wasn't raining any more.

She was inside and sitting in a hospital bed. She had been put on a ward and had eaten and was feeling a lot better. The medical staff were pleased, following her physical examination. The tender abdomen was to be expected, apparently. She tried to impress the doctor by telling her a fact Ash had told her, about a stomach lining renewing itself every few days.

Then a nurse came and sat on her bed with a clipboard and went through reams of questions relating to her state of mind. Nora decided to keep her experience of the Midnight Library to herself because she imagined that it wouldn't go down too well on a psychiatric evaluation form. It was safe to surmise the little-known realities of the multiverse probably weren't yet incorporated within the care plans of the National Health Service.

The questions and answers continued for what felt like an hour. They covered medication, her mother's death, Volts, losing her job, money worries, the diagnosis of situational depression.

'Have you ever tried anything like this before?' the nurse asked.

'Not in this life.'

'And how do you feel right now?'

'I don't know. A bit strange. But I don't want to die any more.'

And the nurse scribbled on the form.

Through the window, after the nurse had gone, she watched the trees' gentle movements in the afternoon breeze and distant rush-hour traffic shunt slowly along Bedford ring road. It was nothing but trees and traffic and mediocre architecture, but it was also everything.

It was life.

A little later she deleted her suicidal social media posts, and – in a moment of sincere sentimentality – she wrote something else instead. She titled it 'A Thing I Have Learned (Written By A Nobody Who Has Been Everybody)'.

A Thing I Have Learned
(Written By A Nobody Who Has Been Everybody)

It is easy to mourn the lives we aren't living. Easy to wish we'd developed other talents, said yes to different offers. Easy to wish we'd worked harder, loved better, handled our finances more astutely, been more popular, stayed in the band, gone to Australia, said yes to the coffee or done more bloody yoga.

It takes no effort to miss the friends we didn't make and the work we didn't do and the people we didn't marry and the children we didn't have. It is not difficult to see yourself through the lens of other people, and to wish you were all the different kaleidoscopic versions of you they wanted you to be. It is easy to regret, and keep regretting, ad infinitum, until our time runs out.

But it is not the lives we regret not living that are the real problem. It is the regret itself. It's the regret that makes us shrivel and wither and feel like our own and other people's worst enemy.

We can't tell if any of those other versions would have been better or worse. Those lives are happening, it is true, but you are happening as well, and that is the happening we have to focus on.

Of course, we can't visit every place or meet every person or do every job, yet most of what we'd *feel* in any life is still available. We don't have to play every game to know what winning feels like. We don't have to hear every piece of music in the world to understand music. We don't have to have tried every variety of grape from every vineyard to know the pleasure of wine. Love and laughter and fear and pain are universal currencies.

We just have to close our eyes and savour the taste of the drink in front of us and listen to the song as it plays. We are as completely and utterly alive as we are in any other life and have access to the same emotional spectrum.

We only need to be one person.

We only need to feel one existence.

We don't have to *do* everything in order to *be* everything, because we are already infinite. While we are alive we always contain a future of multifarious possibility.

So let's be kind to the people in our own existence. Let's occasionally look up from the spot in which we are because, wherever we happen to be standing, the sky above goes on for ever.

Yesterday I knew I had no future, and that it was impossible for me to accept my life as it is now. And yet today, that same messy life seems full of hope. Potential.

The impossible, I suppose, happens via living.

Will my life be miraculously free from pain, despair, grief, heartbreak, hardship, loneliness, depression? No.

But do I want to live?

Yes. *Yes.*

A thousand times, yes.

Living Versus Understanding

A few minutes later her brother came to see her. He'd heard the voicemail she'd sent him and had responded by text at seven minutes after midnight. 'You okay, sis?' Then, when the hospital contacted him, he'd caught the first train from London. He'd bought the latest issue of *National Geographic* for her while waiting at St Pancras station.

'You used to love it,' he told her, as he placed the magazine beside the hospital bed.

'I still do.'

It was good to see him. His thick eyebrows and reluctant smile still intact. He walked in a little awkward, head cowed, hair longer than it had been in the last two lives in which she had seen him.

'I'm sorry I've been incommunicado recently,' he said. 'It wasn't about what Ravi said it was about. I don't even *think* about The Labyrinths any more. I was just in a weird place. After Mum died I was seeing this guy and we had a very messy break-up and I just didn't want to have to talk to you or, recently, to anyone about it. I just wanted to drink. And I was drinking too much. It was a real problem. But I've started getting help for it. I haven't had a drink for weeks. I go to the gym and everything now. I've started a cross-training class.'

'Oh Joe, poor you. I'm sorry about the break-up. And everything else.'

'You're all I've got, sis,' he said, his voice cracking a little. 'I know I haven't valued you. I know I wasn't always the best, growing up. But I had my own shit going on. Having to be a certain way because of Dad. Hiding my sexuality. I know it wasn't easy for you but it wasn't easy for me either. You were good at *everything*. School, swimming, music. I couldn't compete . . . Plus Dad was Dad and I had to be this fake vision of whatever he thought a man was.' He sighed. 'It's weird. We both probably remember it in different ways. But don't leave me, okay? Leaving the band was one thing. But don't leave existence. I couldn't cope with that.'

'I won't if you won't,' she said.

'Trust me, I'm not going anywhere.'

She thought of the grief that had floored her when she had heard about Joe's death by overdose in São Paulo, and she asked him to hug her, and he obliged, delicately, and she felt the living warmth of him.

'Thanks for trying to jump in the river for me,' she said.

'What?'

'I always thought you didn't. But you tried. They pulled you back. Thank you.'

He suddenly knew what she was talking about. And maybe more than a little confused about how she knew this, when she had been swimming away from him. 'Ah, sis. I love you. We were young fools.'

Joe nipped out for an hour. Picked up the keys from her landlord, collected his sister's clothes and phone.

She saw that Izzy had texted. *Sorry I didn't get back last night/ this morning. I wanted a proper discussion! Thesis antithesis synthesis. The whole works. How are you? I miss you. Oh, and guess what? I'm thinking of coming back to the UK in June. For good. Miss you, my friend. Also, have a TON of humpback pics coming your way. xxx*

Nora made a slight noise of involuntary joy at the back of her throat.

She texted back. It was interesting, she mused to herself, how life sometimes simply gave you a whole new perspective by waiting around long enough for you to see it.

She went on the Facebook page of the International Polar Research Institute. There was a photograph of the woman she had shared a cabin with – Ingrid – standing with the field leader Peter, using a thin measuring drill to gauge the thickness of sea ice, and a link to an article headlined 'IPRI research confirms last decade warmest on record for Arctic region'. She shared the link. And posted a comment: 'Keep up the great work!' And decided that when she earned some money, she would donate.

It was agreed that Nora could go home. Her brother ordered an Uber. As they were pulling out of the car park Nora saw Ash driving into the hospital. He must have been on a late shift. He had a different car in this life. He didn't see her, despite her smile, and she hoped he was happy. She hoped he only had an easy shift of gall bladders ahead of him. Maybe she would go along and watch him in the Bedford half-marathon on Sunday. Maybe she would ask *him* out for a coffee.

Maybe.

In the back of the car, her brother told her he was looking for some freelance session work.

'I'm thinking of becoming a sound engineer,' he said. 'Vaguely, anyway.'

Nora was happy to hear this. 'Well, I think you should do it. I think you'd like it. I don't know why. I've just got a feeling.'

'Okay.'

'I mean, it might not be as glamorous as being an international rock star, but it might be . . . safer. Maybe even happier.'

That was a tough sell, and Joe wasn't entirely buying it. But he smiled and nodded to himself. 'Actually, there's a studio in Hammersmith and they're looking for sound engineers. It's only five minutes from me. I could walk it.'

'Hammersmith? Yes. That's the one.'

'What do you mean?'

'I mean, I just think it sounds good. Hammersmith, sound engineer. It sounds like you'd be happy.'

He laughed at her. 'Okay, Nora. Okay. And that gym I was telling you about? It's right next door to the place.'

'Ah, cool. Any nice guys there?'

'Actually, yes, there is one. He's called Ewan. He's a doctor. He goes to cross-training.'

'Ewan! Yes!'

'Who?'

'You should ask him out.'

Joe laughed, thinking Nora was just being playful. 'I'm not even one hundred per cent sure he's gay.'

'He is! He's gay. He is *one hundred per cent gay*. And one hundred per cent into you. Dr Ewan Langford. Ask him out. You have to trust me! It will be the best thing you ever do . . .'

Her brother laughed as the car pulled up at 33A Bancroft Avenue. He paid, on account of Nora still having no money and no wallet.

Mr Banerjee sat at his window, reading.

Out on the street, Nora saw her brother staring in astonishment down at his phone.

'What's up, Joe?'

He could hardly speak. 'Langford . . .'

'Sorry?'

'Dr Ewan Langford. I didn't even know his surname was Langford but that's him.'

Nora shrugged. 'Sibling intuition. Add him. Follow him. DM him. Whatever you have to do. Well, no unsolicited nude pics. But he's the one, I'm telling you. He's the one.'

'But how did you know it was him?'

She took her brother by the arm, and knew there was no explanation she could possibly give. 'Listen to me, Joe.' She remembered the anti-philosophy of Mrs Elm in the Midnight Library. 'You don't have to *understand* life. You just have to *live* it.'

As her brother headed towards the door of 33A Bancroft Avenue, Nora looked around at all the terraced houses and all the lampposts and trees under the sky, and she felt her lungs inflate at the wonder of being there, witnessing it all as if for the first time. Maybe in one of those houses was another slider, someone on their third or seventeenth or final version of themselves. She would look out for them.

She looked at number 31.

Through his window Mr Banerjee's face slowly lit up as he saw Nora safe and sound. He smiled and mouthed a 'thank you', as if simply her act of living was something he should be grateful for. Tomorrow, she would find some money and go to the garden centre and buy him a plant for his flowerbed. Foxgloves, maybe. She was sure he liked foxgloves.

'No,' she called back, blowing him a friendly kiss. 'Thank *you*, Mr Banerjee! Thank you for everything!'

And he smiled broader, and his eyes were full of kindness and concern, and Nora remembered what it was to care and be cared for. She followed her brother inside her flat to start tidying up, catching a glimpse of the clusters of irises in Mr Banerjee's garden as she went. Flowers she hadn't appreciated before, but which now mesmerised her with the most exquisite purple she had ever seen. As though the flowers weren't just colours but part of a language, notes in a glorious floral melody, as powerful as Chopin, silently communicating the breathtaking majesty of life itself.

The Volcano

It is quite a revelation to discover that the place you wanted to escape to is the exact same place you escaped from. That the prison wasn't the place, but the perspective. And the most peculiar discovery Nora made was that, of all the extremely divergent variations of herself she had experienced, the most radical sense of change happened within the exact same life. The one she began and ended with.

This biggest and most profound shift happened not by becoming richer or more successful or more famous or by being amid the glaciers and polar bears of Svalbard. It happened by waking up in the exact same bed, in the same grotty damp apartment with its dilapidated sofa and yucca plant and tiny potted cacti and bookshelves and untried yoga manuals.

There was the same electric piano and books. There was the same sad absence of a feline and lack of a job. There was still the same *unknowability* about her life ahead.

And yet, everything was different.

And it was different because she no longer felt she was there simply to serve the dreams of other people. She no longer felt like she had to find sole fulfilment as some imaginary perfect daughter or sister or partner or wife or mother or employee or anything other than a human being, orbiting her own purpose, and answerable to herself.

And it was different because she was alive, when she had so nearly been dead. And because that had been her choice. A choice to live. Because she had touched the vastness of life and within that vastness she had seen the possibility not only of what she could do, but also feel. There were other scales and other tunes. There was more to her than a flat line of mild to moderate depression, spiced up with occasional flourishes of despair. And that gave her hope, and even the sheer sentimental *gratitude* of being able to be here, knowing she had the potential to enjoy watching radiant skies and mediocre Ryan Bailey comedies and be happy listening to music and conversation and the beat of her own heart.

And it was different because, above all other things, that heavy and painful *Book of Regrets* had been successfully burnt to dust.

'Hi Nora. It's me, Doreen.'

Nora was excited to hear from her, as she had been in the middle of neatly writing a notice advertising piano lessons. 'Oh Doreen! Can I just apologise about missing the lesson the other day?'

'Water under the bridge.'

'Well, I'm not going to go into all the reasons,' Nora continued, breathlessly. 'But I will just say that I will never be in that situation again. I promise, in future, should you want to continue with Leo's piano lessons, I will be where I am meant to be. I won't let you down. Now, I totally understand if you don't want me to be Leo's piano teacher any more. But I want you to know that Leo is an exceptional talent. He has a feel for the piano. He could end up making a career of it. He could end up at the Royal College of Music. So, I would just like to say if he doesn't continue his lessons with me, I want you to know that I feel he should continue them *somewhere*. That's all.'

There was a long pause. Nothing but the fuzzy static of phone-breath. Then:

'Nora, love, it's okay, I don't need a monologue. The truth is we were in town yesterday, the two of us. I was buying him some facewash and he said, "I'm still going to do piano, right?" Right there in Boots. Shall we just kick off where we left off next week?'

'Seriously? That's amazing. Yes, next week then.'

And the moment Nora came off the phone she sat at the piano and played a tune that had never been played before. She liked what she was playing, and vowed to remember it and put some words to it. Maybe she could turn it into a proper song and put it out there online. Maybe she would write more songs. Or maybe she would save up and apply for a Master's. Or maybe she would do both. Who knew? As she played, she glanced over and saw her magazine – the one Joe had bought her – open at a picture of the Krakatoa volcano in Indonesia.

The paradox of volcanoes was that they were symbols of destruction but also life. Once the lava slows and cools, it solidifies and then breaks down over time to become soil – rich, fertile soil.

She wasn't a black hole, she decided. She was a volcano. And like a volcano she couldn't run away from herself. She'd have to stay there and tend to that wasteland.

She could plant a forest inside herself.

How It Ends

Mrs Elm looked a lot older than she had done at the Midnight Library. Her formerly grey hair was now white and thin, her face tired and lined as a map, hands spotted with age, but she was as adept at chess as she had been years ago in the Hazeldene school library.

Oak Leaf Care Home had its own chessboard, but it had needed a dust down.

'No one plays here,' she told Nora. 'I'm so pleased you came to see me. It was such a surprise.'

'Well, I can come every day if you want, Mrs Elm?'

'Louise, please call me Louise. And don't you have work to do?'

Nora smiled. Even though it had only been twenty-four hours since she had asked Neil to put up her poster in String Theory, she was already inundated with people wanting lessons. 'I teach piano lessons. And I help out at the homeless shelter every other Tuesday. But I will always have an hour . . . And to be honest, I have no one to play chess with either.'

A tired smile spread across Mrs Elm's face. 'Well, that would be lovely.' She stared out of the little window in her room and Nora followed her gaze. There was a human and a dog Nora recognised. It was Dylan, walking Sally the bullmastiff. The nervous one with the cigarette burns who had taken a shine to her. She wondered, vaguely, if her landlord would allow her to get a dog. He'd allowed a cat, after all. But she'd have to wait until she'd caught up with the rent.

'It can be lonely,' Mrs Elm said. 'Being here. Just sitting. I felt like the game was up. Like a lonely king on a board. You see, I don't know how you remember me, but outside of school I wasn't always the—' She hesitated. 'I've let people down. I haven't always been *easy*. I've done things I regret. I was a bad wife. Not always a good mother, either. People have given up a little on me, and I don't entirely blame them.'

'Well, you were kind to me, Mrs . . . Louise. When I had a hard time at school, you always knew what to say.'

Mrs Elm steadied her breath. 'Thank you, Nora.'

'And you're not alone on the board now. A pawn has come and joined you.'

'You were never a pawn.'

She made her move. A bishop sweeping into a strong position. A slight smile tugged at the corners of her mouth.

'You're going to win this,' Nora observed.

Mrs Elm's eyes sparkled with sudden life. 'Well, that's the beauty, isn't it? You just never know how it ends.'

And Nora smiled as she stared at all the pieces she still had left in play, thinking about her next move.